The Red Nightingale

The Red Nightingale

A Novel by Richard Hargis

Ashland, Oregon

Type set in 10.75 / 14.4 Baskerville
Printed in the United States of America

ISBN-13: 978-0-615-33409-7

Book packaged by Ink & Paper Group, LLC
Book designed by Bo Björn Johnson
Edited by Laura Meehan

Rimer Resun Books
Ashland, OR

For Dave Parry,
who reached the edge of evening

I, like Aeneas, raise anchor, hoist sail and depart;
Return to my land, a broken heart.

—Samantha, 384 CE

Prologue

The female is running out of options. She sees an outcropping of three cinder stones and scurries between them, turning her back against the middle stone and facing her attacker.

She had ventured into this rill creased into the desert floor by a flood ages ago, smoothed flat by sandstorms, and set down in geodesy by three large stones. She felt drawn to the place by an emotion of which she was unaware.

The denizens of the sand come again and again to the same spots, to mark them with a lore known only to them. These are places unmarked on maps, enfolded quietly into a dimension at the edge of the desert. She has found such a place, one known by more than one species and used for more than one purpose.

The male appears, his body flushed with purpose, and sees her backed against the stone. As he surges down the promontory, he feels something with his leg—a strand planted in the ground; it disappears away from him to something beneath the surface. His sense of it diminishes as he approaches the female.

Undaunted, he presses his attack. The female arches her abdomen over her head like a night beacon, stretching two claws forward for a final defense. The male clasps her claws in his, and the chase is over. This will be the place of their mating; as others of their kind have done, they scuttled here as adversaries, then became lovers.

Beneath them, a box containing plastique vibrates in counterpoint to their dance.

1

The Wedding Rite: Day One

The din in the marketplace, where the woman has come in search of cloth for the wedding, reaches a crescendo. She feels a faint foreboding. What could be wrong in this? She did accede to her first marriage, and to the divorce. After all, for ages in the Kabylia, the first Berber marriage would end that way. However if a girl divorced, she may have to wait another eight years for the next marriage ceremony to be organized, or seek her fortune in another land.

† †

With Milan at her back, Samantha made her way to Rome and boarded a swift wherry down the Tiber, the parallel waterway to the High Road. Augustine had booked passage for her to Carthage from Ostia. Their son had stayed with him.

Samantha was on the deck thinking about her son when she was chilled back to the present by the wherry heeling over and the Tiber washing her sandaled feet with yellow water.

The narrow craft found smoother water downstream, occasionally passing small ranches whose denizens' clucks echoed into the little villages nearby. Grand villas stood beside cleared land, farms worked by senators or wealthy men on weekend escapes from the *vox populi* of Rome.

† †

After she had met Augustine and wrapped her legs about his torso in passion that first week, they found an apartment adjacent to the wealthy neighborhood where his students lived. He was a brilliant professor and taught her much of what she knew of the history of Mauretania and of Rome, and Latin conjugations. He taught her about the Greeks: their language, how they did things, and what gods were important to them.

When Augustine came home from work, they would sit at the table and speak Punic, the common language spoken in Carthage and the language of the courts. Occasionally they would speak in Latin or Greek to catch the right word or phrase, or to relieve boredom.

"This is but a short stay," he would tell her in his clipped Punic dialect. "Tomorrow we will sail for Rome."

"No matter; I love you," she would say in Berber, as a reminder of whom he really was. Not long after they had rented the apartment, and after several more wrappings despite her multilingual chidings to him, her belly began to swell. "It's a boy; I can tell by the way he kicks me."

Augustine laughed and said, "A future senator, no doubt."

And indeed Samantha did give him a son. She wanted to name the boy Apueleius, after the Berber author who wrote *The Golden Ass*.

"Nothing doing," he told her. "The boy's name must aspire to the purple robe, *Adeo*—what is more—*ducem hostium intra moenia atque adeo in senatu videmus!*"

"You're saying, 'He charges in on horseback?'"

"'Into public life,'" he concluded.

She laughed, "I think we get between our horses."

"No more than between the sheets."

"Who knows what language our future ancestors will speak here in a thousand years. We can only dream of it, but the tribes will be here long after the Empire has vanished, and these conversations have a habit of repeating themselves."

"We might as well leave it to the horses, then."

She stretched over to kiss him, saying, "We must not forget our tribe, Augustine. But *Adeodatus* will do."

† †

When she debarked from the boat at Ostia, the town was as she remembered it: a merchant harbor with intricate labyrinths of breakwaters, basins, and docks. Tall ships laden with cargo reefed sail and nudged their way into the inner channels.

Samantha passed the moored Egyptian corn ship, *Ptolemica,* which dwarfed an imperial trireme alongside her. What Samantha searched for was a smaller vessel, the *Junia Secunda,* and she found her three docks over.

Stevedores trudged up the gangplank, hefting ampullae bound for Carthage. She gave fifty sesterces to a stevedore standing alongside the ship to heft a small trunk that had accompanied her on her trek from Milan. Once on board, the man set the trunk down beside the ship's sails that had been spread on the deck to dry. Steam rose from the dank cotton, pressing against her face and curling up beneath her dress with the smell of the sea.

I must remember to tell my people of this voyage. My people. I shall tell them all of Milan and of Rome, and of the Mediterranean that separates us—part reality in the passage to North Africa, and part dream of that foreign place from whence I came. I will speak of this to the local saints; it was they who told me to go.

I was convinced Augustine would be my final husband. We eluded the tribal marriage rite. That was our error.

Samantha's gaze wandered back to the deck, now empty with rolled-up sails. Only the ampullae remained. Clay jugs shaped like figure eights, they looked like short men bound together for the voyage.

I left my child behind; should I speak of him? She looked at the spot where the stevedores had been, and brushed back her mop of hair. *Have I been away too long to dream on the saints' sarcophagi or talk to them? Will they forgive me my transgression?*

At the tribal fires, Augustine spoke about a strange religion he had discovered, one in which you enter a dimension of life after death. He spoke of this to the Jamai, *our tribal leaders. That was ten years ago.*

I fell in love with him and fell away from my tribe. I thought he was of my tribe, but he was Roman all along, my Latin teacher.

Samantha folded her hands in prayer and brought them to her face, then unfolded them and cried, "Oh God, into what part of his spirit was I arraigned before this Punic injustice? Will I see Adeodatus again?"

Monica told me to join the convent; according to her, Christus would come and show me the way. Monica said He was the way to forgiveness and making my soul clean. I have much of which to be forgiven.

I shall go to the Cave of Dreams, where time changes everything and everything changes time. We spoke of the time of reincarnation when our spirits would move through mirrors of polished brass; now as Augustine goes to his destiny in the Church and I to mine in the cave, is it so easy to wriggle free of these thoughts? I will stand with the fire at my back again and tell them all. May the flames purify me and anneal me to the spot should I ever think to leave the tribe again.

She found a hollow amid the ampullae on the wooden deck and curled down into the light of her dream.

2

The bakers knead dough for the wedding pastry that will measure a good yard in length. They begin to wag their tongues as a bride nears the open hearth they have fashioned for the baking of the ceremonial loaf.

Men stoke the fire while others beat the ground with sticks to ward off spirits attempting to beguile any bride on her second or third marriage into a perpetual state of virginity. If she remains a virgin, a state unpardonable among the Berbers, she will become an outcast.

AZOUZA, ALGERIA, 1973

The Muslims laid claim to the Cårtobé family's land in the name of Islam while the bureaucrats officially marked it into record as *habus*, land donated to the communal state. It was common knowledge among the Berber tribe that the Cårtobés had worked their Maghreb lands some three hundred years after the death of Christ, while the Donatists were still dancing about the tombs of their saints.

Augustine, it seemed, had spent a great deal of time chasing after these Donatists, to bring them to their senses about the folly of elevating ancestors to sainthood and return them to the kneeler of the confessional. Meanwhile, he tried to provide sanctuary for those escaping the whip of the slave merchant—but when Rome turned a blind eye, the tribes revolted. And when the Arabs came, the cold stare of rebellion looked out from beneath the Berbers' pointed hoods as they stood before the fires and talked of glory days.

However, long before the Muslims took their property in the Maghreb, Sol rolled up her sleeves, packed all their worldly possessions that could easily fit on the hand-drawn cart, and took the family to the foot of the Djurdjura Mountains with the rest of their tribe. And all the while, she admired the strength with which her husband, Fortola Cårtobé, pushed back his crop of curly auburn hair, unfurled his brow, and hefted the greatest load as they hiked up the mountain and settled into a cave one hundred and fifteen kilometers east of Algiers, in Azouza.

Fortola had fought alongside the *pieds noirs* and French Foreign Legion in support of a French Algeria, but the Cårtobés fled to the Djurdjura before the conflict ended in 1962. All of the others Berbers simply vanished from the sacred lands as well, many moving to higher ground—perhaps their last refuge for the millennium. The Arabs who came to the Maghreb and witnessed their departure described the tribal ties among the Berbers as *assabiyya*, loyalties that no religious or secular force could break.

After Fortola abandoned the fields, he earned a little from odd jobs, but he and Sol were poor. In the Maghreb, they had had bounty on their dinner plates and a nice house to give them shelter. Now they shared a half-cave, half-hut perched above the mountain city with two Muslim families. Their Berber heritage provided the galactic glue needed to keep the three families from spinning off into space, no matter how heated the arguments among the infidels became. It was a hovel politics of survival that drew no quarter for religious intolerance. In time, the ways of the cave settled somewhere between Christian and Muslim, as Augustine might have sanctioned with a sweep of his scarlet cape.

Fortola knew there were practically no other Christians left in Azouza, but he saw to it that the Cårtobé Catholic heritage held fast, at least on his side. Unfortunately, the Cårtobé *nif*, their public esteem, may have suffered because of this. Fortola was not shunned from tribal functions; he nevertheless had to struggle for bragging rights at the *Jamai*, recounting his exploits during the Berber uprising, which gave him a glimmer of esteem in the eyes of the men who professed Islam. Sensing his plight, Sol persisted in the family's cave-dreaming legacy. She repeated her dream interpretations to Tashoda, the old marabout, giving the family a better foothold in the tribe and offering a balance to their otherwise-teetering *nif*.

In the spring of 1981, Sol bore Fortola a daughter, Tamia, the first of the sacred heritage. Three years later, in a fit of passion in their semi-private quarter of a cave, they conceived Malena.

From the start, Fortola insisted that his daughters be baptized. Sol wasn't a believer, but acceded to his wishes—yet secretly vowed the girls would cave-dream, abhorring the Church's belief in redemption. *There's nothing to redeem*, she thought, preferring the enlightenment of the cave.

"The girls will be baptized," Fortola averred. "I don't want them in the cave; Augustine would have forbidden it."

"Cave-dreaming goes way back." Sol retorted. "I admit I feel kinship to Augustine, poor thing—practically conscripted into the priesthood, and half-Berber at that." She stood and stretched her five-foot frame up as far as she could. "In my heart, I know he loved his people, but I owe allegiance to Samantha, our true matriarch."

Fortola pushed his hair back. "That's blasphemy! And Samantha's dead, you know."

Sol puffed out her ample chest. "Of course she's dead; that's why she's a saint. I've spoken to her many times." She continued stiffly, "She came back from Rome, returned to the tribe, and remarried—a number of times. Nevertheless, Fortola, she brought forth a dynasty of cave-dreamers: the Cårtobés."

"Along with a lot more family names that have passed under the bridge before the Cårtobés. And what of my bloodline? What did Augustine to do with that?"

"Never mind. Our bloodline holds true; Samantha told me. 'After all,' she said to me, 'he *is* one of the saints.'"

† †

In 1990, Malena was in her sixth year, and Tamia was a striking girl of nine. Like the rest of the Cårtobés, they both had ruddy skin, a pointy nose, and grey-green eyes. Tamia leaned toward Islam, as most of their friends were Muslim. She had begun dreaming in the cave, but produced less-than-favorable results; the interpretations of her dreams were coming in a bit thin.

"Are you making up the dreams?" Sol asked. Tamia shook her head and swore she had repeated them back just as they happened. Sol was not convinced, and began instructing little Malena in the practice of cave-dreaming.

That same year, Fortola got Malena to the baptismal, but Malena ran in terror to Sol as the priest doused her with holy water. "Renounce the devil," proclaimed the priest, running after her—though as a Berber himself, he took her flight for a good omen.

"There, there, little cave-dreamer," said Sol, and looking at Tamia, said, "Stop that snickering." She never asked Tamia to return to the cave.

Later the church was burned by Muslim extremists, who said it was a house of devil-worship. Much to Sol's irritation, Fortola still carried the rosary a missionary had given to him years earlier, in the fields of the Maghreb. Five times a day, as the Muslims were called to prayer, Fortola would thrust his hand into his pocket and find the crucifix, move down to the first bead, just above the cleavage of the chain that formed a circle of *Ave Marias*—and for him it was unbroken.

† †

By the time Malena was eight, Sol had reserved the privilege of cave-dreaming for her. Malena was aware of the special status that went with the cave; she was now the favored child and she knew it. Sol sent Tamia to work in the city.

One morning, as they prepared breakfast, Tamia confronted Malena. "I'm trapped!" she exclaimed.

"Trapped how?" Malena cooed, continuing to slice a cucumber.

"Here," Tamia said, "within the confines of my own family—my own tribe."

"But you live here, Tamia," Malena insisted innocently.

"I'm a trapped Berber female, nothing more than a slave," Tamia whined. "I don't understand why Mama has banished me from the cave and let you take my place. It's not fair."

Malena shrugged. "I haven't a notion what you're talking about," she said, and continued to carve up the cucumber. It was true that she whiled away her days listening to a hand-cranked Victrola Fortola had found in an abandoned farmhouse, and Tamia toiled in the marketplace, sorting vegetables and sweeping garbage from the street.

Tamia vowed revenge.

An opportunity fell into her lap one morning when Malena told her about a dream wherein she had asked if Sol's close friend was pregnant. "The symbols don't make sense," Malena complained.

"Let me think about that," Tamia said, closed her eyes, and proceeded to cook up a convincing explanation, telling Malena the dream's obvious meaning was that there was to be no baby.

"Thanks Tamia," Malena yelled, and ran posthaste to Sol. The dream's prediction, however, produced a furrow so deep in Sol's brow, it reminded Malena of the canyon beside the city where dead cats were thrown. Sol, caught in a severe pinch between truthful dream outcomes and her friendship, reprimanded Malena for her obvious inattention to the dream, and sent her back to the dismal cave to do better.

Malena realized she had allowed Tamia to dupe her by twisting the dream's symbolism. The next time, upon emerging from what amounted to a bad night's sleep, and sans Tamia's counsel, Malena ran to Sol and blurted out her vision: "Snakes! I saw snakes with skinny tails swimming up the river!"

Sol's mind raced. She clasped her hands together and raised them over her head, crying "The sperms, wriggling their way up to the egg!" She left at once to tell her friend to go forth and bear fruit. Tamia's plot to soil Malena's prowess in the cave collapsed, for indeed the woman became pregnant.

Retreating from her sibling problems, Malena spun records on her turntable, releasing the switch to her other world; when it spun seventy-eight times a minute, musical dreams emerged. Aside from the tribal meetings in town, the family's sole entertainment was the record player, echoing its strange American tunes into the cold night of the Kabylia. Fortola did tell Malena to keep the volume low, so as not to offend his neighbors—or God.

Malena particularly liked the Cinnamon Caruthers records. "She sounds like the desert bird, Papa," she said, moving her arms in time. "The one who flies south over that water."

"The Mediterranean?" Fortola sat next to her, his elbow on his knee and his reddish hair in his fist.

"Yes Papa, Mediterranean," she nodded, pushing back her mop of hair, a gesture she had picked up from her father. She scooted close to him.

"It is the red nightingale that flies south."

"Yes south; it lives outside our place in a scrub tree." Malena closed her eyes and thought of the bird. She began to sing as the record spun. Curling her lips around a curiously phonetic lyric, she sang in a clear Berber inflection. "Yes, Papa, it stays here until it is too cold outside and then it flies further south. Who is the woman who sings?"

"The American, Cinnamon Caruthers."

"Papa?"

"Yes."

"What does the nightingale do in the desert, when it is not here?"

"It finds itself a place for a home, builds a nest of whatever it can find, then finds a good mate and has baby nightingales."

"Papa?"

"Yes, Malena."

"When the nightingale returns, does it bring its babies with it?"

"I don't know. Next time they come through, I will look."

"I will look too, Papa. Papa?"
"What is it Malena?"
"American Cinnamon, does she nest?"

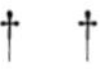

Ten-year-old Malena could only dream of the Maghreb's golden harvest from the tales Fortola and the old men related in Azouza's city center, where the men of the village went to exchange their stories like wares. Neither Sol nor the girls were allowed in the *Jamai*, as custom forbade their attendance, but Malena and Tamia would follow Fortola to the meeting place and hide out within hearing distance. And after listening to sagas that wafted up from the central fires, they stole away and invented war games, emulating Fortola's exploits by chasing each other with sticks.

"I'll be Fatima; you be Messouda," ordered Tamia.

"I know Messouda's song," Malena exclaimed:

'Twas on her wedding night
She saw her plight.
Oh, Country!
Oh lovers!
Come back,
Come back to fight—

"But it's not fair Tamia; you were Fatima the last time."

"You're not old enough to be Fatima. You're not even old enough to get married."

"You're thirteen and married once, but that doesn't give you the right."

Tamia had adhered to the Berber tradition of the marriage-divorce ritual twice, though Fortola said he hoped she would settle on a husband the third time around. She corrected Malena: "Twice. I was married twice. Anyway, you can't play Fatima, and that's final."

"Then I don't want to play." Malena stomped back inside the

hovel to the Victrola, and put on a Cinnamon Caruthers record. She vowed to one day travel to Algiers, where she would sing like a desert bird, find a place to nest, and make lots of money and have babies. She had been making this vow since she was six, when the priest had nearly drowned her in that cave of a church. She repeated the vow while hitting the high notes square-on and moving in rhythm to the seductive parts of the song. She wished for a time machine to keep up with the spinning record on the old Victrola, one which would record everything just as it happened.

Malena found paper and scribbled Tifinagh characters on it. She folded the paper evenly into ever-diminishing squares and hid it beneath her bed. When she was alone in the hovel, she recovered the paper and opened it, and music burst forth; she kept in tune with the magic notes. She did this constantly, except for when she was playing outside with Kaarem. But it was when she heard the music that she was the happiest.

† †

Everyone called Malena "the romantic," but they were forever calling her one thing or another. This may have been because of the lore in the tribe that anyone who did not cry was devoid of emotion, and therefore was predisposed to move on.

If it were true she was a romantic, as it was true she could not cry, there was no way she could explain the condition; her practicality simply kept it inside of her. She wondered if she would meet other romantics, and how she would recognize them. Would they show signs? Perhaps she could spot them by the way others acted toward them, unless they infected others and stole out quietly to cry outside, where no one could see them.

As far as she could tell, Malena had not infected anyone with her dry eyes, not even Kaarem, with whom she played daily, and saw cry whenever he was hurt or bothered by something. She always thought that one day her condition might bear her away from him, her family, and her tribe.

† †

One afternoon when Tamia returned to the hovel from work, Malena sat on a rock outside the entrance, absentmindedly prodding a hapless scorpion with a stick and dreaming of cheering audiences and white flowers. Being situated in squalor outside the ruttish city of Azouza did not dissuade Malena from her daydream.

Tamia stopped and watched her for a moment. "Why aren't you inside, fixing something for us to eat?" she snarled.

"Don't feel like it I suppose," Malena sighed.

Tamia darted into the hovel. Within earshot of Malena, she moaned, "Mother, Malena's wasting time again."

Sol only said, "Daydreaming or singing—I tell you, at both pastimes she's a natural."

Malena ducked into the hovel. "Can I help with supper?" she asked.

Tamia snapped her fingers at her. "You should get married; then you'll see what for."

Fortola, who was lounging on an old chair, was amused. "I like her singing," he said.

Malena's sister looked at him with disdain, then turned to Sol. "Don't you think so, Mother?"

Sol continued to mix some vegetables she had purchased at the open market. "Think what?" she asked.

"That Malena should get married the next time the marriage rite comes around."

Sol shrugged again. "I suppose—yes, if the opportunity presents itself. We'll see." She paused and looked up, as if trying to imagine Malena in a marriage. "Maybe Malena's too impudent to marry yet."

Tamia pointed at Malena again. "A good husband will straighten her out."

"You've been married twice. Has it helped?"

"You know I divorced both times right away. There was no consummation."

"Exactly. So how will it help Malena?"

Tamia exploded, "Malena's impudence goes far beyond the tribe's lenience regarding a young woman's attitude, and that will cost her dearly when she accepts the final marriage arrangement—pity the husband."

Fortola nodded patiently, saying, "That's enough talk about the subject for one night."

But change was in the air and Malena could feel it. She would consider any attempt to marry her off as an enchantment used to break her spirit. She had no intention of participating in an asinine ritual of mass marriage and divorce to secure her place in womanhood; her heart had already been reserved for Kaarem. Her scorn for the mass marriage, however, nearly always provoked a fight with her sister, who was a good six inches taller—but Malena was a fierce fighter and nearly always victorious.

In one family dispute, however, Tamia found a way to get at Malena. Malena had been stealing food from the communal cache that the families shared, and Tamia began to suspect her. Malena happily justified the thievery to herself because of her empty stomach.

One morning before leaving for work, Tamia caught her in the act and told Fortola. To Tamia's glee, the exposé produced Malena's first and last beating. Fortola told her it was wrong to take food from the cache, no matter how hungry she was. He hit her repeatedly with a wisp of stick that stung her bare bottom.

"Why don't you cry?" he yelled.

"Because I'm mad!" she yelled back, rubbing herself. She was blessed, as was said of Caruthers, with a set of pipes, and singing and yelling came easily. "Besides, I may be here, starving in the hovel, but my heart is outside with Kaarem!"

The commotion brought in Sol, who, upon seeing Malena stretched out with her dress pulled up in front of the smiling Tamia, yanked her from Fortola's lap and cried, "Unforgivable! Unforgivable!"

Malena smoothed out her dress. "One day I'll leave this miserable place. Why won't I cry? Because I sing instead!" Then she said to herself, *Maybe when I can no longer sing, I will cry.* The beating turned her against Fortola and Tamia. None of them ever did see tears from her, though her right eye smarted as she vowed revenge against them.

† †

The Cave of Dreams was two miles south of Azouza, and as they journeyed, Malena told Sol about a place she had never seen, a sandy creek bed with three stones, and what Caruthers sang.

The woman paid no attention. Instead, she spoke of the Cårtobés and countless days of incubation. The twelve-year-old girl had been daydreaming already, and gave the woman a sleepy look. "Cave-dreaming is a gift not to be wasted," the woman concluded, "like time wasted singing into an old Victrola or dreaming outside the cave."

"What's incubation?" the girl asked.

"When you sleep atop the saint's tomb, wisdom will come to you, passing into your body—incubation is the purifying ceremony beforehand, to open your mind to the answer of the question, then the dream, and finally the testimony."

"What question?"

"Whatever needs to be answered."

The girl was not so sure she wanted this sort of wisdom. The girl wondered if dead people thought at all, and what it felt like to have their thoughts pass through one's body.

After a day's purification, clearing her mind, and forming the question, the woman led her into the burial chamber and told her to lie down. "Go to sleep now. I will come for you in a while." The girl did as the woman asked, and started to dream in the tomb.

Malena was still sleeping when Sol came for her. "Did you dream?" she asked.

"I've been dreaming in the cave," Malena replied.

"What did the saint tell you?"

Malena felt the coldness of the rock in her bones. "I'm sleepy. She told me something."

"Whom did you say? The woman who spoke. Who?"

"Said her name was Samantha," Malena replied, shaking off the cold.

"You spoke to Samantha herself?"

"Mm-hmmm; she said to go to the cave where Saint Fatima is buried and ask her about my sister's marriage."

"What else?"

"She took me to a place where a woman was singing music in the dark; it was a room filled with people standing up and sitting at tables. She was above them."

"How do you mean?"

"On a raised place. Behind her, men sounded horns and beat drums. Some horns sounded like the woman. When she was done, the people at the tables clapped their hands together. I don't know why they did that–couldn't they ululate?" Sol was silent. "The woman bowed to the people and said something I could not understand. I remember the color of her skin."

"What about it?"

"It was beautiful, the color of dark gold. She wore two white flowers on her head. I didn't understand her words, but I understood her song."

"How did you come to know the song, but not the words?"

"It came through my body, just as you said it would. The woman was sad." Sol took the girl from the cave.

They did this many times. The girl wondered what the woman did with all the dreams she told her. The woman didn't say, but the girl suspected she told the old Tashoda, the marabout who owned the auburn goat.

† †

When Malena turned thirteen, Sol told her, "Now you will not only fast before dreaming, but will also have to purify your mind from sex." The girl didn't quite understand what her mother meant, but it sounded like what the Church had told her—that sexual thoughts were impure and sinful. Sex, therefore, had no place in her consciousness. She simply thought of it as an inevitable outcome of marriage.

However, fasting the night before a dream only made Malena hungry. And when she placed henna and fruit for the spirit of light who dwelled within the cave, she was always tempted to take a bite of the fruit.

Malena much preferred daydreaming to cave-dreaming, since she also had a mortal fear of closed spaces. For Malena, the cave held a special terror. Within its darker regions, Malena had connected with the local saint in her dreams.

Despite Malena's fears, Sol persisted, and Malena spent longer and longer periods in the cave. Finally one day Sol said, "You are to remain the night," and made Tamia escort her.

Since she was a strapping girl, Tamia proceeded to close the entrance of the cave with a stone, entombing Malena and her saint within. Terrified, Malena curled up on top the crypt.

She smells the desert and the body odor of a man who stands beside her, amid three stones. She feels his breath at the back of her neck, and she shifts her position on top of the stone, but the man tries to lie on top of her and touch her breasts. She bolts upright and the man disappears.

Malena sat up, rubbed her eyes, and shivered. She got up and inched her way along the wall of the cave toward the entrance. She bumped her head on the lowering ceiling. Getting down on her hands and knees, she crawled toward where the entrance ought to have been, scraping her knees on the jagged rocks of the cave floor.

She smelled the dust curling up to her face as she inched forward. Stretching out her right hand so that she wouldn't run headlong into the wall, Malena felt the rounded sides of the entrance and reached beyond—but there was something solid blocking it—a rock.

Scooting up and crossing her legs beneath her bottom, she began to dig. She cut her fingers on the jagged rocks surrounding a larger one, which she could not move. Still she continued to claw at the rocks. The dirt embedded itself in the cuts on her fingers, and she shrieked in pain. She pushed her shoulder against the large stone covering the exit, but couldn't move it.

Finally, exhausted, she gave up and crawled back to the tomb. She crawled up on it and reclined again, in an effort to sleep.

She eventually dropped off.

She hears a woman singing:

Girl, singer of my dreams,
Why do you come?
Men will kill you
For dreaming in tombs.
The City of man
Has no need for two singers.
The Cave of Dreams
Will show you what you must do.
Respect this holy place;
Our saints lie here.

† †

Malena had taken up with the boy Kaarem from the moment the families had agreed to share the hovel-cave. They would go outside into the Sun and lie on a patch of grass growing beside a thatched porch jutting from the cliff-side hovel. For as long as she could remember, she had loved his black hair "I wish my ugly hair were the color of yours, Kaarem."

"But I like your hair, Malena. I think one day I shall color mine to match yours."

"Don't say that."

"But it's beautiful, like the coat of Tashoda's angora goat."

"Just the same, I would like to have the black hair."

Kareem reached down and scooped up some mud from a puddle beside the entrance. “Maybe we could trade. We could cut some off and stick it on our heads with mud. If we did it carefully, it would grow.”

“You can’t put mud on your head—are you crazy?”

“How would you do it?”

“If there is a way, Tashoda will know; surely he knows the secret of angora. Maybe he will tell us.”

They walked the two miles to see the marabout, considered the wisest man in Azouza. When they got to the front of his hut, his auburn goat was standing at the stoop, munching a wicker basket.

The two children looked at each other, but neither said anything. After a period of silence, Malena threw up her hands in disgust and blurted, “Tashoda, come out.”

A scraggly old man poked his head out of a window. “Yes, what is it?”

Malena looked at Kaarem, but he still would not speak, so she did: “Tashoda, what can we do to make Kaarem’s hair red and mine black?”

Tashoda gazed at them for a moment. “Just a minute.” He emerged, wearing a drab red robe, and sat on the ground with them. “Kaarem, your hair is already the same as Malena’s, but darker. Her hair is the color of yours, only lighter. So there is nothing left to do. Accept what you have, and get on with the other things you’ll find more important.”

The boy and girl nodded as if they understood, thanked the marabout for his wise words, arose, and walked back to the hovel. As they went, Kaarem took Malena’s hand and asked, “How does the marabout come by answers to everything?”

“I think he gets them from his auburn goat.” Malena said seriously. Kaarem giggled and she continued, “Father says goats are the wisest animals on earth, and will be here long after the tribes have passed.”

The children finished the rest of their walk in silence, lost in

Fortola's lore. When they reached the hovel again, Malena announced, "Father says Berbers will outlast all the others."

"When do you think my tribe will pass?" Kaarem wondered. Malena shrugged.

† †

They grew and played together in the mixed wisdom of the tribe, and Malena loved Kaarem. When the heat and their curiosity got the better of them, they went to the Aissi River to swim, disrobing in full view of each other. She convinced herself that swimming together in the nude might be a prelude to marriage, and therefore was not sinful. And indeed, "One day I shall marry you," Kaarem pronounced.

"And on that I day, I shall ask Father to say yes."

"What if he says no?"

"I will run away."

"Where will you run?"

Malena smiled. "With you."

Kareem reached for her hand, saying, "Promise?"

Malena grabbed his hand and kissed his cheek. "I promise."

The day after their vows, Kaarem's father, Abdul, ran past them into the hovel and yelled something at Kaarem's mother, Syth. The children heard her scream something to Sol, finishing more loudly, "They cut his head right off, Sol, right off!"

Sol screamed, "Right off, right off!"

"Shut up, woman!" cried Fortola, "The children will hear!"

"Yes, shut up Sol," cried Abdul.

"It's not your place to say shut up to Sol," Fortola yelled back at him.

"It's not your place to tell me what to do, Fortola," yelled Abdul.

"What are you two so upset about? The Marabout Tashoda is killed," said Sol.

"And what of his goat?" asked Fortola. "Where is his goat?"

"No one has seen it," said Abdul.

"Then it survived," Fortola concluded.

Abdul sneered, "What do you know?"

"More than you, but less than the marabout, who apparently knew less than his goat," Fortola proclaimed.

They moved on to speak of others whom had been slain, as if that would console Syth, who according to Kaarem cried every night after that. Fortola explained his belief that it was a man called Fezzan Kelbeau, one of the security police, who did it. "By God, he was the one," he said, striking the table.

Apparently Fortola carried his suspicion to the fires of the *Jamai*, which proved a grave error on his part, for within the week his body was found in a ditch, his severed head a few feet away.

"But how could this happen?" yelled Malena, then withdrew to a corner of the hovel with Cinnamon Caruthers, vowing to kill Kelbeau at first chance.

Not wanting to become involved in further trouble, Kaarem and his family moved to Algiers to live with his aunt without so much as a good-bye. This outrageous act of impoliteness so angered Malena that she vowed to find Kaarem and give him a piece of her mind. Tamia took the opportunity to push Sol more than ever to include the fourteen-year-old Malena in the upcoming marriage rite, to stand beside her on her third. Sol agreed to arrange a gift exchange with another Berber family to cement Malena's betrothal.

Malena overheard the conversation and placed Tamia's name at the top of her vengeance list. She wanted more than a sedentary family life; she wanted to sing. With vendettas piling up and arranged marriages looming, she planned her exodus to Algiers to find a singing job. She would search out Kaarem and force him to make amends, and they would be married.

Two days before the henna celebration, she reminded herself of these things as she hid beneath her bed a white blouse, an embroidered cape, and a red full-length dress bearing the tribal colors in a repeat of vertical yellow and black stripes. She thought she might be sad to be leaving, but dismissed the feeling as conjuring. Over the week prior, she had hoarded enough goat jerky to sustain her for the hike ahead.

† †

In the early afternoon on the day of the celebration, she pulled the cache of clothes from under the bed. She amassed what she could carry and left the hovel for good, avoiding the dust on the floor, as evil spirits could trace footprints, while reminding herself that the Church forbade her thoughts of revenge as pagan and sinful.

She backed out the door, her footprints pointing into the hovel, not in the direction of Algiers. She did not look back to see if she was being followed, for this too could conjure evil.

As the attendants anointed the brides with henna, Malena slipped out of the bridal chamber and scrambled down the hill to the south; keeping Aït Hague Village off her right shoulder, she hiked down the Aissi. From there, she proceeded west toward the Mediterranean and Algiers, unaware her path was taking her to the capitol of the province, Tizi Ouzou.

She continued along the river until she came to a large lake winding about the surrounding hills. When she came to the edge of the dam, the noise of the water falling to the rocks below was deafening. Spray arising from the chasm fell on her, cooling her face and hands. She thought about Kaarem and the promise he had made at the water's edge back home, and how his promise seemed to fall as well.

She surveyed the countryside below that opened up into farmland, the houses perched on the lower rolling hills. She saw the people had bordered off their lands with rocks formed into uneven fences that cut up the land into lopsided squares and triangles.

Finding a trail, Malena clamored down the slope and came upon more houses; then there was a flood of them. She wandered down more organized streets; the houses grew until she was in canyons of buildings shutting out the Sun's rays. There, she saw a woman approaching. Malena thought she might be Berber but was unsure. She took a chance and spoke to her in Berber. "What is this place?" she asked.

The woman gave her a startled look, then smiled. "Well child, you are at the *Gare Routière.*"

"I don't know what that means," replied Malena.

"It's the commercial district."

"Is that the name of this entire place?" Malena persisted.

"The entire place is Tizi Ouzou," replied the woman, waving her arm. Then she asked, "Are you lost?"

"No," Malena replied, "I just didn't know the name of this place. Thank you."

The woman hesitated, but then nodded and went on her way.

Fortola had talked about such a place, *Tizi Uzezzu*, giving it the Berber sound.

"What does Tizi Uzezzu mean, Papa?"

"View of the flower."

Malena walked another block and came to an open-air market, similar to the ones in her village, but much larger. She was reminded that she did not have any fruit or vegetables to eat. The street was lined with hundreds of tents. Townspeople moved among them, picking up pieces of fruit and vegetables that captured their fancies. Malena thought it might be a good idea to do the same.

She had dropped two apples, eight dates, four carrots, and three figs into her tote when she heard a loud cry issue from behind her: "Thief!"

She turned around to see what the yelling was about and saw a short swarthy man wearing a brown apron pointing his finger directly at her, a rude gesture, she thought. But then she saw two other vendors take off their aprons and start toward her and the swarthy man.

Instinctively Malena broke into a run in the opposite direction, the three men in pursuit. Zigzagging, she wound her way up one street, then down another, not knowing precisely where she was heading.

She charged down several long streets at a steady pace. Rounding a corner, she stopped and leaned against a building to catch her breath. She looked back down the street and saw that the men had given up. When she looked the other way, she saw she was at the edge of the city.

While she rested, Fortola's warning from the day of her beating echoed in her mind: "Malena, you must pay for what you take." Malena vowed never to take anything again without paying for it, and rubbed her bottom, which seemed to be stinging just then. She brought her palms up and stared at them, as if to capture the reality of the moment, then turned her hands over. Several scars were still etched onto her right index finger and left thumb, reminders of her frantic dig to escape the cave.

When she looked up again, she saw the Sun was dangerously close to the horizon. "I must find a place to sleep," she said, realizing this was to be her first night away from the safety of her family and tribe. *Being sealed in the cave with incubus on top of me might be safer than a night on the road alone.* She shook off the thought and found her way back to the river.

She found a spot under a willow, sat down, and took out the fruit and washed it. She washed her face, neck, and arms. *The fourth day of the marriage is for cleanliness*, she thought, meditating on the henna plant's pigments and how the application of its tattoos could have enriched her body, making it clean of evil. She shrugged off her disappointment.

I should look for flowers—where are the flowers? Papa said they were here. She replaced the fruit, keeping one apple into which she sank her teeth.

Finishing her apple, she reached into her tote and pulled out a woolen black-and-white striped robe that had belonged to Fortola. She threw it over her head and pulled it down. She stretched its pointed hood over her head and clasped it with her hand beneath her chin, leaving just enough of an opening for her high-bridged nose and a lock of auburn hair to protrude. Then she tucked her arms into each opposite sleeve, and drew her legs up under her.

The first day is for sanctity, the second is for good fortune, the third is for purification of the mind, the fourth—cleanliness, and the fifth, well, that's tomorrow. She brought her hand up to her nose and held it with the index finger and thumb. She had no dots or arrows painted on them, her nose, her chin, or her cheeks for luck. Instead she carried a tune and enough water to take her to the next watering place on the way to Algiers. All that she knew of her future she carried in the form of the Cinnamon Caruthers records wrapped in goatskin and cradled on her hip in a tote. She had had no room for the old Victrola, and hoped she could find another in Algiers.

In the mornings, she imagined, she would dust off her dress and walk into the Sun with no thought of retracing her steps along the artery that had brought her there. She brought her hand back down, reinserting it in the sleeve, and soon was asleep in a seated position, like a Chinese monk.

The next morning, when the Sun rose, she stood up and stretched. Pulling off the Berber robe and folding it, she placed it in the skin tote. *Today is the fifth day—the brides' day.* "Today is my *freedom!*" she said aloud, then poured some water from the jug into her hand and washed her face with her hands. She dried her face on her sleeve and looked down the river. Taking out a comb her father had made for her out of bone, she combed out her hair, which had not been washed in four days and was becoming darker red as it hung down in large looping curls to her shoulders.

"Today is *my* freedom," she said again, knotting her mane into two braids, interweaving a scarf with her hair to signify her virginity. She pinned the braids on top of her head, and poked around in the tote to make sure the records were still there. She was allowing that somehow Cinnamon's records would help her become a singer.

She started out on her second day of the journey. As she walked, she mused the old record player had sung a different tune than those she had heard from her mother, or from Tashoda the Marabout's chant. She begged forgiveness for claiming the Caruthers records as repayment for the beating.

By the time she had turned fourteen, she had formed serious

doubts about the lore she heard at market, believing allusions to the spirit were somehow connected with Church angels, whose plaster faces she could not see in the cave. The Church had taught it was to her benefit to believe in angels, and she paid homage to them if for no other purpose than to bolster her fortitude for the journey ahead.

As she journeyed, she kept to the western bank of the river leading closer to the Mediterranean coastline and on a more westerly track to Algiers. She passed two large cities and gave a thought to looking for another commercial center, but thought about the promise she had made about stealing, and she cut to the outskirts of every settlement she encountered. *Maybe,* she thought, *if I can keep this promise, Kaarem will keep his.*

In the evening she found another weeping willow tree and collapsed beneath it. She pulled off her sandals and examined her feet for red spots, a ritual her parents had drilled into her and her sister, Tamia. She found nothing, and took it as a good omen. She rubbed the crease between her shoulder and her neck that was rubbed raw from the weight of the tote, feeling the subtle muscle spasms beneath her skin. She took off her blouse and pulled down the straps to her slip, letting it drop to her waist. Her nipples stood erect from the cold air.

Rummaging in her tote, Malena pulled out an envelope made from coarse paper. She carefully unfolded it and dipped her fingers into a salve she had mixed from lard, henna, and crushed pulp from a succulent that grew outside the hovel entrance. She massaged the salve into the tissue between her shoulder and neck. The remainder she massaged under her arms and onto her breasts, for no other reason than that it felt good to have such a wholesome fragrance and color on her skin. Besides, she didn't have a spare rag with which to wipe her hands. She pulled up her slip and put on her blouse.

After dark, she pulled out Fortola's rosary, retrieved from his coat pocket on the day they discovered his body. Holding it in her right hand, she began to shiver; she felt the cold night for the first time. She pulled out her father's hooded robe and shimmied into it.

Now returned to the stillness of her situation, she began her prayer. She prayed for her abandoned family, ruing the shame she had brought upon their *nif,* and that Tamia would find a permanent husband on her third attempt. She begged God to forgive Kaarem for being such a donkey and to force him to keep his promise. She prayed that Sol would live a long life. She asked that he would provide a better singing voice to Sol, as she couldn't hit a note. Finally she begged forgiveness for keeping such a long vendetta list, vowing to shorten it just as soon as the debts were repaid.

They're dancing the Ahi Duce, she thought, touched her auburn braids. She carried half the privileges of an adult with her; a raised scarf piled atop her knotted hair was the sole sign she had participated in the marriage ceremony, since only once did she espy the groom-in-waiting, and she never had the chance to dance the Ahi Duce. She might have tripped her way to a more permanent basis had it not been for nagging doubts as fleeting as the blowing ashes from the marriage pyre or spoken history of her tribe.

† †

On the third day of the trek, Malena left the comfort of the river and began following a road. In May, temperatures in the Kabylia hovered at ten degrees Celsius. At the lower altitudes they could be three times that, so Malena had dressed to bear the heat. She avoided two more cities and felt grateful her feet were holding up. However, each day, no matter how many times she switched the tote from one shoulder to the other, the muscles beneath were giving out. *Maybe,* she thought, *I could figure out some sort of backpack to shift the weight away from the soreness.* In the end, she gritted her teeth and bore the pain as she inched across the map to Algiers.

On the fourth day, with the Sun in front of her to the west, she came to a steep bend in the road, and upon rounding it, heard the sound of water. The journey had been difficult, so she moved through the grove of scrub toward the sound, hoping to find refreshment.

On the other side, she found a miraculous grotto filled by a waterfall. After surveying the place to make sure she was alone, she waded in, lifting her dress as she went. The water encircled her thighs, and her breasts partially lifted, the skin around each tightening. She shivered.

She pulled her wet dress and slip over her head as she moved deeper, twisting them into a cylinder of white, red, and yellow stripes. She rolled onto her back, and kicking with her feet, held the dress over her head, squeezing water out of the roll. She made her way over to a rock and set the rolled dress on it. Climbing out onto the rock, she unrolled the dress and slip, laying them out to dry.

She slipped back into the water and submerged herself completely, then stood up with a burst. Climbing back out onto the rock, she sat beside her dress, combed her hair with her fingers, and sat for a time.

She gathered up the dress, now nearly dry, and pressed it to her face. It smelled of lanolin and yellow ochre and the cochineal insects which had been crushed into a crimson dye.

She stood up and threw her underskirt on, then unrolled the robe she had slept in. Yanking it over her head, she looked at her reflection in the water. She convinced herself that she looked manly enough, if not like a distinguished wizard; she wrinkled her nose and giggled at the thought. After carefully folding away her striped dress, she walked back to the road and turned west toward Algiers, carrying the skin tote slung and a hope that she would find Kaarem.

As she trudged along beside the road, she took out a record jacket. There seemed to be a strange wisdom embedded in the breakable disk that expelled the specter of enchantment from Malena, replacing it with the mortality of Cinnamon's music. She stopped momentarily and ran her hand over the woman's face, and wondered if the two white flowers in her hair were for her wedding.

Her eyes were also dry; perhaps she too could not weep for her father.

Malena removed the record from the jacket and caught the grooves with her fingernail. An energy coursed up her arm, a sonic rill that split her between the east and Kabylia and the west and Algiers.

When the Sun slipped behind the junipers on the hills, she put away the record and reached for her water jar. She stretched down to fill the clay pot and sang:

Dreams and nightmares,
We feed them
To stay alive—
Terrified by our pasts,
We're afraid to die.

She thought in French of the English lyrics Fortola had translated for her from Cinnamon's records. Were they Cinnamon's interpretation of the Bible? Malena was startled by the fact that she was thinking in French in the first place, and couldn't recall when she had begun. The long shadows of the trees took on the look of figures and Malena daydreamed of angels standing in the Church.

† †

Meanwhile, in the Cave of Dreams, Sol had gone to ask for Malena's return, and to beg forgiveness for the insult dealt to the marriage rite. In her dream, she said, "I will recant my marriage wishes for Malena if only she will come home."

Then she saw the light, and in the center of it stood a figure who was either Samantha or Augustine. Sol lay on the tomb for some time before her breathing became shallow, then intermittent. And then, sometime during the night, it ceased.

† †

The jerky lasted the five days it took to reach the eastern edge of Algiers. Malena consumed the last carrot she had liberated from the market in Tizi Ouzou and drank water from the clay jar. She bit into the last piece of jerky as she surveyed the dusty street lined with crumbling one-story buildings. Suddenly she stopped chewing and removed the meat from her mouth. *Could this be Tashoda's missing goat I have clasped in my teeth?* She shrugged, put the meat back in, and consumed it.

She crossed the city into the *Kasbah*, the place of Arabs. It was a dangerous sector to be in, but she would not know that until later. She began to repeat the street name she had overheard Sol say Kaarem lived on with his aunt. She said it in her best Arabic. Maybe saying it aloud would change the printed characters on the metal signs into something she could understand—for she could not read them. She half-whispered the word to passersby, but they brushed past, silent as the street signs. Maybe the street signs would come alive and speak. In the heart of the Kasbah, she was not ready to admit she was lost, or to acknowledge the night closing in around her.

Suddenly she heard popping noises, something akin to the Berber muskets fired into the air over Azouza during celebration. The sounds were more rapid now, unfriendly. Through the walls of the *Jamai* she had heard Fortola describe the deadliness of repeating guns, and how he had used them to kill rebels during the Revolution.

Malena heard rapid footsteps and then a scream—a woman's scream. She began to walk quickly down the street, then broke into a run. She turned onto another street, and heard more gunfire, more screaming. At the last turn, she came upon three men who were holding a young woman, the one who had been screaming, down on the street. Two of the men grasped the girl's arms as the other stood over her, unbuttoning his pants. He pushed up the girl's dress and cut off her undergarments with a long curved knife.

Malena backed into an unlit alcove, concealing herself in the shadow of its notch. She saw the youth drop down on top of the girl, who struggled, rolling from side to side. But the others held her fast and he drove into her, and the girl shrieked. Malena let out a shriek of her own at the sight.

The man atop the girl stopped and sat upright. The others turned toward Malena. Then the one on the girl raised his long knife and drove it into the girl's chest; she arched her back and cried in Arabic, "Long lives the Almighty!" He stood up and pulled up his pants in one motion.

Malena heard the men mutter, "Two for the price of one!" and "Bear no witness!" They strode toward her. One man had a long scar down the right side of his face, put there by a knife or sword. He was the first to reach out for her.

She was still screaming when the door behind her opened and an arm encircled her, pulling her in. She was still screaming when something came from the darkness, striking her face. Then she was flat on the ground, taking dust into her nostrils and mouth. She tasted blood and thought she was inside her clay jar, or perhaps an Egyptian tomb.

3

Fezzan Kelbeau spread out his prayer blanket, faced east, and joined in the midday prayer. His skin hung in layers as testimony to his devotion to eating; he felt it was a corporal reward to him for his steadfastness to Islam. *It's no vice at all,* he would tell himself, *to reap the fruits the Almighty places before me.*

Before 1980, when he took over the Head of Security position, he had openly abhorred the politicians' greediness. He was covertly instrumental in the '80s in bringing to power *le Front islamique du salut,* whose aim it was to bring all of Algeria out of the secularists' grip. Although the FIS had been outlawed in 1992, Kelbeau still served as one of its furtive leaders, serving as a cell leader of the FIS's military enforcer, *le Groupe islamique armé.* In turn, the GIA had gathered strength and had garnered no less than 100,000 deaths in Algeria and spreading its tentacles abroad, established bases of operations in France, Belgium, the United Kingdom, Italy, and the United States, killing a passel of Islamic dissenters along the way.

As Head of Security, he now protected the very politicians he hated and had as yet managed to elude exposure. *Politicians use Islam as a mere backdrop for their hypocrisy. They are treacherous and untrustworthy men.*

Facing east, Fezzan Kelbeau touched his head to his rug and prayed, *Almighty God, give me strength to make them mend their ways. In the depth of their evil, they cannot see the light without you.*

Help me find the turncoats who aided the French Secret Service. And grant me the fortune to ferret out the infidels and put an end to their putrid lives, to your greater glory, Almighty Lord!

Since the French killed his father in 1952, Fezzan Kelbeau's life had been filled with hatred for anyone with foreign blood—*pied-noir, petit blanc,* Harki, Berber, Muslim secularist—no matter. He had killed 175, severing their heads from their torsos, slicing away any chance of an afterlife. Occasionally, in a last-ditch effort to convert them, he had tortured them before the killing.

Lord, he continued, *give me the strength to make the best plan for rounding up the Arab traitors, along with their foreign blood-brothers who help them.* He considered the infidels' deaths, this genocide, a monument to his faith.

Kelbeau got up from his rug, neatly rolled it, and placed it in the large desk drawer. Pressing a key on the intercom, he said, "Tell Piton I want to see him." He pulled out a dossier with the name *Isaac Haroom* aka *Arago Sidu* embossed on the tab and opened it.

A dingy man with a scar down the right side of his face slipped into Kelbeau's office without knocking.

"There you are, Piton."

"What's that?" Piton smiled, wiping a mouth full of warped teeth with his coat sleeve.

"Sidu..."

"Do you want him killed?"

"Of course not. Maybe later..." He slid the folder into a drawer. "Now I picked up on some rumors about another, Chumie Radak, a secularist they call 'Dack.' He's up to something; I'm not sure what, but he may have been in on the thing with the one you took care of—Hassan.

"I do know that Dack drinks, and when he drinks, he talks. Get to our contact at The Black Owl; maybe one of the whores can get him to talk. Watch him yourself. Who knows where he may lead us—hopefully to the infidels who are working with the French.

"I myself will go to The Black Owl too, as usual. Sidu thinks he's doing me a favor, serving me watered-down drinks and letting me pet his whores. When the time is right, thanks to the Almighty, we'll make our move."

† †

Malena remembered her head hitting the floor and her body letting go. She thought she was dreaming.

She sees the juniper tree outside the hovel, and the Victrola beside it, a record spinning. "She sounds like the desert bird," she says to Fortola.

"The red one that flies over the sea?"

"Yes Papa, red. Sometimes, in the juniper tree, it sings the nightingale's song."

Fortola's gone mad now. "Why do you sing?"

"I can't cry."

He shakes her. "Cry! Why don't you cry?"

"The record's playing."

Fortola grabs the record and smashes it. "Now will you cry?"

"I can't. Don't make me go in!"

"Where?"

"There! There!" She's looking at the tall, arched building.

Fortola grabs her. "You have to; it's time."

She breaks free and runs toward a huge striped curtain and she is in its folds; she entwines her body into the cloth and comes up against something solid—a leg! She wraps her arms around it. Something is prying at her hands. "No! Don't make me!" She loses her grip, and is pulled from the safety of her mother's dress.

She sees Kaarem, and cries, "Help!" The boy doesn't hear her, and she screams again. He turns and disappears down the road. Something keeps her from following.

Fortola is shaking her again, "You'll do this!"

Malena opened her eyes and saw a different man, fat and balding, but with kind eyes.

† †

Arago Sidu was born into the Haroom clan, Sephardic Jews descended from the tribe who fled Spain for Morocco in 1610. Eventually his family had moved from Rabat to Cherchell, Algeria, where they set up an acting studio.

For his twelfth birthday, Sidu got a stake from a rich uncle to begin his own production company, as long as it wasn't in Cherchell. By the time he was eighteen, Sidu was a young lion; his family began reminding him of his uncle's monetary legacy and the production company. He found it necessary to leave the pride and get on with business. He thought about the huge population of Algiers he could bring his productions before, and as soon as he had finished secondary school, he caught a bus east to the big city.

Sidu surveyed the latest catch Nuluna had pulled in from the street. No raving beauty, but she had a rugged sensuality that excited him. He liked her auburn hair, and wondered if she could make a unique addition to his burgeoning harem. He stared at his one artistic asset, hung on the wall—a Picasso print of a misshapen but nonetheless nude woman. Rendered in homage to Delacroix, the figure burst from the confines of her apartment.

Sidu stared at the print and then at the girl on the floor. *They both struggle for freedom,* he thought, and in that instant decided he would never allow Malena to enter those apartments of The Black Owl reserved for his more depraved clientele.

Unfortunately, at that moment the girl screamed, hurting Nuluna's sensitive ears, and she smacked her into unconsciousness. She said, "I dislike this young Berber." One look at Nuluna's face told Sidu she was visualizing the girl in the pungent rooms upstairs, her young body draped in flimsy wrappings, so stitched to tie any customer into a knot of desire.

Sidu looked down at the girl, whose nostrils were caked with dust from the floor. "I'll warn her that if she is to stay or be thrown to the wolves is entirely up to her. If she stays, she will bathe and learn silence and—God willing—respectability."

The girl's eyes flickered open. She shook her head and looked at Sidu and then Nuluna standing beside him. Getting up on one elbow, "What happened?" she asked.

"She…"

"You hit your head when you fell through the door," Nuluna claimed.

The girl looked around at the shelves of cans and cartons with pictures of food imprinted on their labels. "What is this place?" she asked.

"The Black Owl," Sidu replied. The girl raised her nose and sniffed. "Time to get up," Sidu said, and helped her to her feet. As she dusted off her robe, Sidu regarded her attire and rubbed his head as if massage would somehow restore its destroyed follicles.

The girl stared back at him unflinchingly, and then made a slow turn, wiping the dust from her nose and taking in a deep breath. She closed her eyes, apparently taking in the odors emanating from the kitchen, where a cook was preparing lamb and red peppers in garlic sauce. The aroma rose to the tin ceiling, mixing with scents of cinnamon, ginger, and coriander that lingered there.

"Where did you come from?" Sidu asked.

The girl stared at him, her green eyes turning gray. "From the east," she answered tentatively.

"From where in the east?"

"Tizi Ouzou—might I have some food?

"You need a name," Nuluna stated.

"You may have food," Sidu replied, then turning to Nuluna, added, "She's not to be one of your flock."

† †

After Isaac Haroom withdrew his uncle's money from the bank and moved to Algiers, he created Sharman Productions. The company flourished and made him rich by local standards with its theatrical contrivances. He changed his Jewish name to the more neutral sounding Arago Sidu.

He married a lithe *pied noir* with snow-white skin and an angular face, from which dark brown eyes peered out at him. Her name was Ester and she worked for a French general named Salan; in the course of her duties, she secured good political connections for Sidu. They built an elaborate dig in the Jewish sector in Constantine, and established themselves there among the other Jewish settlers.

Ester had always felt vulnerable at Sidu's kosher table when the guests scooted their chairs up to the lamb entree. The questions always began with the meal.

"So Ester, you were raised Catholic, no?" a fat man to her right asked.

"True," she said, "but that was ages ago." She picked up her knife and cut through the tender lamp chop.

"Your priests prayed for our conversion to Christianity at every mass."

"Yes." She poured herself a glass of concord wine and took a swig of it.

"You have your Messiah, the Christ."

"Yes, and you are awaiting yours, I suppose."

"You married Sidu. What do you suppose now?"

"I suppose I don't know anymore. Years ago, I was quite sure, but now..."

"And now, the afterlife looks more distant?"

"Yes," she said and swigged down more concord. "In Constantine, everything looks a little more distant."

"You're among friends, then."

"Yes, but then I can't breathe such secrets." And they all laughed.

Over time, it had become something of a bitter revelation that being Catholic didn't necessarily guarantee wonderful things in an afterlife she could no longer see, or in which she no longer had faith.

Ester simply shuddered at her guest's apocalyptic suggestions, gulping down another glass of concord wine. She submerged her psyche into the last bottle of *vin perdu* for the remainder of the evening. Oddly enough, upon hearing such tenets of faith, or rather the subtraction of them, she at once felt refreshed and terrified. While the priests prayed at the foot of the altar for the Jews' conversion, she was becoming a Good News exile.

† †

Salan had tasked Ester to find out what the Communists were doing in Algeria. In a constant state of paranoia, she persevered, becoming the cleverest person on the general's staff. She was Salan's ferret, seeking out identities of the Egyptian Nasser's guerrillas, who spoke Arabic; she spoke none. French words from her informants sailed across demitasses and eggs-on-brioche in street cafés, sticking in her like Roman arrows. From what she was hearing, she deduced what Nasser sought was nothing more than to link communism with the greater peril: Arab revolt.

When Ester presented Salan with her findings, he remained stoical. Whether or not he trusted the intelligence, he never said, but Algeria might have lasted another decade—or millennium—if he *had* acted on it. When General De Gaulle made it clear that he was ready to throw Algeria to the wolves, Salan and the other four generals went forward with their plot to assassinate him. Precisely who the lobos in the streets really were, neither Salan nor the other four had a clue. They never got around to suspecting that the Arabs could really do anything.

However, Ester did meet a man who was not like the others, and with whom she had spoken to at many furtive meetings. This one had sought her out, and neither Salan nor any of the other generals knew of him. Yet he came to her, telling her he had been observing her for a long time, and for a long time had recorded what she discovered from the informants. "Are you an informant?" she asked.

"I pass along information," he had said.

"What would you tell them of me?" she inquired.

"I would say that you are wise and a good citizen of France. You must not tell the general of my presence here."

"Eh bien," she said. "And whom will you tell?

"Only the one who matters," he would reply.

When the plot failed, Salan and the other conspirators went into hiding and Ester was out of a job. Without being told, Ester knew French Algeria's days were numbered, along with hers; she counted them in terror.

Ester pleaded with Sidu to flee the country with her, and he found himself remembering his rich uncle in Cherchell had told him things always went badly for anyone married to the ethnic French. Sidu told her he might have thought leaving a good idea were it not for the need for profit.

Instead of fleeing, he borrowed from the principal interest in Sharman Productions, fired most of the actors, and purchased a dilapidated cabaret, which he renamed The Black Owl. While Ester cowered at home, Sidu remodeled the cabaret with an upstairs to sate the subterranean appetites. Sidu said to her, "Whether Christian or Muslim, one can enter the place and aspire to sainthood or sin with impunity."

After the Evian Accord of 1962, Ester broke and fled with the rest of the three hundred fifty thousand *pieds noirs* to France. She left a note:

14 Avril 1962
Dear Arago,

I have begged you to join me in a new life in France, but you have chosen to ignore my pleas. Had we children, I might have thought twice before fleeing, or you may have thought twice about remaining. But this is not the case. I wish I could muster the courage to stay, but life for me here is intolerable. I have tried to be a good and faithful wife—maybe when you think about out short time together, you will still change your mind after all and come to France. I have left my new address in your top bureau drawer, just in case.

There is one other matter, which I have kept secret from everyone, but now I shall tell you. I met a man, a spy, who is a friend. I asked him if I could tell you about him; and at first, he said no. But I explained that you were a good and honest man, and might be of further use to him for information you might gather in your enterprise—what is it? A cabaret? No matter—you'll meet a great many people and can still be helpful to France. He tells me of a wadi at the edge of town where the city ends and the desert begins. It's unusual because it has three stones in the middle of it. I have also left the directions to it in your drawer.

If you want to contact him, leave a message buried at the base of the middle stone. Wait a week and return to dig up his answer from the same spot.

He pays well for information. I must confess, I financed my escape by telling him of Salan's plot to kill de Gaulle, among other seditious things the four generals had levied against France. You may address the note to the Jeweler.

Take care my love,
Ester

Sidu was disgusted by Ester's departure, but kept the letter and did bury an overture for the Jeweler. He then took up with an Arab trollop he named Nuluna, because she said she was born on a new moon. Nuluna moved into the Constantine house with him, and became head *fatma* of The Black Owl's upstairs concession. With her blue-black hair, snow-white skin and slithery torso, Nuluna so resembled Ester that in a Semitic sort of way she could have been her twin. Whether or not Sidu doted on her countenance, he never considered. He did tell her she would enjoy the comforts of the Constantine house just as long as she tended to business at the cabaret. She told him that hers was the genus of "good business," and she would muster the most productive *fatmas* the world had ever seen.

The Black Owl's interior was defined by its clientele. It was a pot into which Algiers poured her hungry men to boil and blacken the insides; it was a wall with a thousand voices in it, ground to grist on the dark tile floor, poured onto the street after the place closed.

Sidu admonished Nuluna not to have liaisons with downstairs clientele. Those who aspired to the upper reaches of The Black Owl would be allowed to levitate of their own volition, and not as a result of any proddings or pokings from the *fatmas* descending the staircase, especially at showtime whilst the patrons were being treated to song and performance.

"What's the difference," asked Nuluna, "if a girl opens her mouth or her legs?"

"The difference between heaven and hell," he replied, really believing God may have intended this part of Algerian history to unfold, dividing the good from the evil within the confines of the cabaret.

† †

One thing from her past Malena was not able to shed was her contact with her ancestors. Samantha tenaciously pervaded her sleep in whorls and historical snippets of Rome and Carthage. Malena heard whispers of her break between Augustine and his mother, Monica. Monica had forsaken the pagan ways of her tribe and joined the Judeo-Christian sect that had vexed her Roman husband so much that he lamented after his own conversion, "There's no turning back to the Pantheon now."

As Samantha intoned in so many ribs of Malena's dreams, things had gone south once Monica arrived on the scene.

"She's neither a Christian nor a cave-dreamer," Monica complains.

Samantha says to Malena, "That is true: I'm neither Christian nor cave-dreamer."

"What are you then?" Malena asks.

"I'm lost between my dreams," says Samantha, then adds, "I'm banished from him."

"From who?" asks Malena.

"From him—him." She points behind her.

Malena squints at a distant figure. "Why can't you say his name?"

"Because he is lost to me." Samantha's voice breaks. "And she calls me 'the Berber slut.'"

Monica's opinion was akin, Malena supposed, to Nuluna's view of her caste.

In another dream, Augustine and his mother were boarding a boat, when Monica slipped off the gangplank and fell headlong into the murk below, striking her head on a piling. Malena saw a head, broken and bleeding, bob up momentarily, but the face was that of her mother, Sol. It was then she knew her mother was lost.

† †

Malena's freedom, as Nuluna put it, began when she, like the other twelve who had happened into the cabaret, become a permanent fixture that stayed behind long after the two o'clock rinse. Her hide, Nuluna reminded her, was up on the wall along with those of the other *fatmas*. "Truly, that's what you are, just like the rest of us who entered Sidu's domain; don't forget that."

Despite the threats Nuluna kept issuing, Sidu provided special treatment for Malena. When he asked her to proofread a revision to the menu one day, he discovered she was illiterate. He made arrangements for her tutelage with Madame Gertrude Schmidt, an American turned French linguist, who took in sewing with her ancient Singer to augment the earning she eked out from her underground French school.

Sidu told Malena Nuluna had bragged about having a driver's license early on in their relationship, so he would loan her his old Jaguar Mk V to chauffeur Malena to Madame Schmidt's. Unbeknownst to him for a time, however, Nuluna took advantage of being alone with Malena by threatening to press into service certain little pink parts of Malena's anatomy, punctuating the name of each little pink part with a quick jab to the Jag's pointed horn cap on the steering wheel to warn the gaggle of pushcarts struggling out of the way.

"This," she said, with another jab on the horn cap, "will happen at first opportunity." Malena was terrified by Nuluna's threats, and tried to disappear into the pleated leather seat next to the *fatma*, covering her face with her veil, save one triangular opening for a green eye staring straight ahead. She always kept her knees pressed tightly together.

† †

When Sidu caught wind of the threats, he wanted to oust Nuluna for her behavior, but then chose not to, owing to a reminiscence of their bedroom's theatricals:

Nuluna transforms into a enemy submarine beneath the brocade comforter, slithering ever so close to the one uncharted island off the coast of Oran, with a lone Zahidi palm bearing prodigious fruit: her quarry. In what is described in warfare tactics as a "pouncing maneuver," she grabs the prize fruit, which produces a loud call to prayer on his part, "Mon Dieu!" *Game over.*

And crediting Nuluna with a no less tangible assessment, he was reminded that he was indeed enriched by her contribution to The Black Owl's cash flow, which was in the black.

Sidu gave Malena chores of a more honorable kind: scrubbing and running errands. While he did his utmost to see that Malena remained insulated from the ravages of the upstairs rooms, he named her after her chores: "Scrub." He counseled her in the wiles of avoiding fundamentalist patrols while not wearing the veil, and avoiding secular patrols if she did wear it. Malena explained that a proper Berber woman does not wear a veil, as it was a sign of ownership and deference to the male. Being independent, she should be treated as such.

"Well," he explained, "if you want to live long enough to enjoy such independence, keep it in your pocket and use it when you must; then take it off when you must. What's the point of losing your head over a trifling piece of cloth?"

Malena chose not to bare her face, yet at the changing of the guard, or when the shadows veiled her entire body, she would discard her veil as she made her way through the curving streets of the Kasbah and out into the city.

† †

When Malena was sixteen, Sidu commissioned her to start running errands to his contacts in town. Malena became a cat, avoiding the secularists and fundamentalists with the shadowy stealth of a lioness, and everyone, even Nuluna, marveled. Thus she became known as "Dark."

One day, as Malena was on her knees cleaning the dining room tile floor, she mused, *I'm like one of the twelve who followed Christ, but follow Sidu. I take on names describing what I do for his pleasure.*

Although she was one of the twelve girls in The Black Owl, Malena was isolated, since Sidu forbade her to go upstairs. *The others must think I'm snooty,* she was thinking, when she saw a young girl floating down the stairway on a cloud of veils.

"I'm not!" the girl exclaimed, to Malena's confusion.

"Not what?"

"Not Egyptian."

"Who said you were?"

"The ones upstairs say I'm from Egypt."

"What's your name?"

"Little Egypt."

Malena viewed the girl, who stood slightly shorter than herself. Her face was rounder than Malena's and she had a flat nose, which gave her look a moonlike appearance. "Where do you come from then?"

"From Tizi Ouzou."

"How did you end up in The Black Owl?" asked Malena.

"By foot along a river that led here. I saw a woman yelling at some young girls who were sweeping the street in front of this place. I was hungry and I asked if I could work for something to eat. She gave me a job." Little Egypt smiled wryly.

"Who named you 'Little Egypt'?"

"Nuluna. She said Little Egypt is what to call me here. My real name is Cassandra." She inspected Malena's face. "You're light-skinned and have a pointy nose," she giggled. She placed a finger on the tip of Malena's nose. "So how did it get so pointed?"

"By my sticking it where it doesn't belong," Malena laughed.

"Mine's flat, probably caused by the just the opposite."

Nuluna heard their laughter and flew downstairs like a banshee. "Back up!" she shouted, thrusting a finger in the direction of the seraglio, and in a lower growl said, "Geeet, Leeettle Eeegypt."

Little Egypt's shoulders dropped, and her smile vanished. "Till sometime," she said.

"Till sometime," Malena repeated.

Little Egypt trudged up the stairway. Nuluna glared at Malena. "Sometime, one day, you will follow her." Nuluna wheeled around and tromped after Little Egypt.

† †

The next day, when Malena was cleaning tables and softly singing a Caruthers song, Sidu came into the room and asked, "Is that you singing?" When she nodded, he said, "Sing more." She dropped her rag and did as he asked.

He was astounded by her clarity and range. He told Nuluna to stop what she was doing and get Malena into some appropriate costuming. Thereafter, Malena lost her handles of "Scrub" and "Dark," and took on a far more glorious *nom déposé.* Ten years after being relieved of her cleaning duties—la, la—she was thrice nightly *La Chanteuse de la Black Owl.*

Even were it not for her singing career, she had always done as Sidu asked because sometimes it got her away from the shadow of Algiers and into the desert beyond to temporary freedoms, in the case of the migrants.

One night, mid-song, she saw some men in one corner of the cabaret. *Not the usual clientele,* she mused. Then Sidu was standing offstage—not in his usual spot. When Malena finished her song, he motioned to her, and she approached.

"I have a job for you." His eyes were cold.

"You always have a job for me."

"Not now, Malena."

"Okay, what is it?"

"There are some men in the cabaret."

"I saw them."

"Good. I want to you to escort them to the wadi..."

"of the Three Stones," she finished.

Sidu shot her a glance. "I've arranged for a lorry. Go with them on it. Someone will meet you."

"Who?"

"A Moroccan. He will take the men off your hands."

From that night on, she would periodically take migrants to be met by the Moroccan, who led them through his country to the edge of the sea. There, the migrants boarded a soggy boat for Spain where they would work for a pittance, especially after sharing their wages—a sizeable percentage—with Sidu and the Moroccan.

There was more. While delivering the migrants to the wadi, she often carried a "package." This she would bury at the base of the center stone, as Sidu had instructed. She saw no harm in the migrants' ventures, and took no money for her part in them. *But what of the packages I bury?* she wondered. *What do they contain? Who digs them up?*

† †

Little Egypt made it a habit to come downstairs and visit between Malena's shows and Little Egypt's "tricks." They went to Malena's dressing room, which had become their sanctuary, but they kept an ear to the door. There, they shared their childhood memories.

One night, Little Egypt told her story: "Malena, I came from a good family and my parents were wealthy, but the extremists killed them. They came at night and crashed through the door. They were local kids from poor families, parading about under the guise of Islam, but they didn't fool anyone—they were evil thugs." She shook her head, "They moved into our home and took everything."

"Did they rape your mother?" asked Malena.

"Yes, I saw them do it; they tore off all her clothes, and…" Little Egypt bowed her head and sobbed.

"You don't have to finish; I've seen it for myself," Malena said consolingly.

"I should have helped her, but I ran instead. Isn't it funny," she added, "that those who say they are pure have to get rid of the evidence that they're not? Anyway, after that I was on the streets, getting money or food any way I could."

† †

Three years later, Nuluna commissioned Little Egypt to entertain several sexual partners simultaneously. A fight had erupted between the men, and when the authorities were called in, Little Egypt was beaten for her part in the orgy.

Squinting into the dim light through her swollen eyes and dabbing her raw upper lip, she headed backstage. Her hair hung down in dreadlocks matted with blood, and the mascara she had so carefully applied to her eyelashes in the early evening streaked down her cheeks in black rivulets. She hid in the folds of sequined dresses hanging on a rack backstage. She listened to Malena's song, heard the applause, and cowered further back into a bulging rack of costumes.

When Malena came into the wings, Little Egypt emerged and grabbed her. "I can't do this anymore," she sobbed. "This night will be my last trip down—or up—that stairway."

Malena put her arms around her and asked, "Can't do what—what's happened?" They headed to Malena's dressing room.

"I had to do things," Little Egypt began, but her voice broke.

Malena took her over to a small couch and held her for a minute. "Lie here and rest." Going over to her sink, she put some water on a washcloth and gave it to Little Egypt.

Someone banged on the door. Little Egypt recognized Sidu's voice: "Next show—what are you doing?"

"I'm coming," Malena yelled. She touched Little Egypt. "Stay here. No one will bother you. I'll be back...just wait here." She went out, turning off the light behind her.

Little Egypt waited in the darkness, vowing to escape. *Maybe Malena will help. No matter—I will leave this place tonight, one way or another.* She could hear Malena singing through the door, then faint applause.

Several minutes later, the door opened and Malena turned the lights back on and came over to sit beside her. "Help me escape this place." Little Egypt said.

"Where will you go?" Malena asked.

"Back to Tizi Ouzou."

Malena closed her eyes, lost in silence for a moment. Then she nodded her head. "I'm taking some immigrants to leave for Spain after the place closes tonight." She got up, and going to her clothes rack, she pulled out a black-and-white striped Berber robe. "Try this on," she said, holding it out to Little Egypt.

Little Egypt stood up and put on the robe. Malena pulled the pointed hood over her head. "It's a little long, but it will work," she smiled. "It served me well. Now let's get you cleaned up."

When Malena went back onstage, Little Egypt was lying in the dark on the sofa in Malena's dressing room when she heard Nuluna's raucous voice ask, "Arago, have you seen Little Egypt?" She heard a muffled response, and the door swung partially open.

Sidu yelled, "No, Nuluna!" and it slammed shut. Little Egypt slumped back and let out a gasp.

After closing, as the immigrants assembled in the dining room, Malena instructed Little Egypt: "Wait here in the wings until Sidu finishes talking to them. He'll collect their money and leave. When we start out of the building, fall in behind us. No one will notice, and the immigrants won't say anything; they will be too frightened."

Little Egypt did as she was told, and waited while Sidu finished talking to the immigrants, walking among them and collecting his fee. Malena stood up and all the immigrants followed suit.

When they moved to the side door, Little Egypt fell in behind them, and the group walked out into the shadows of the street. In half an hour, they got to a wadi with three squatting stones. Malena lagged back and motioned for Little Egypt to hide behind one of the stones, whispering, "Wait here."

It was a crisp night and Little Egypt shivered as she hunkered down behind the stone. The immigrants stood beside Malena, stamped their feet and crossed their armed across their chests.

Then out of the darkness appeared a man in a woolen Moroccan djellaba—a long, loose, hooded garment with full sleeves. The hood lay on the man's back, and he wore a tarbouche on his head. After he and Malena exchanged a few words, the man motioned to the immigrants, and the little group moved off toward Morocco.

When they had begun to recede into the distance, Malena quietly called, "You can come out now." She gave Little Egypt a jug of water, and a bag of food and money. "This will get you to Tizi Ouzou," she said.

Little Egypt grabbed Malena and they hugged tightly. "Till sometime," Little Egypt whispered, then crept out into the darkness. She thought she heard Malena say something like, "Find your way, Little Egypt," but she was already busy heading back to the east, and wasn't sure she had heard anything.

† †

In 1998, when Malena's friend Kaarem knew his family would leave the hovel for good, he had felt uneasy about not telling Malena their plans, but his aunt had made him keep his silence. Algiers was no place for a Christian Berber in those days, so any thought of Malena joining them was out. Kaarem minded his aunt and, up to the day they left, said nothing of their departure. They followed roads used for centuries by their ancestors, who had for one reason or another abandoned their nomadic ways and stayed where all roads end: in civilization.

Now, more than ten years later, he had made a life for himself. He received a political science degree from the University of Algiers, then accepted a position under two diplomats: Nim Hassan and Chumie Radak. The three of them had grown close, so much that Kaarem called Hassan Nim. No one ever called Radak by his first name, but simply referred to him as Dack. From the first day he walked into their building, he could tell he impressed them and everyone else with his tan hawkish face and dark eyes exuding intelligence that added to his five foot, ten inch frame.

At first, he typed reports and filed the myriad of papers generated by Hassan and Radak. However, they soon discovered he had an analytical mind, and they put his problem-solving abilities to use, giving him an office of his own with an increase in salary to match, enough that he was able to move from his old flat near the college to an upscale condo on the *rue du Lobo.*

Not that it mattered, but he often thought of Malena. He had remained single all those years, even after college. Somehow he still felt connected to her, and would often muse, *I wonder where she is and what she's doing.* Perhaps out of respect for her memory, he avoided other women.

Hassan and Radak were grooming Kaarem to be a full-fledged diplomat. Dack frequently invited him to the seraglio where he sated a thirst for brandy and sexual exploits. Kaarem declined these offers. Citing the backlog of his political analyses with *les affaires d'état,* he stayed at his office late into the night, creeping silently along the dangerous streets to his condo.

He still considered himself a Muslim, but vehemently disapproved of the terrorism levied upon his fellow citizens by the extremists. He kept the delicate balance between religious beliefs and his position in the diplomatic service as a political necessity. He could define himself as a secularist, but to do so publicly would bring a price on his head.

One morning, as Kaarem was unlocking his office door, Dack appeared behind him and followed him in. Dack's face was ashen. "Nim's been killed," he said, shaking his head.

Kaarem collapsed into his desk chair. "My God, what happened?"

Dack paced about Kaarem's desk. "Officially, we are going to call it a random act. He was found lying on the sidewalk outside his house. He was stabbed repeatedly, apparently the victim of a thief, according to the police."

Kaarem rubbed his forehead. "I've known him two months and yet I feel like I've known him all my life."

Dack nodded. "Nim was like that." Then his voice broke. "He was on that damned sidewalk all night—his housekeeper found him this morning when she came to work." He paused, regaining his composure and becoming taller than Kaarem had ever seen him. Leaning over the desk, he peered into Kaarem's eyes. "Be careful. I suspect Kelbeau's GIA cohorts are behind the killing."

Kaarem felt a chill run down his spine, and Dack turned toward the door, muttering, "I only hope Nim's assassination wasn't the result of the oath he swore to Faberg shortly after the Evian Accord." Looking back over his shoulder, he extended his index finger, and pointed at Kaarem. "Keep this to yourself, but keep your guard up." Then he disappeared through the door.

† †

A month later, Dack stuck his head, flushed with drink, into Kaarem's office and said, "Want to join me at The Black Owl? I'm leaving." Without waiting for a response, he ducked back out.

Getting up, Kaarem followed Dack back to his office and took his jacket down from the hanger by the door. Dack turned away and extended his arms toward him, asking, "Well?"

Kaarem slid the coat onto Dack and said, "No, I have much work to do."

Dack turned around to face him again. "I suspect that someone on the inside of the diplomatic corps is talking to the radicals." Kaarem stepped back and inspected Dack to ensure his clothes were in order. "We have kept one foot in their camp, all the while looking none the wiser. Now al Qaeda has begun bombing in the streets. What I hear is that they are using the city streets as a training ground for future bombings abroad—probably in Spain."

"I'm preparing a brief covering on just that topic tonight." Kaarem felt the tightness start up between his shoulder blades, and stretched to relieve it.

"I await your pearls of wisdom." Dack patted him on the back. Then he stood up, his round face glowing in the dim light as if he had laughed too long. He turned and shuffled down the hall.

Halfway down, he yelled back, "All right, young man; don't say I didn't offer."

Kaarem ignored his comment as that of a blasé secularist, and hid his disdain for Dack's unsteady gait like that of a blind Muslim. After Dack had disappeared down the hallway, Kareem turned and locked Dack's office door.

He walked back to his office and sat at his desk, unlocking the bottom drawer and pulling out a box. A note was attached: "For Kaarem Khedda—to be opened in case of my death. Hassan."

† †

As he stumbled out to his car, Dack mused, *The affairs of the state are something of a crisis in the making.* "Or dis-affairs of the state, rather," he mumbled aloud, chuckling. *Years ago, Hassan and I made a promise to Faberg to take certain actions when the time was right. Now that Hassan is dead, is that time close at hand?*

In 1992, President Bendjedid had been ousted from power and the FIS seized control of the last strands of what might be called "government." Extremists were everywhere, stalking what remained of the old regime, killing anyone who was doing any good for Algeria.

First came the FIS; we threw them in jail; then came the GIA. Murder —no—chaos is their middle name, Dack thought to himself as he opened the car door, shuddering at the thought of the myriad of groups fighting to gain control. *And now, al Qaeda. As bad as the situation is, it could get much worse. A fundamentalist victory now would be a catastrophe. It would embolden the other extremist groups throughout the world.* That he could not allow, no matter how much the danger lurked in the shadows of the street. "The damned Chinese are probably behind it all," he said aloud, within the cover of the Peugeot.

Driving through the back streets toward The Black Owl, Dack thought of the oath he swore at Evian. *How long before the forces in France call in my card?* He still had the dagger, worth a fortune in jewels, but worth much more when used for its intended purpose.

What if I am found out by a militant mole? Should I tell Kaarem before it's too late?

He parked around the corner from The Black Owl, slipped through its stained door, and slid his ungainly frame into an easy chair.

Looking around, he thought, *Maybe I should take a woman home.* There was at least a measure of security there.

† †

On the evening of her thirtieth birthday, no one celebrated, and Malena slept at her makeup table, head down among the vials.

A big woman lies across a bed. She moans and rolls onto her back. Reaching up, she touches a bruise over her left eye. "That'll teach that son of a bitch. Crap, I'm either belting songs or men; get hurt just as bad from either performance."

She rolls onto her stomach. "Shit, woman, why can't you be like you was once? If you copying someone else's singing, you working without feeling. Without that, you ain't ever going to amount to nothing.

"I can't never sing a song the same way. Same with people. Decided one day I'd never do anything unless it meant something. Truth is, singing became a habit. Can't dance; may as well sing. Can't cry; may as well sing."

The big woman swings her torso around so she faces Malena. "Hey, girl! You got a problem with that?" Then she smiles. "No, you in the same fix."

Malena escaped the dream. She buried her face in her hands, then shook her head and raised her shoulders to shrug off the sleep before finishing her makeup.

Somehow she had made it through the last ten years without so much as a whisper of *fatma* duties. She had heard Nuluna and Sidu arguing countless times over the matter, but she had eluded the gambit. It was not that she didn't know what the bed was for, but for her, it was not for the love or the money. And since she could only muster platonic feelings for men, she just dated decent patrons when it suited her interest, to ease her isolation and loneliness. And that night after the dream, she felt very lonely and whispered, "Little Egypt."

† †

Dack found a table near the front of the lounge to watch the floor show. Malena came onstage, wearing a black wig adorned with two white flowers. The house lights went down and the crowd grew quiet. She began to sing, then to croon.

Dack thought with a start, *It must be Cinnamon Caruthers, come back to life!* The woman shimmered under the klieg lights. Red and blue light filtered through the transparent gel onto her skin. The feeling of the song crept into his mind. *It* is *her,* he thought. After the gig, she put down the mike and disappeared offstage.

The song had put him in a relaxed state, and Dack ordered another drink. After several minutes, the singer reemerged, and headed straight for his table.

"Is this seat taken?"

"Sit down. Like a drink?" Dack held up his glass to the waiter. "Was that you or Cinnamon up there?"

"What do you think?"

"I think you're beautiful, and she's dead."

"The dead sing so long as music lives." The drinks arrived, and they each took a sip. "How long have you been here?"

"Minutes, hours, days."

"We should figure out how we can while away time's passage."

"Come with me"

"To your house?"

"Yes."

She nodded, set down her drink, and excused herself.

† †

Malena found Sidu, and told him she was going out with Dack. She could see he was troubled. "What's wrong?"

"He's a diplomat and a secularist. Be careful with him."

"He seems harmless enough."

"I've heard stories. If you go, find out what you can; it could be in our interest."

"I'll do what I can." She returned to the table.

Dack had become talkative with drink; he motioned for Malena to lean closer, and she bent in. "I'm with the diplomatic service, and a vital choice has to be made," he whispered and took a sip of his drink. In a louder whisper, he said, "There's oil wells and daggers afoot."

She stopped him. "Not here; let's go."

"Oil and daggers..." He threw money on the table, and they got up and weaved their way between the other tables to the door. Outside, Dack leaned on Malena as they lurched along toward the Peugeot. She looked at him suspiciously as they piled into the car, wondering if he was fit to drive. He fired up the car and noticing her glance, said, "Not to worry; I've driven home in worse condition." He herded the black sedan toward Villa Tagarins, where General Salan used to meet with the other traitors from the 1962 rebellion.

† †

The man's entrance into the cabaret went unnoticed. He was used to making such entrances. He found a seat and ordered a drink, settling in to watch Malena sing.

After her gig, Malena walked past to his table on her way to Chumie Radak's. He watched as the fat man reached into his pocket and gave her money. He was laughing, wagging his finger back and forth. He whispered something else and laughed again. She simply looked stoic. The fat man began to tell her something else, but she put her hand up and said something. He threw some coins on the table, and they left.

The man took a sip of his anisette.

4

NEW YORK CITY

It wasn't his bladder that awakened Jean Reynard at three a.m., but the phone. "What the hell…"

"Jean?" a gruff voice asked.

"Yes, Claude? Is that you?"

"Oui, c'est moi, Jean."

"For God's sake, where are you? You sound like you're in the next room!" Reynard rubbed his eyes, listening to Claude's request, then said, "My schedule can't permit it; I'm in the middle of negotiations."

"No matter, it's urgent. Negotiations can wait," Claude said with authority. "You're booked on the red-eye to Paris. Be at JFK at six. A car will meet you at Orly and take you to the old meeting place."

"Eh bien." Reynard replaced the receiver. Half-awake, he mumbled, "Okay." He lay back down, trying to focus on a streak of light bleeding through the curtains onto the ceiling. He hated the red-eye, especially to Paris. Anyway, it was done.

Getting up, Reynard shuffled to the bathroom. He looked down into the toilet. "God, how the past catches up with you."

He made the plane with minutes to spare. When he found his seat and flounced into it, he felt rumpled, like an unmade bed. Looking down at his blue suit, he combed back his salt-and-pepper hair with his hand. He fumbled in his coat pocket for his Zippo lighter, but knew he couldn't smoke. *Why am I wearing this damned suit?* Reynard let go of the lighter, but his hand lingered in the pocket. He flashed back to dangerous times in Indochina and Algeria, the secret meetings and resultant questionable acts he wanted to forget. He thought he had distanced himself from the Service. *You're never completely out.*

He thought about Claude—that was what he called himself. He had been in those same places with Reynard. Reynard mused on their cleverness: the two of them had financed the SDECE's mission, *Hamlet,* with drug sales. He cringed even while he admired his own cunning. It had been a montage of deception; the agency conducted a false investigation to ferret out drug dealers, while sanctioning and promoting the production and sale of heroin to young French soldiers, who melted it down and filled their cigarettes with the distillate. *We created an army of addicts in order to finance our operations.*

Reynard shook his head. He needed something to fall back on. *What's Claude up to now?* He tried to remember their last project, but his mind was blank. *Did Claude support me, or was I left out in the cold? If so, it wouldn't have been the first time—is this to be the next?*

The airplane plunked down at Orly Airport at eight in the morning. After clearing customs, Reynard shouldered his bag and made his way out of the terminal into a crisp April morning. He spied a black SUV waiting at the curb.

He opened the door and said, "Reynard," then got in. The driver steered the Peugeot onto Route Nationale 7 to avenue de Fontainebleau and made his way to the rue des Deux Îles, crossing the bridge on to Île Saint-Louis.

Reynard studied his driver. The man wore a black pullover sweater. About Reynard's height, curly black hair, plain features. *Something of myself fifteen years ago,* Reynard thought.

After a couple more turns, they pulled up in front of the Hôtel des Deux Îles. "Go inside and wait," the driver said.

Reynard entered the hotel, went to the restaurant, and ordered a table in the back. Once he was seated, the waiter brought coffee. Claude, a tall, white-haired man wearing a dark blue suit, slid through the front door.

"There you are. I see you remembered," he said as he drew near, reaching out and tugging at Reynard's lapel.

"Perhaps too old a lizard to change my stripes." said Reynard, standing up. They hugged, patting each other's back.

Claude frowned. "Zebras have stripes! Lizards...though in that regard, I think you are a chameleon."

"Here you go, about to dazzle me with that magnificent colloquy of yours, verbal remnants from those midday teas you hosted at the HQ. After the shakeup in 1982, the agency changed its name—what's it called now?"

Claude massaged the soft redness around his neck, saying, "*Direction générale de la sécurité extérieure*—DGSE."

Reynard continued, "All those infinitely long reception lines. The banality of it all!"

"You never understood," said Claude, scratching furiously at his neck, which was turning a deeper shade.

Reynard pressed the attack: "Those charades under the guise of official protocol. But I do miss the brandy."

Claude kept scratching. "And while we sniffed brandy at those starchy ceremonies, they were unleashing new whirlwinds throughout your world." Claude sat down, and Reynard followed. "Life-shattering incidents called history. How many began? How many ended? You *are* an old lizard—and I'm glad you came."

Reynard was aware the meeting was more of a mandate than an invitation. *The mission is open and I'm being sucked into it, whether I like it or not.* "So...here we are together once again to face a harsh test..."

"I remember that line. *De Gaulle et Algérie, n'est pas?*"

"There is nothing either good or bad, but thinking makes it so, but then you are full of slogans—what's the new one?"

"*D'accord*: 'In every place where necessity makes law.' The Service remains vital only so long as we leave the morality up to the philosophers, eh?"

"So what are we talking about, this time?"

"We need an operative in the Algerian oil field."

"Are the Algerians defaulting on their royalty payments?"

"We suspect the extremists who are killing businessmen, journalists, and *le gendarmerie* are stealing the royalty money to finance their *jihad* against us."

"So you need someone to steal it back, *n'est pas?*" Reynard asked cautiously.

"More importantly, our agents. The oil company itself lost one of the high-ranking members. I can't tell you how much the Service wants to find out who's doing the killing—but there's more at stake than that."

"I'm in show business now—how can I help?"

"Precisely, Jean. You're in show business, and that's why I'm here. The Service knows about your deal with the Americans to do the propaganda film in Algiers. You're in the right place at exactly the right time..."

"Wrong time, don't you mean," Reynard interrupted.

Claude continued as if he had not heard, "...to create a documentary on the atrocities in Algeria, pointing out that things have worsened since the takeover in 1962."

"My God, Claude, that's an understatement."

"There's more at stake than what has happened in Algeria," Claude said. He picked up a table knife and began turning it over and over in his hand, catching the overhead light and shining the reflection first at his own face, then at Reynard's, and then back again. "France is at a crossroads: we're seeing the dawn of a new European economy and the growth of the euro against the dollar. The United States has held the reins as the prime economic power for long enough." Claude flipped the knife and its reflection fell back on Reynard's face. "Reins that should have belonged to France following World War II. But there was the U.S., at the height of its military strength, yet still in the infancy of its diplomacy." Claude laid the knife down beside his empty bread plate and gave Reynard a straight look. "Now the Americans are embroiled in a battle of attrition in Iraq, and with their new president's sentiments and trouble brewing in Afghanistan, we believe they'll pull their troops and redeploy. It's only a matter of time."

The clinking of the knife caught the attention of the waiter, who came over and asked, "Are you going to order, or would you just like more bread?" Claude cast him a dirty look and he shrugged and left.

Reynard shifted forward in his chair. "Well, France pulled out of Algeria, leaving the fundamentalists to their own devices there—and just regard that bloodbath." Claude blanched, but said nothing.

They moved on to discuss the sore issue of the petroleum holdings stolen by the National Liberation Front when they nationalized the Maghreb's oil fields in 1971. Large holdings represented billions of francs stolen in the scant eight years following the Evian Accord. Petroleum flowing in Algeria flowed from a wound in the ground that belonged to France, and she wanted it back. The line that joined North Africa and Europe had become a vital link for France once the euro was involved.

"Big money kept those channels open all those years," Reynard said.

"Old money. And it's offering considerable reward to the Service to regain control."

"You're talking about insurgency then."

"Another way."

"Infiltration?"

"C'est ça," Claude told him. "That is where your documentary comes in. Tell the world how France has reformed from her colonial days. How she champions human rights, and how the present government in Algeria is indirectly killing a hundred thousand people, Arabs and Berbers alike, all because they cannot rule themselves in an honorable way. I'm talking about live shots here, Jean."

"For God's sake man, humans are being disemboweled in the streets of Algiers for being the wrong race. Women are killed just for not wearing a veil. And now the bombings in the street. What more do you need to know?"

"Just a minute, Jean, remember to whom you are speaking."

"I know who I'm talking to. The expert on the subject of Algeria. Now you want me to go back and tell your story, this time through the lens of the camera." Reynard's voice had risen to a frantic whisper, not so loud as to be heard over the din in the restaurant, but forceful enough to get his point across. "Cameras need voices—the voice of the people! What people do we have? Right here, right now, in France, we shutter out the Algerians and their kids. What about their chances?"

Undaunted, Claude told Reynard that only a handful knew what went on behind the scenes of the negotiations at Evian, and of two envoys, the real players in a position to keep oil flowing to France once the royalty payments had stopped.

Reynard looked puzzled. "Where do the envoys fit in?"

"We believe they hold the key to the location of a secret valve."

"A valve?"

"Yes. One that, when turned on, will bypass the Algerians' meters, and oil will flow unimpeded to France through a dedicated spur. There is another possibility outlined in the brief I'll give you, but this is our best guess."

"But who financed such an undertaking?" Reynard persisted.

"I don't need to remind you that the real balance of power in the world lies within the pages of a well-oiled checkbook."

"I quite agree...but whoever speaks the language speaks for them."

"That's what you're going to do—speak for them. But it's equally important that you find out who is targeted by the Algerian government, whose head is on the chopping block."

"My dear Claude, I'm in the film business, not the spy business."

"What if I told you that the film was guaranteed to be a success at Cannes? That wouldn't look too bad on your list of credits."

"But I'm in the middle of the American deal—what about them?"

"We'll buffer the Americans through diplomatic channels."

"I'm talking about the private concerns."

"We'll pay them off."

"When would we start?"

"We would like you to be on location June 14."

Reynard slumped back in his chair in silence for a full minute, then sputtered, "Truth is stranger than fiction! We'll probably be killed at the outset."

"What we are thinking is that you will organize a ruse, like we did in Indochina—the play-within-the-play."

"Hamlet?"

"Yes." Claude laid out the strategy with utter simplicity. He told Reynard to continue negotiations with the Americans to do a documentary on how well United States dollars were being spent in Algeria, just as before. "Go to Algiers, do the film, then give it to France, who becomes the heroine to international fancies.

"There will be two contacts. An operative called Sidu, who runs a cabaret as a front, will help you with the production. The other is in deep cover—the Jeweler. Sidu gets intelligence and gives it to a runner, who buries it in a safe place near the city. The Jeweler digs it up, screens the information, and gets it to us. Sidu will be your first point of contact. Go from there. He will arrange security and put you in touch with the envoys.

"Well, Claude, who are these envoys?"

"That's where your detective work comes in." Claude leaned closer to Reynard. "We know who the players are. Once you start the production, you'll launch into the second phase of the plan—to contact the envoys and get them to tell you where the valve is located—then turn it on."

Reynard shook his head in disbelief, saying, "It comes down to one valve."

"Right. Once you're in, we will help all we can, but success depends on finding the envoys. We're in hopes you can get some intelligence before you deploy to Algiers. If you're not successful with the attempt here, by the time you get on station the Jeweler may have shed some light as to whom and where they are. Once you accomplish the second phase, get out quickly."

"I know the Jeweler—good with explosives. He was in Indochina from the outset...and you say these nameless envoys are those from the Evian conference?" Reynard asked. "Judas, Claude, how can you not know their identities?"

"We did have them, but a hacker broke into the computer and that history was stolen. When we repaired the computer, the information was gone. Because of the level of classification, we were not allowed to make backup files."

"But I don't understand. If you have two people already there, why go through the trouble—and risk—of planting more people in such a dangerous place?"

Claude shifted uncomfortably. "Well, we had three. We were getting *communiqués* from the Jeweler, saying he was close to getting names when his contact disappeared—an informant we think, who possibly knew the identities of the of the envoys, but something happened to him. The Jeweler transmitted that the Algerian Security may have got wind of the company's plan. We fear the agent was killed. As you can see, it's urgent to get in and sort things out."

"Someone must know..."

"That's where your local intelligence gathering comes in. There is a key player who dates back to Evian and before. He owned many of the oil wells in Algeria and was instrumental in the construction of the secret valve and spur oil line. As a final part of his plan, he arranged a meeting at his castle across the lake, in Lausanne. There were five delegates who went to Evian, but only two who met alone with the old man."

"A rather big wager to make on two foreign diplomats," Reynard mused.

"Maybe so, but he was in the oil business and used to taking such risks."

"Who is this man?"

"Gustav Faberg."

"So we contact him?"

Claude leans back in his seat. "There's the problem. He's dead."

"Someone at headquarters must know."

"Too much time has passed. All the agents who were involved are either dead or missing."

"Then who?"

"That's what I'm getting at. Gustav had a daughter. She was there at the time of the meeting. Be careful. We have Algerian agents in the company. We don't want be responsible for her death. Just the same, we must take some risk. I want you to go to Faberg Castle at Lake Geneva."

"What's her name?"

"Anna. And there's another point of contact: Lamar Talka, a former cinematographer of yours. He lives in Lausanne."

"What's his connection to Anna?"

"He's married to her."

5

THE WEDDING RITE: DAY TWO

A bride stretches out her left foot, holding it just over the bread; a knife cleaves a groove around her foot, leaving an outline in the dough. She removes her foot and the knife cuts into the outline, making a smaller piece of bread in the shape of her foot, to be devoured by the groom later. The bridal procession arrives at the edge of the village to a small pile of rocks. It circles the pile of small white stones three times.

The night bore through the arch of the veranda into the living room where Malena lay naked under the comforter, having deposited Dack into his own bed. She felt the radiation from her body rise over the sofa and mix with the humid air. She ignored this discomfort as she had ignored the heat rising under her dress from the road to Algiers. She endured it because she believed in the promise of the inevitable parting, not so much from the discomfort but from necessity.

She heard Dack moving around in the next room, perhaps going to the bathroom. Malena's mind drifted: *When I dream, sometimes I wish I would wake up, so it would be real, the here and now. Sometimes when I'm awake, I wish to dream. In dreams, I see myself as different people. I must be dreaming now, because I'm looking at myself, and I'm another person.*

Suddenly awake, she opened her eyes wide, realizing a scream had awakened her. Getting up, she pulled on a robe and rushed into the bathroom to find Dack lying facedown on the floor, his body twitching in a pool of blood.

How can this be? How can I be outside my own body? Am I awake now? Am I awake! But she was awake.

She stooped down. "Dack!" she called, and pulled up hard on his arm; his rotund torso sloshed over on its back. His lips began to move; he was still alive. Malena leaned down to listen.

He pulled himself to the bathroom doorway and pointed to the coffee table in the living room, saying, "There…go there…"

"Go there? You want me to write something?"

He shook his head. "There. Lift the rug beneath…safe. Turn… three, thirty, twenty-seven…right, left, right…skip the middle once…" He fell back and muttered, "*poignard…poignard…*"

Malena ran to the table and slid it roughly to one side, then whipped back the Oriental rug. She saw nothing but ceramic tile. "There's nothing here!"

Dack rose up a little with a great effort. "Lift it…lift the tile."

Malena felt along the edges of the tiles; one felt deeper, with no grout. She dug her fingernails under its sides, and pulled up. Beneath she found the safe. "Three, thirty, twenty-seven," she repeated, and spun the dial right until the three was under the index. "*Skip the middle*"—*what does that mean?* She tried spinning the dial past the thirty, stopping it at the index the second time. *I hope that's right,* she thought, then spun it back to the right again, stopping at twenty-seven. She tried the handle next to the dial, and it yielded as steel pins retracted into the bowels of the door. She pulled the door open.

Inside, Malena found a wooden box, and pulled it out into the light. Its wood exuded a pungent odor, and two white elephants were inlaid on the top. "I found it," she shouted, running back to Dack.

"Kaarem…worked for another…Hassan. Murdered last month… they found nothing…Kaarem may have what they were looking for…find him…find the truth…"

"I don't understand; Kaarem who?"

Dack nods, gasping, "He...knows...Khedda knows."

My God, she thought, *is he saying "Kaarem Khedda"?* "Kaarem Khedda—where can I find him?"

"Market...small street...rue du Lobo, number twenty-one...find him."

"What truth?" she asked. He stared straight at her without blinking. "What truth?" she yelled, shaking him. Nothing. "What truth?" Malena was breathing as hard as if she had just sprinted down some back street; she felt light-headed. She rubbed her hands together but she couldn't feel them.

She opened the box and withdrew its contents. She held the poniard as if she were going to use it. She moved over to the lamp by the table and rolled the instrument back and forth; the jewels in the hilt caught the rays from the bulb, splitting the spectrum into its many colors.

She placed the dagger back in the box. *Whoever killed Dack might still be lurking about,* she realized with a shudder, glancing into the next room. She picked up the box and found her way to the door.

Outside, she dodged a patrol, fading into the shadows. She stroked the wooden box hidden in her robe. *My ticket to France,* she thought.

Every now and again, between the buildings, she saw a faint glow from the east. *It's morning.* She finally came upon the street where she and Dack had staggered to his black Peugeot a few hours before. She slipped through the doors of The Black Owl.

Sidu was sitting at one of the tables. "You're late."

"It's just morning—you said, 'by morning.'"

"What did you learn?"

"Not much. The fat man is dead."

"What?"

"Dead. I can't make it any plainer."

"What did you do?"

"I took him home, isn't that what you wanted?"

"I didn't want him dead. What happened?"

"He got up and went into the other room."

"That's all?"

"No, not all—after a while I heard him scream, and I found him dead."

"Nuluna tells me he was very talkative when he was here just before you two left. What did he tell you?"

"Nothing."

"You're lying."

"I've told you what happened—no more, no less."

Sidu got up from his chair and towered over her. "You bitch. You're lying!" he shouted, and slapped her across the mouth for emphasis, knocking her to the floor.

"You bastard! What are you, anyway? You're not Arab, Berber, or French. What are you, besides a bully?"

Sidu softened. "You should have been more careful." He tried to help her up, but she shrugged him away. "Can't you understand that I'm just trying to protect our interests?"

Malena wiped her mouth. "I only see that I am bleeding."

"I'm sorry I hit you, but it was for your own good. Besides, I told you before, don't go out without your veil."

"I hate the veil—it's a sign of ownership, and nobody owns me."

"Think not? Wear the veil for your own sake then."

"Let me see if I understand what's happening. If I go unveiled, the fundamentalists will kill me for disrespect. But if I am caught wearing it by the secularist patrols, I'm arrested and killed for knuckling under to the fundamentalists."

"You're talking nonsense; just carry it with you."

"That's something on which we both agree. It *is* nonsense."

"Wear it."

"I'll wear it—at night, when no one can see it." They were like the young lions who spar on the African beaches for position; the fight was quickly over.

He told her the Americans were coming to town to do a documentary. "There may be an acting part in it for you."

"How is it possible?" she wondered. "The fundamentalists have created a *fatwa* to kill all foreigners."

"I have arranged for a secure place, Hôtel Fleur de l'Âge on the quay, and an armed security guard. The documentary is about how well Algeria is spending U.S. dollars. Where there's oil, there you will find the Americans. Who knows—maybe they can grease the tracks for you all the way to Paris."

"Sounds dangerous."

"These are dangerous times, but there could be big money in this. Stick with me and you will become rich."

"What choice do I have?" *I still have the poniard, you bastard.*

"You don't. Accept your opulent fate." They both laughed, and then Sidu became serious again. "Try out for a part—you're good enough. You will land it."

Malena nodded, remembering her audition with him years ago.

She finishes scrubbing the floor, while humming a tune from Cinnamon Caruthers's album.

"You know American songs," he says.

"I know some."

"Sing one for me."

Malena stands, smoothes out her soiled dress and pushes back her auburn hair, then sings.

† †

Reynard returned to his office that night. He closed the door and opened his briefcase, removing the large double-sealed manila envelope Claude had slid over to him. When he opened it, he found a smaller envelope inside, stamped *TOP SECRET.* Slicing it open, he removed a brief, summarizing Gustav Faberg's plan to reclaim the oil reserves in Algiers:

Faberg hedged his investment by bribing two Algerian envoys to facilitate the continued flow of crude back to France, should the secularist government nationalize the oil and gas fields. When the Algerians reneged on the royalties it had agreed to pay through a state-owned holding company called Saladin, Faberg's envoys would move into action.

Faberg invited each envoy to the castle at Lake Geneva to cut

A DEAL, WHICH INCLUDED MONEY DEPOSITED IN TRUST AT A SWISS BANK FOR FINAL PAYMENT WHEN THE DEAL WAS COMPLETE. THEN, TO EACH ENVOY FABERG PRESENTED A JEWEL-ENCRUSTED DAGGER. THEY WERE INTENDED TO GUARANTEE LOYALTY.

Reynard put down the report and pulled a cigarette from the pack on the desk. He licked the cigarette tip, which was not filtered, and lit it with the Zippo he had flipped open with his other hand.

Old Gustav was smart in giving daggers. Nothing better for them to swear upon. He picked up the papers again.

HOW THE ENVOYS WOULD AFFECT THE OIL FLOW TO FRANCE REMAINS UNCLEAR. HERE IS OUR THEORY: A PIPELINE ALREADY EXISTS, AND THE ENVOYS KNOW WHERE IT IS AND HOW TO TURN IT ON, TO START THE OIL BYPASSING THE EXISTING METERING SYSTEM. THE WELL THE SPUR PIPELINE IS LINKED TO WOULD DICTATE THE QUALITY OF THE CRUDE AND THE PRESSURE AT WHICH IT WOULD TRANSFER.

Reynard blew a couple of smoke rings. He took another drag on his cigarette and rubbed his hair. *Maybe there is some sort of code associated with the daggers themselves. When the time is right, the envoys produce the daggers to our agent in charge of Messouda Drilling and decipher the codes. The combined code would lead them to a high-pressure valve's burial spot, and they could simply turn it on.*

Oil would flow to France through a secret spur off the main pipeline connecting Africa to Europe. Once the pressure came up, a meter on the European side would sense it and send off the euros to Faberg Industries and to the Faberg receiving station in France. Since their meter would not be on the secret spur, Saladin would be none the wiser. Reynard nodded, and read on.

THE AGENCY BELIEVES THE DAGGER PRESENTATIONS AND OATHS DID TAKE PLACE. UNFORTUNATELY, BEFORE THE REMAINDER OF THE PLAN COULD BE ACTIVATED, ONE OF THE OPERATIVES WORKING FOR MESSOUDA DRILLING was found out by Algerian security and eliminated. Then the other operatives in the company were rounded up and killed or simply vanished; the company eventually evaporated.

As part of your cover, enlist the services of Lamar Talka, married to Anna Faberg, and offer him a job filming the documentary.

Reynard was to use the Talka relationship to gain access to Anna, who may have held the key to the envoys' identities.

The brief summed it up at the end:

The mission is to locate the envoys, and thereby the two daggers. We believe the daggers may have relevance to the valve's location, in the event the envoys do not.

Reynard returned the papers to the envelopes and locked them in his briefcase. He leaned his head back and thought about the rest of Claude's oral brief:

"We want you to accept for your principle narrator an actor here in Paris, Nicole Soutane. She was born in Tunisia, but moved to France after her mother was killed and her father sent to prison."

"Why her, does she speak—is it Berber?"

"No, but she's half Berber."

"What else?"

"Joseph Soutane, her father, was a dissenter in Toulon. During the Algerian Revolution he ran an underground pro-independence Algerian newspaper. Later Joseph was imprisoned by the Tunisians for his subversive activities. Nicole's mother aided Algerian guerrillas in a border town, and was killed in one of the French air raids over the area. When Nicole came of age, she left for Paris and never returned."

"If her father's a dissenter, how do we know she can be trusted?"

"We did the usual background check, and we've been watching her movements."

"And..."

"And she's just a struggling actor."

"*If* she's to be trusted."

"Post a job offering and we'll make sure her agent gets it first. You'll be looking for someone to portray a reporter for a documentary 'to be shot on location.' We won't tell the actors where that is." Claude scooted a little closer to Reynard. "Do you see the beauty of it, Jean? Can you produce a script that can be acted out for the Americans, but is to benefit the French?"

"I have a good writer, Philippe Dupont."

"Good; he's done research there, I am told. Writing a book about it—not necessarily favorable to France. We should keep an eye on monsieur Dupont."

"He'll do what needs to be done."

"Tell everyone you've landed a plush contract with the Americans. Tell your writer only what he needs to know to furnish the script. We provide some stock footage of attacks in surrounding cities. Sidu will arrange the other stuff. You have to trust him."

"I trust no one," Reynard muttered.

Claude continued, "We'll provide the cameraman. All you have to do is provide the scripting and production. You'll set up in an old French hotel at the edge of town." Claude searched Reynard's face and added, "Totally secure."

"That's too easy. And this—struggling actor—what does she look like?"

"Half-Berber…forties, good-looking. Better than that, she has a presence—what do you call it—'X factor'?"

"That's what they call it," replied Reynard.

"This documentary—"

"The universe…"

"Your avant-garde stuff?"

"Just next door. And let me tell you something my friend: 'next door' isn't all that easy. The industry is specialized. What I do, what you call the 'avant-garde stuff,' is the documentary; that's something I know about," Reynard asserted.

"Isn't avant-garde nothing but an extreme aspect of truth?"

"A perspective of the present," Reynard said. "What's in front of the camera."

"Where's that?" Claude began scratching at his neck.

"Somewhere between the past and future—we lay it at your feet."

Claude stretched his neck, trying to shrink away from the starchy collar. "Well...yes...there you have it. Even a documentary can be at the front lines of cinema."

"Everything we have ever done together, Claude, was extreme. It'll be hard to maneuver these secularists to our way of thinking though."

"Greed, Reynard, will be our ally. Having control of the oil fields since 1971 has made wealthy men out of some of them. We cut a deal—in the event of a turnover to France, they will become even wealthier. You'll be well-compensated as well, I assure you."

"I'm not assured of anything. And one other thing: how do we physically turn on the valve? It must be huge."

"To be sure, and it's a ways beneath the surface. But it's hydraulically opened, by way of a pump that is quite near to the surface in a concrete box, much like that which contains the water shutoff to a house. There's a crank handle inside with the pump. One simply has to pry open the lid, insert the handle into the pump, and turn it until it stops. Then the valve opens."

"That does make it easier, but we haven't discussed terms."

Claude handed Reynard a dossier. "I can tell you there's big money in this. Your award at Cannes won't hurt either."

"I hope so, my friend, I hope so."

Reynard started with a phone call to his travel agent, for arrangements to get to Lake Geneva. He looked forward to seeing Talka and meeting Anna there. Not only from what he had read in the dossier, but from her photograph, he thought Anna was a woman to be savored. *A woman like that—what if* I *had married her?* he wondered. *Ah, I would have only hurt her one way or another.*

He glanced down at the list of players, and picked up the phone. Nicole's profile was even more fascinating. Born in Tunisia, educated in Paris. An actor, a solid character. He studied her photograph. She jumped off the glossy print with her pale blue eyes and a tall, slender build. Her blonde hair was pushed back to reveal a high forehead, and knotted into a ponytail in the back. Her face was amazingly youthful, with a straight-bridged nose. He put the phone down again. *What a presence! Claude was right; she has the X factor. Good at language—that should come in handy. No particular political ties—thank God. I don't need an agenda on the shoot.*

6

Évian

Sonja was making love with him for the second time, and it was only two in the afternoon. Lamar Talka was a man of fifty-two with a twenty-four-year-old's sex drive. But she loved him, and had been with him for two years.

He arched his back and uttered a loud cry, which could probably be heard down in the lobby, but not as far away as the street in front of the hotel.

He relaxed and she slid her body up and nestled her head next to his. "I love you, darling."

"So do I."

Sonja lifted her head and shook her blond curls. "What? Love yourself?"

"But of course, though you as well," he laughed.

"Better," she said, and laid her head back down. "I'm hungry!" she pleaded.

"I suppose I could nibble on something."

"Darling, you have nibbled, but I'm thinking of food."

"That's what I was talking about. Sonja, wherever do you get these strange ideas?"

"From you, *mon chéri.*"

"You want more then."

"Not now, I'm famished. Please, call room service."

"It was all a jest." he assured her.

"Come on Lamar, I *am* hungry!"

"Okay, call room service."

Sonja rolled closer and kissed him on the mouth. "I knew you'd see it my way." She rolled back the other way and picked up the telephone.

Talka looked at his Rolex. "*Merde!* Sorry darling, I must go; I have a train to meet." He got up, dressed, and then raced down to his convertible parked at the curb below.

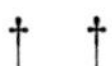

Reynard caught the evening train connecting to Lake Geneva. The train arrived at the station precisely at *14h,* and Talka was there waiting for him.

Talka was the outdoors type, and sported a tan. Reynard could see he had aged, but with his casual dress and crop of copper-colored hair, he somehow seemed even more alive now than he did fifteen years ago. By comparison, Reynard knew he was pale white and wore dark circles beneath his light brown eyes; he cringed.

It was clear day, but Reynard took little notice of the beauty on the twenty-minute drive to Lausanne and Faberg Castle; he was busy planning his approach, as he had not seen Talka in ten years. Reynard glanced over at him as he skillfully wheeled his convertible over the two-lane road. *How has he changed? Does he have enough of* l'aventurier *left in him for the project?*

Talka glanced over. "Not bad, eh?" and ran his hand over his hair, which in places stood on end in the air flow.

"You're a regular Fangio, old man." Reynard arched his shoulders back. He felt the strain of uncertainty creeping up between his shoulder blades. The stretch was one way to cope with the old, familiar pain. He suddenly felt certain Talka would go along with it.

The late afternoon sunlight crept in the castle windows, warming Anna as she leaned against the great room window sill. She was painfully aware of Lamar's whereabouts—with Sonja at Hôtel

Évian on the opposite bank. The last of her teatime friends had departed, and Anna clinked her cup down onto the bone saucer, making a noise like a violin's E.

She walked to the sofa and sat, pulling her left leg up beneath her bottom. With her dress spread over the knot of her legs like a tablecloth, she gazed out the oriel onto Lake Geneva. The fading sun on the water reminded her of Italy, and she leaned back and closed her eyes.

It's 1966. She's married to an American Navy flier in Naples, but is seeing another American Navy pilot, Brad, in Rome. Brad's credo is, "Fly, make love, and drink—not necessarily in that order." He is twenty-five, and she is thirty.

Opening her eyes, Anna thought, *God, we were great in bed together.* She shivered at the thought of it. *Where is he? Where's the touch of him now?* She rubbed her eyes and looked out onto the lake. The sun was low, and its reflection radiated through the great room's oriel window like a welder's torch. Anna allowed herself to slip back into the past.

Brad's will-o'-the-wisp ways are starting to prevent their relationship from traveling any further than her bed. He discounts things she cherishes: poetry, art, and la saveur *for life itself. These are the things she brings along whenever she makes for Rome because life at the lake has become intolerable. And these are things Brad doesn't understand, and therefore ignores.*

When Anna recites the poems she has written on the insistence of their love, he listens but does not respond. In moments like this, her love turns to hatred. He is insensitive to poetry and the fire it brings, its small word islands that would have been theirs to keep, to beach their boat on. Bright rhymes, whiting out life's details, encircling them as the sun comes around and the wind changes direction.

The two suns she saw when she closed her eyes, as the setting sun blinded her now.

Even if he didn't get what she was saying, they enjoyed life in those evenings at her family's hotel in Rome. Even though their relationship swirled about a failed marriage to another pilot, it was something they didn't discuss.

There was always something breakable about him. How could she have helped? He was a man who needed women. He cried out his need, but she could not define it beyond the bed. This knowledge Anna now held was that which comes with age and pain, after experience goes bad. Experience holds some good despite the pain; one only has to survive it to benefit.

Anna sighed and pictured her last night with him in Rome.

They lie in bed in her suite in the hotel, having just made mad love. Caught up in the emotion, she recites a poem she had written about absolute love. A lengthy discussion somehow ensues about parallel universes, killing the shared moment.

She bristles and tells him something like, "All of us move through our own universe in our own idioms; the wine gets lost…"

When he yells, "What lost wine?" she realizes it's over.

The sun had set and the sky turned mauve. Anna saw the pine trees above Evian move furtively up the arête, cutting a jagged edge into the blue horizon, marching up into the darkness. Lights from the chalets flickered in the forest like those on the castle's Christmas tree.

Sometimes as a child, when no one was looking, Anna would scoop the ashes of winter oak from the hearth, creep off to her bedroom, and spread them beneath her bed.

In the evening, she was always in for a letdown. She uncrossed her legs and stood erect, heaved, "Nothing lasts," and left the room.

The morning sun cast long shadows across the still lake. Talka sat across from Anna on the garden patio where they customarily took their breakfast. He peered over the newspaper at her. "I picked up a friend from the train station this morning; he's here now."

"For what?"

"A visit."

"A visit. Why?"

"He'll stay a few days."

"Where is he now?"

"In the south wing. Is that okay?"

"Wherever you like—what difference does it make now?"

"None whatsoever. Tell Charles."

"You tell Charles," she said with an edge reserved for him, and went back to reading her section of the newspaper.

As if on cue, Charles, the head butler, led Reynard from the huge arching entry door to where the couple sat. Talka jumped up and approached them. "There you are, old man," he said, shaking hands with Reynard. "Have you had coffee?"

"Yes, Charles bought me something"

"Great. I'd like to show you around."

Reynard shot a glance at Anna, who returned his look with a poker face, then shook out her paper and went back to reading it. "Uh—sure, I'd love to see the place."

Talka showed Reynard the Faberg grounds. The whole time it felt like they were playing some kind of cat and mouse game, but near dinnertime Reynard finally told him what was on his mind, describing a film project.

"With your talent and eye, Lamar, you're the man I need. With your thirst for danger, I don't have to worry about timidity."

"I would like to show you the garage." Talka knew what Reynard proposed probably hid some other intrigue. He saw it in his face, and read it between the lines. The two men walked along the path leading toward what used to be a large stable.

Going through the door, they ended up in a full-scale machine shop. Talka showed Reynard around, saying, "Anna has a fondness for old cars. Can't get spares for some of them anymore, so we mill them out here."

Reynard stopped to take a last look as they walked back toward the door. "I'm impressed."

Talka dropped his smile. "What the hell are you really getting me into?"

"There is some local stuff to help with the expenses, that's all."

Reynard said, and stepped through the door. Talka followed and shut the door behind them. "Let's talk about genre," Reynard continued. "I want to do a film on location in Algiers that brings the audience out of their seats and onto their knees."

"Do it without dialogue then. With all that we have to work with in Algiers, I can do what you are thinking in short order."

Reynard shifted his weight. "I promised Philippe he would have a say in this. But we can shoot our footage raw right up to Camus's little chamber of horrors: *Theatre of the Absurd* with a minimum of dialogue."

"Camus, eh? Let me tell you something: I never had any time for that guy, or Sartre, or any of those other existentialist bastards and their abstractions of life."

"There's the rub. It's the abstractions that people fall into. According to Philippe, Camus says people opt out of reality by side-stepping into abstraction: war is no longer horribly real. And that's a human condition the wrong people can use to rally the citizens around their agendas."

"That's a lot of bull. I can put onto film more horror than anyone is truly capable of—without a word of dialogue."

"People begin immediate rationalization from the time it starts."

"I don't believe that," Talka insisted. "They just go into shock. Show them someone getting their head lopped off, and they feel the sword going through their own skin. They feel the warm blood run down their throats, and the numbness that comes with death.

"They shut it out."

"Jean: imagine sliding down a banister and it suddenly turns into a razor blade—there you go. No abstraction, the scene is shuttered closed; the mind simply opts out of the carnage."

"Well, we're getting nowhere. Are you in or out?"

"How much control do I have over what's coming into the camera?"

"You can shoot whatever truth is out there on the street and I won't water it down or spin it into something else. That I can promise."

Talka paused, then asked, "And whatever else you're up to won't interfere with what I'm filming?"

"You have my word."

Talka trusted Reynard, and knew he had come to invite him into a vital piece of filming, so thought, *Be damned whatever else the trip to Algiers will be. What's the worst that can happen?* He couldn't think of a solid reason not to go, not even Sonja. "Okay, count me in," he replied with a final certainty.

Eventually Talka escorted Reynard back to the castle, saying, "You must meet my Sonja sometime."

"No thanks, my friend. One woman at a time is quite enough, and we have Anna."

Talka and Reynard entered the dining room, where a formal service had been set. Anna stood at the far end of the table, dressed in a full-length satin dress. Reynard thought, *Indeed, a princess in the castle.*

Talka stretched his arms out first to her, then to Reynard. "Anna, here we are: Jean Reynard, my old comrade-in-arms and best film producer present. Jean, let's toast the lady of the house: Anna."

Reynard picked up his glass and eyed Talka. *He's mocking me!*

Talka smiled broadly, with a *That's right!* look. They clinked glasses, saluted Anna, and drank.

Anna made a slight bow and extended her hand. "Now that's what I call a proper introduction."

Reynard walked past the six empty chairs that separated them, and took her hand, kissing it and saying, "I've heard many splendid things about you, Anna."

Anna pulled her hand away, and cast a sour look toward Talka. "I'm sure you have."

"No, really—splendid things." Reynard retraced his steps along the table, gazing at the maze of plates, silver, and crystal on the table, looking for his place.

"Sit wherever you like, Monsieur Reynard; they're all the same," said Anna.

Reynard selected a chair halfway between Anna and Talka, who had already seated themselves at opposite ends of the table. "Please call me Jean," he said, pulling out the chair. Its legs screeched along the floor.

Charles and two other butlers came through the arched doorway leading from the kitchen, bearing large serving dishes. Reynard gazed at the food and felt ill. He was torn in two. He wanted to solicit Talka for the project, but felt inexorably drawn to Anna, wanting to make love to her. He gulped down the food set before him.

"You like it then?" asked Talka, on the verge of a laugh.

Reynard tried to answer, but his mouth was still full. He simply swung his steak knife in a circle and nodded. The food was trying to come up; he dropped his silverware with a clank against his dish, and covered his mouth with his napkin.

"Are you all right?" inquired Anna.

He nodded again and managed to squeeze, "Bien," between the rebelling morsels. After that things seemed to settle down, but the conversation was unpleasant at best; worst of all were Lamar's constant sexual innuendos, which Anna and Reynard ignored.

After dinner, Talka excused himself to "run an errand." Anna and Reynard went to the great room to view the sunset. As they entered, Anna smiled and hooked her arm in his. "I come here in the evening and sit on the divan." She turned to Reynard, and said, "Sit with me awhile," gesturing to the sofa. Charles brought in two aperitifs, set them on the coffee table and departed.

Reynard threw his drink back like it was a shot of whiskey he didn't really want to taste. Anna looked amused and did the same. "So that's the way it's done," she said, leaning over and pressing a button. Charles appeared in the doorway, still holding the tray with the bottle on it. "Quite so, Charles, bring it here and leave it." Charles brought the tray around and set it firmly on the coffee table with a slight sniff. Anna looked disdainful. "That's all, Charles, thank you."

After slugging back several more drinks, Anna inching toward Reynard with each slug, she murmured, "Tell me, Monsieur Reynard, why do you come here?"

Reynard uncrossed his legs and turned toward her, allowing his knee to touch hers. "Why don't you call me Jean?"

"Jean," she responded, pressing her knee back against his ever so slightly, "Why *do* you come here?"

"To, uh, see...to see if Lamar is interested in a project."

"Jean, shame on you—really," she said slackening the pressure. She picked up her glass and sucked out the remaining liquid, then, feigning an inquisitive stare out the oriel, said, "'Splendid things'?"

Reynard picked up his glass and emptied it. He turned toward her again, this time pressing his knee hard against hers.

She looked back at him coyly. "What are you doing with my knee, Jean?"

Reynard paused, leaned over, and kissed her lips. "Just following the script."

Anna recoiled slightly, then leaned into him, putting her arm around his neck. "Let's ad lib."

† †

It seemed like an eon since Reynard first felt her slender fingers against his bare skin. It seemed like an eon since he had felt *any* slender fingers against his bare skin. He gazed at Anna's bare legs, which she now held gracefully together. How long ago had it been that he had caressed them?

Anna picked up an earring from the coffee table and attached it to her ear. "You *are* the passionate frog, Jean. It's been awhile for you, *n'est pas?*" He nodded. Anna slipped her hand from around his back and stood up, pulling her skirt back down across her hips, smoothing it properly over her legs. She walked over to the large window.

Reynard fastened his belt and got up from the sofa and walked to Anna and stood and they looked out into the darkness of the lake. He kissed her cheek. "That was unexpected," he said.

"I live for the unexpected these days," she replied, taking his hand.

"There's something I have to ask you," he said.

Anna pulled her hand away. "And now you want to talk turkey, is that it?"

Reynard was somewhat abashed. "Well, wrong country, but not far from it. Let me tell you what I know, and maybe you can fill in the blanks." She walked back to the sofa and he followed.

After he recounted what he knew of the Faberg history, Anna nodded. "Yes, Father lost his Algerian assets; how did you know they came to be lost?"

"I guess I know low people in high places. I've been asked to help you get them back—that's where your husband comes in."

Anna jumped up. "*Merde!* You'll never get him away from that little whore—what's her name, Sonja—across the lake. You're barking up the wrong trunk, old man."

"Wait a minute Anna," Reynard said consolingly. "If this thing works out like we hope, your Algerian investment could be regained with royalties coming back into the Faberg estate."

"Well, that would be something for my time with him," she said, gesturing toward Evian. She paused, then sat down beside Reynard. "Okay, this not just for the money; I'll help because I consider it return of stolen property.

"I hadn't been out of school all that long, and took up with an American Navy flier I met in Naples—at the San Carlos Opera," she laughed. "He was a helicopter pilot based there, and he looked splendid in his mess dress and medals. We eloped. We soon found out things weren't going to work out for us, and I came home on a trial separation in February of '62. I was thirty and tired of life already. I came home to get away from it all," she said, chagrined. She told Reynard of two meetings at Faberg castle, but couldn't remember names or faces.

On the day of the first meeting, a man appears at the front door in the early afternoon, holding two packages. Charles accepts them and takes them into her father's study.

That evening, her father can't find his cufflinks, and calls Anna to help. When she goes into his bedroom, she discovers two narrow boxes made of polished wood on his dresser, each inlaid with ivory in the shape of African elephants.

Thinking they are jewelry boxes, she opens one. Inside, she finds a dagger, encrusted with sapphires and rubies shaped into curious symbols on a golden haft. Its blade is slightly curved, and has the number three stamped close to the hilt.

Anna quickly closes the box and retrieves the cufflinks, which she spies hidden behind it. "Here they are," she said, coming out of his room and holding them out to him. "I found them for you."

"Thank you, Anna. Since your dear mama died, you have been my greatest asset."

Anna ignores his comment. "There were some boxes on the dresser, and I opened one, thinking to find the cufflinks there."

"You saw the contents?"

"Yes."

"Never mind; it's a gift."

"For your guest tonight."

"For our special guest tonight. Anna, keep the box and its existence to yourself."

"Why the secrecy?"

"Vitality to family interests, and frankly, our guest's life. You must never breathe a word of it."

"What about the other box?"

"Not a word."

"But what about the other box?"

"Not a word; it's for our other guest who will be coming tomorrow."

"Oh, another?" Gustav gives her a look. "Okay, Papa, not a word."

"Good, Anna—my Anna." She did as her father asked, and never spoke of the visits or the daggers again.

Anna lifted her hand from the divan and caressed Reynard's knee. "In fact, it wasn't until you reminded me of the oil situation that I thought about this, Jean. Now I can put two and two together —the meetings, the boxes, and the envoys are all tied to the oil debacle, aren't they?"

"We think they are," he said. "By the way, how did you know the elephants were African?"

"They had big ears," she mused.

Reynard pressed Anna for the names of the two visitors; she told him she never knew them. She did mention that their old cook kept a diary of all visitors and their preferred entrees, however, in case they would be coming back to the castle.

"Do you know where the diary is now, Anna?"

"In the kitchen pantry, I think." She got up and led Reynard into the large kitchen, which he noted was the size of a small house and had white tile floors and walls. Copper pots and pans hung on hooks around a central stove and preparation area.

Anna walked over to a large wooden door and opened it. She switched on the light— the room was as large as his living room. Its walls were lined with shelves of what looked like recipe books. Anna walked to the end of the room and stretched her hand up to the top shelf. She ran her finger along a row of a dozen large blue binders. She stood up on her toes, peering at the labels on the spines. She said, "1962," and pulled out a book. "It would be in this one." She opened it and began paging through. "January, February, March—it may have been in March."

Reynard moved in beside her. He looked at her blonde hair. *It would be down to below her shoulders*, he thought, *if she would undo it.* He gazed down her back. She still had her figure. No children. She was handsome.

Anna turned, holding the book up between them and looking up at him inquisitively. "You have a nice back," he mused.

"You're not thinking about business, are you?—This is the name. What do you think?"

Reynard refocused on the page to which she pointed. Two

names beneath were different from the others; they were foreign–*algériens*. Reynard pulled a small notebook out of his inside coat pocket, along with a pen, and scribbled them down. Anna reached for the switch.

"One moment—what *did* they like to eat?" he asked, at the same moment she flicked the switch. The light went out and the two of them were standing in the darkness. She had turned toward him; he felt her breath on his face. He ran his hand down her back and unzipped her skirt, whispering in her ear, "What do you think was in the other box?"

† †

The next morning, Reynard was still too groggy to give notice to the rush of scenery through the window of Anna's Mercedes 300SL. Anna shot through the curves of the two-lane road to the train station with the touch of a race-car driver.

"You and Lamar should compete," he mumbled.

"We do," she said curtly. "I've been thinking about the situation, and will make some calls after you leave. There are real dangers waiting for you and your crew in Algiers. The damned French haven't planned this out very well. You need another way out. Leave that part to me; I have a plan."

"That's been on my 'loose ends' list. I agree on the necessity of an alternate escape route," Reynard said.

"Tell me where you can be reached, and I'll let you know the particulars."

Reynard gave her a secure telephone number and cautioned her to commit it to memory. Reaching into her purse, she pulled out a gold ballpoint. Clicking it open, she imprinted the number onto the inside of her hand, along the thumb line. Reynard gave her a quizzical look, and she said, "It's an old trick I learned from a pilot I knew once. I'll memorize it on the way home, then wipe it off before I get out of the car. See—no evidence."

Reynard pointed to Talka's convertible in front of the hotel as they passed, saying, "He's going to be out of your life for a while."

The big Mercedes turned the corner and pulled up to the train station. Leaning over, Anna kissed him, murmuring, "Make that a permanent arrangement, won't you?"

Reynard pulled back and stared at her. He took her hand, turned it over, and read the number she had written down. "I'll return the dagger."

† †

When Reynard arrived in Paris, he immediately went to a public telephone and contacted Claude to arrange a meeting at the La Fontaine. Reynard told him he had confirmed most of the brief. "I don't know what we will find in the end," he concluded

"You've done well, Jean—I knew you would. The Agency is prepared to give the go-ahead on the Algeria documentary as long as you can convince the Americans that you are doing a film about the wonderful things their president has accomplished with one billion of their foreign-aid dollars. That being the case, you have my word, Jean, that you will have complete artistic license to do the film as you see fit."

"Awfully decent of you, old man," Reynard said wryly.

"Get that valve open, and we'll keep our part of the bargain and see to it that the documentary gets favorable position in Cannes, the Academy in the U.S., and any other place you like."

"What about the money?" asked Reynard.

"The sum of one million euros has already been deposited in a bank account in Switzerland. Another one million euros will be deposited upon successful completion of the mission. Should the mission fail, the documentary deal will nevertheless go forward."

"That's a real comfort—we'll all be dead," Reynard said. "We need to talk about an escape plan, in case we should be uncovered."

† †

After Anna dropped Reynard off at the train station, she returned to Lausanne, parking the Mercedes in the stable next to an old

Rolls Royce opera coupe. She went inside and immediately picked up the phone. "Charles, get me a secure line to Hong Kong."

† †

Something had been eating at Reynard, and it wasn't the oil job. As he stared out the office window, he wondered why no documentary film of any note told the story of Algiers.

Why should there be one? Is it not a monstrous embarrassment to France, so who wants to be reminded of it? Maybe the extreme right; maybe the extreme left. We've got to make this look good. I am in the film business, and even though I have a mission, I am going to make this real. If the documentary is sound, it might make it to Cannes.

With the current pull of events in Algeria, Reynard instinctively knew there *was* a story, it *had* to be told, and he was the best one to do it.

He returned to his desk, pulled his chair up, and brushed back his greying hair. He focused on the blank tablet in front of him, then stopped to pull out his Zippo and light a cigarette.

He thought about Nicole, how she would help the documentary along, and wondered how well she would work with Philippe. Nicole was such a wolf in the city; Philippe was such the idealist. Nicole had the hard-bitten personality to carry off a reporter just doing her job. Philippe was another matter. He was writing a contemporary history on the subject of Algiers. From what Philippe had told him, from Camus's point of view.

Reynard remembered something Philippe had told him over drinks one evening, a something that had frightened Camus as well:

"Once the populace is confronted with atrocity, it becomes abstraction—the numbing condition abetted by the media, spun and made more political, reasoned away, made to look in the best interest; thus the horror becomes easier to chew. Once this is done, anything is possible. Under such spells of self-hypnosis or mass hysteria, humans seem capable of anything. Any heinous deed is possible; all guilt is put aside. Humans deal with the guilt later—that's another matter. And so long as he believes in what he is

doing, an amateur soldier can levy any monstrous act against another. Man kills with impunity." Philippe had been less drawn in those days, and looked happy as he rambled on, pounding his fists on the bar.

Reynard shook his head, thinking, *We are using this production as a smoke screen for the real reason we're going to Algiers. When it comes to Philippe, I must exercise caution. Should I tell Claude about my reservations?*

He picked up the telephone, then changed his mind and replaced the receiver. *We're about to really piss off the Americans.*

He began to write, his lean frame hunching closer to the pad, as if getting closer would somehow assure the truth of what he put down.

Producer's Role:

Create a film about the religious refugee in Algeria and violations of human rights. Cover events since the Evian Accord, especially since 1992 and the renewal of atrocities. Depict the debilitating effects of secular rule vis-à-vis a religious imperative to destroy individual freedom for the sake of religion. Who wades in midstream between the two extreme banks? Uncover violations on women's rights—the veil thing.

Use Nicole Soutane's talent to portray the female news reporter telling it like it is. Philippe writes a script that makes the Algerian women's plight Nicole's plight; she becomes a surrogate the audience will sympathize with. Back it up with violent scenes—on location!

Ambiance of Docudrama:

Handheld, 16mm, and digital Cam- and Palmcorders; everything small enough to be concealed as necessary on location.

Female commentator, authoritative and dynamic; fill in shots with local color, street scenes, violence if we can get it. If not, then create with local talent. Death and destruction

Script:

Expository, narrative. Writer who knows about Algeria—Philippe DuPont is writing a nonfiction on Algeria, knows scripting.

Mise-en-scène made to seem extemporaneous
Old hotel to serve as a fortress

On location:
Street scene in Algiers
Berber village scene?

Research:
Secularist: National Liberation Front
Government complicity in local terrorism
Connections with outside influences
Connections with international terrorism movement
Fundamentalist : Islamic Salvation Front, Iranian, Syrian, etc.
Religious precepts for the Muslims: The Koran
The World Religious Organization
Religious extremists
The Islamic Law Charter, 1976
Neutral: United Nations
Information from the United Nations Human Rights Council

Funding Sources / Front Organizations
France—Sun King Productions's slush fund
U.S.—State Department, NEA, NIH
Canada—Québec Libre Productions
Personal Funding—Secured (in trust)

Reynard put down the list. He knew he had a lot of phone calls to make, but he was just too tired. He lit a cigarette. Satisfying his habit gave him some inexplicable energy, which welled up as he exhaled the smoke. *All I need is time and a good camera.* His thoughts turned to Lamar Talka. *Up there on the lake, he's sleeping with someone other than Anna. I slept with Anna.* He didn't know quite how to feel about that.

He and Talka had talked about lots of things: Indochina, the Suez. France was always getting into scrapes and the Service smoothing things over. He and Talka had been through a lot as a camera team and as comrades. It had been Talka who talked Reynard into going into the motion picture business once the Cold War was over. They had worked well together, and they would again.

Reynard looked at his list, thinking, *No one can ever see this.*

7

Beneath her veil, the girl wears a single braid interwoven with a scarf. She raises the foot she used to make the outline in the bread; she must not stand on it for the rest of the night, for dust from its footprint would point the way to her undoing. Her attendants carry her and place her against the wall of the bridal chamber.

Other brides are brought in one by one, and each girl is propped up against the wall with one foot raised. Soon the walls are lined with one-legged women in wedding robes.

† †

At the corner table, the man was sitting just outside the light. He paid a waiter to give a message to the singer who had just finished.

In a few moments Malena emerged, and approaching his table, flashed him a tired look. "You wanted to see me?"

"Have a seat." He motioned to the empty seat beside him. When she asked, however, he refused to buy her the obligatory tea. When she tried to leave, he kept her down with the strength of one hand. Looking into her green eyes, which he could barely make out in the dim light, he said, "If you want to know me, it'll take more than warm tea to fetch it."

She wrenched free. "*Et alors?*"

He had watched her change costumes and seen her moves in the shadows along the streets; he had followed her to where she left the migrants at the wadi. There he decided he had seen enough of her beauty, and wanted to know her.

At their table, he was within her aura and the smell of her hair. In that instant, she was a daughter lost to gunfire in the street, in the next, his victim-paramour in flames. "You go out after dark... and you are trying to get out of this place, heading for a better one."

She gave him a straight look and resumed her seat.

He lifted a glass of milky anisette, "For Paris." She watched him cautiously. He told her he liked her Caruthers renditions. Malena relaxed, and told him she would one day leave for France to sing where Caruthers had sung. He told her he saw no reason why she couldn't make it. The prospect of an arrangement began to formulate, how he might help her. He told her this and thereby drew her to him. She said she pictured herself being *La Chanteuse de Paris.*

† †

That night she went alone to his room. She was frightened. That was the first night. After that, she found herself wanting to slide between the sheets, having become *his* addict. The lost tonic he found begged him to take her with him to Paris. To get out, while there was breath in their bodies.

She always kissed him and promised to make love, and he always promised he'd take her to Paris. Each time when his hands touched her between the legs, she cowered. Instead of sensing joy, a deluge of purity poured over her.

Once he managed to pull up her dress and kiss the inside of her thigh. She winced like a colt struck by a lightning and bolted off the bed. "When will you?" he asked.

"I don't know," she whimpered, turning away from him and crossing her arms over her breasts. "I really don't." Down deep she knew it was somehow connected with her inability to cry.

When she slept, she dreamed of the running water she had found while journeying from the Kabylia—the small pond fed by a waterfall. She would wade in deeper, toward the fall itself, pulling her dress over her head as she went, until she swam into nothing.

Words would come to her she had heard before, from within or from someone else:

Each has another,
One who survived
In a house
Or on the land.
One day our paths will cross—
Mine and my other's...

Malena remembered the Berber phonemes to express these words, but thought, *Perhaps I should dream in another language—French or Arabic. But I can't honestly say I dream in any of those tongues, though I speak them.*

She dwelled in her dreams more often these days, awakening to another reality, only to fall asleep and dream again. She wondered why dreams outside the cave were so different.

† †

The apartment is so cold. Nicole shuddered as she looked out of a clouded glass window to the wet streets below, and thought, *This view would have been good for Renoir, but it's bad for tourism.* She usually liked the rain, and would look forward to the seasonal change, when flowers were consigned to grow out of the dead land.

Arnold's flat was not in the nice part of Paris, but in what remained of Montparnasse. Void of the artists and intellectuals of the "lost generation," it had become just a wet street. Nicole tried to ignore its shabbiness like she ignored the drudgery of part-time jobs, alternating between bit acting, waiting tables, and office work uptown. Now, on this rainy Renoir day, she wondered why she had moved in with Arnold in the first place.

The thought put her in a petulant mood, and as she gazed out her clouded window, she thought, *I don't know why tourists think April in Paris is so romantic.*

Her thoughts now turned to finding gainful employment in the entertainment industry. *I need to get better digs. I know I'm attractive enough.* Nicole was forty-three, but had been told she looked more like a twenty-year-old. *Maybe I should get work in the States. How in the hell do they do it in Hollywood?* She answered aloud: "Probably on their backs."

"Do what on their backs?" Arnold asked. She didn't answer, but sat down cross-legged on the floor in front of the television. Arnold was memorizing a script for a play, for which he had been chosen as the second lead. "This is my big break," he said triumphantly when she didn't answer.

Nicole nodded silently and continued to paste up her portfolio with suggestive photos she had collected over her lifetime, showing off what she thought was best about her persona. Eventually she said, "I have some big breaks coming my way, as well."

"Oh yes, what big breaks are those?"

"I have a meeting tomorrow with the people at Sun King Productions. They are looking for someone to do a docudrama—important filming."

"What do you know of docudrama, *ma petite?*"

"Enough to get me hired, I should think. Besides, they say I am the right age, height, and look; if that's good enough for them, it is good enough for me."

"*Bonne chance.*" Then, softening, Arnold asked, "Do you need help with anything?"

"I am capable of handling my own affairs."

"Anything at all now," he sang back.

"Go on with your memory work, then." Then, "*Mange merde,*" she said under her breath.

† †

Before Arnold would have left for his rehearsal, Nicole arrived at the front office of Sun King Productions. "I am here to see Monsieur Reynard."

"And whom shall I say is here?" asked the haughty blonde receptionist.

"You may say Nicole Soutane is here."

"Please have a seat." Nicole sat down. She was dressed for the occasion in a rather tight business suit, open at the collar—something she thought a female newscaster might wear for the evening program. "You may go in now," the receptionist said, motioning to a door marked *Production.*

Nicole got up carefully, and mustering all of her poise, marched to the door and opened it. She was confronted by a tall man who stood to greet her. She announced, "My name is Nicole Soutane, and I am here to fill your position."

The man smiled, saying, "Well then, we can stop looking, Nicole."

"Yes; I am the one you need for this assignment."

"I must see what you have then." She handed him her portfolio she had so carefully arranged the night before. He took it, walked back to his desk, and sat back down in his chair, all the while keeping his eyes fixed on it. "My name is Jean Reynard, and I will be conducting your interview today—is it 'Madame'?"

"I am not married, Monsieur."

"That may be of some advantage, Mademoiselle—or shall I call you Nicole?"

"Call me whatever you wish, Monsieur."

"Fine. One moment please, while I look over what you have here." He filed through her face shots, write-ups, letters of recommendation, and favorable play reviews. "Have you ever done anything with docudramas, Nicole?

"Well, you can see for yourself, Monsieur...um, I once stood in for a television reporter—but I don't think it was representative."

"Put everything down, Nicole; one never knows what will come in handy. As it happens, we are looking for someone who has acted as a news anchor. I would say it is very fortunate indeed that you have done so."

Nicole tried to register little surprise, and maintaining her practiced composure, deftly but subtly arched an eyebrow. "Please go on, Monsieur."

Reynard didn't answer immediately, but thumbed through her

portfolio without really looking at it. Nicole remained stationary in her chair, and kept the good face.

Finally he put down the portfolio, reached into a small cedar box on his desk, and pulled out a cigarette. He fished around in the center desk drawer for a lighter, but then seemed to remember an old Zippo in his coat pocket. He ratcheted the wheel a couple of times, and in a shower of sparks, a slow flame came to life.

Nicole held her breath as long as possible, then inhaled, taking in the incense of the lighter fluid and tobacco. She stifled a cough and continued to look at Reynard. At long last, he spoke. "We're putting together a full-length documentary about Algeria. Do you know anything about Algeria?"

"I know some things, Monsieur."

"Good. We are looking for a mature woman who will take the role of news anchor—"

Nicole felt a welling-up in her abdomen. "Yes, I can do that—"

"—one, you see—how shall I put it? *petit blanc,* or *pied noir* if you like—who fled Algiers at the end of the conflict, and now returns on special assignment to film events—all staged of course." Reynard got up and walked to the window, dragging on his cigarette, and exhaled the smoke through the blinds. "She will show us the ongoing atrocities and the continual tragedy that is today's Algeria in ruin." He stopped talking and looked intently at Nicole. "What makes you think you can do it?"

"I am a professional," she said. "And I am Berber on my mother's side."

"Your mother's side," repeated Reynard.

"From Tunisia."

"You mean to say you are actually a native?"

"That is what I am telling you."

"But to look so fair, your eyes…"

"Truly, Berber stock. Some of us were mercenaries for the Moors in Andalusia. We stayed awhile and returned fair—but then there were other fair people in North Africa, B.A."

"B.A.?"

"Before Arabs. They took everything, even our looks."

He took another drag on the cigarette. "Would you be available for a screen test tomorrow, Nicole?"

Pulling out her appointment book and leafing through the pages, Nicole looked up the date. "I am free then."

"I'll be at the studio; do you know where it is?" She nodded. "Seven o'clock tomorrow—in the morning."

"Yes, in the morning then."

"We get started early; the rest of the crew will be there two hours ahead of that, but your presence will be required at seven for the makeup and the light measurement."

"I will be there, Monsieur, and thank you very much." With that, Nicole stood up and extended her hand. Reynard took it as if it were delicate china. Letting go, he handed back her portfolio and said, "Merci."

"Tomorrow then," she returned and walked out the door. When she got to the haughty receptionist, she gave her a stage smile and stuck out her thumb to Reynard's door, "Tomorrow." Then she turned, marched out the office, leaned up against the wall, exhaled and pulled out her cell.

† †

Lighting another cigarette, Reynard recalled that when he told Nicole he was looking for a mature woman, her eyes had dilated. He picked up the phone and dialed the Agency. "Hello, Claude. Yes, I met the Berber today. No, I don't know how she'll work out."

† †

Nicole set the alarm for five. She slid into bed opposite Arnold and lay perfectly straight on her back, hoping his groping hand wouldn't venture her way. But he was asleep or pretending to be. She would pretend too.

She no longer heard anything soft in his voice. For its soothing effect, she began to recall her Aunt Lalla's stories about her mother, Kristianne. She retreated to these stories when she was alone or when Arnold was busy doing something else, memorizing or sleeping.

She thought of Argenteuil, a place she had visited often, and where the stories stirred with other memories, mixing in with the Seine, waving back its pastel mirrors. Soon the palette bled to her faded youth beside a soccer field in Tunisia, when Philippe would read poetry to her. Those memories were the bulk of the baggage she carried across the Mediterranean when she came to France in 1969 for her education.

Nicole had been allowed to become a citizen, partly because she was Berber on her mother's side, and partly because of France's willingness to concede a place for African refugees into the Parisian strata after the Evian Accord was signed. But the French people were slow to accept anyone who had come over. She was lucky to look so blonde, and she had used her looks to find a niche, keeping her birthplace a secret. She was good at keeping secrets.

She remembered those times in Tunisia, she wrote to her Aunt Lalla, who wrote back about her father, though the family seldom saw him after his release from prison. *Your father was a gay rogue, but he supported the struggle here in Tunisia and in Algiers. He's a good man, Nicole, and you must never forget that. Some say he is the Antichrist, but I must tell you,* ma petite, *he is a true patriot, just as much as Robert DuPont, who flew and fought for France.*

Sometime between midnight and two a.m., Nicole had dropped off. The alarm reminded her of her mistake, and she slapped it into silence and shuffled into the bathroom. She took a shower and dabbed on some street makeup. After dressing quickly and hurrying downstairs, she caught a cab to Sun King Production Studios, arriving at six forty-five. Arnold was probably still asleep at home.

Some grips were preparing the set as she entered. Reynard sat in a director's chair. "You're late! Maria, get her ready if you can."

Maria ushered Nicole to makeup and spent forty-five minutes on her. Nicole thought, *What was wrong with the way I looked yesterday to Reynard—and what is wrong with the way I look today?*

When Maria exclaimed, "*Voilà!*" she ripped off the protective sheet and ushered Nicole to costumes A man with tired eyes, whom Maria introduced as Henri, handed her a beige twill business suit with an open collar. "Put it on," he grunted and pointed a stubby finger to a room divider. Nicole quickly went behind the divider, disrobed, and donned the business suit. When she presented herself to Henri, he picked up a bowl of pins and stuck them into the suit as if he were a picador, tenaciously pulling in the material. When he finished, he pushed her back and looked at her as if he were viewing a dairy cow. He pursed his lips and said, "Go back to studio."

"Back to the studio?" asked Nicole.

"Back to studio," he repeated, and Nicole walked out to the main set, where two large cameras rolled back and forth on massive wheeled tripods, driven by men hunched over the controls. A solitary microphone stood on a small wood dais, ablaze from Klieg lights attached to bars in the ceiling.

"There you are, Nicole," said Reynard. "I was beginning to think you might have changed your mind about us."

"No, Monsieur. I am ready."

"Very well then, here's a script. Study it for a few minutes, then look over here to the camera. Can you see what is over the lens?"

"Yes, Monsieur—it is a teleprompter."

"You know what it is of course, and the precise dialogue you have on paper will appear on this screen. Take a few moments while we finish with the lighting and sound levels." Reynard shouted back over his shoulder, "Philippe? Hey Philippe! Do you have the scroll for the teleprompter ready? We are just about ready out here."

Nicole heard a voice in the background: "It is ready, Jean. Watch, just there, Mademoiselle—uh…"

Nicole faced the camera lens and squinted at the teleprompter above it, "Soutane, Nicole Soutane—I can see the words clearly now, thank you."

"Did you say Soutane?" asked the voice, closer now. Nicole saw a figure step into the light. "Did you say Soutane?" he asked again, coming up onstage.

Nicole felt a vague recognition creep over her. "Philippe...he said Philippe..." She trailed off.

"From Tunisia."

Nicole ran to him and threw her arms about him, crying, "Is it really you?"

"It is, it is!" he laughed.

"You two know each other," said Reynard.

"We were childhood friends in Bizerte," replied Philippe.

"He read poetry to me."

"Well, visit afterward then, on your own time," smiled Reynard. "Places everyone. Now Nicole, read the words just as if you were saying them for the first time, as if you had just witnessed what you are reporting. Okay?"

"Yes," she said and moved back to the dais, still in a daze from Philippe's appearance, and now wanting to show him what she could do.

† †

Nicole got home shortly after two p.m. and slept for an hour before being awakened by the ringing phone. It was Philippe.

"No, I wasn't sleeping. I can meet you, Philippe. Where?" Nicole tried to act nonchalant, and said she would meet him in an hour.

Filling the bathtub, she looked back on the day. She still held a wonderful feeling about getting the job, but wondered if she had oversold Reynard on her talent. She felt she was entering into uncharted waters filled with hungry sharks. She lay in the bathtub, remembering Reynard's final words to her.

"You will work closely with Philippe. It's important that the wording make your commentary sound impromptu."

"Will there be a director?" Nicole asks.

"What I envision is cinema verité."

"And?"

"And I will direct such actions as you may require. But really,

Nicole, you are a professional. I hired you based on your experience, and I expect you to do a professional job. Once you get with Philippe, you will know what to do."

She got out of the tub and put on her evening makeup, which looked like no makeup at all, and slipped into a dress.

† †

Philippe stood in the restaurant foyer, standing rather stiffly, she thought. "Philippe," she said, and kissed him.

"Nicole...I can't tell you what a delightful surprise it all is. After all these years, to meet once again under such bizarre circumstances."

"How long?"

"More than twenty years, I think."

Nicole's shoulders dropped, and she smirked. "How long before we get a table?"

Philippe laughed, "Fifteen minutes."

"Not bad for short notice. I meant to ask about your brother, Michael—how *is* he after all these years—with his heart, I mean?"

He looked startled, and said, "I'm sorry to tell you, but Michael passed last year."

"I am sorry. I shouldn't have asked."

"Not to worry, I'm over it, but yes, I miss him."

"Our dear Michael, how he could run after the ball, no?"

"Indeed, yes," Philippe said.

"I am looking forward to the project, how about you?" They approached the maître d' and he raised one finger, nodding at them. Nicole admitted, "I don't know what to make of Reynard."

"He's not such a bad sort, but full of surprises."

"How many of these docudramas has he under his belt, do you suppose?"

"I haven't worked on anything with him but *avant-garde.*"

"This sounds about as avant-garde as you can get!"

"Sans blague! Algerie," Philippe shrugged. Just then the maître d'

motioned to them, and they followed him to a booth. After they had slid in and gotten settled, Philippe said, "I have been thinking about this. I've even come up with a name for your character."

"Really, what is it?"

"Hélène Demaurie."

"That sounds famous."

"It fits."

"The character."

"More than that, it fits you." Philippe grabbed her hand. "Keep it."

"Maybe it does, but how can you really tell, Philippe? We haven't seen each other since childhood. How can you know what I have become, what I have gone through?"

He released her hand and tapped his temple with his finger, saying, "*Extrasensoriel*—or perhaps it's in your face, those *extra-expérience* lines creeping around the eyes and mouth, darling." Nicole wished she had pasted on more makeup. "I don't mean that in a derogatory way. They give you that something separating you from the rest of the women in the world. They make you special, not ordinary."

"Philippe, it's been such a long time. There's so much to be said—where do we begin?"

"For now, let's begin with the project." But he stopped when the waiter appeared and whisked the table quickly with a slap of his towel before offering them their menus.

Nicole looked around the dining room at the other patrons eating and talking, feeling like she and Philippe were not part of the crowd. "Do you ever get the feeling that you're all alone?" she asked.

"Beg your pardon, Madame?" asked the waiter.

"I was speaking to him," Nicole pointed at Philippe. "And we're not married."

"As you wish, Mademoiselle," the waiter retorted in a snooty tone. "Would either of you care for something to drink?"

"Give us a few minutes, won't you?" Philippe said, and continued as if the waiter had never been there. "After you left yesterday,

Reynard got busy. He gave me one day to produce this." He pulled out a roll of paper and handed it to Nicole. Rubbing his nose, he said, "It's the treatment for, uh, what we should look to do over there." Nicole scrolled open the roll of paper as if it were sacred, and Philippe continued, "As I was saying, this project goes hand in hand with a book I am writing about Algeria. Did Reynard tell you about it?" Nicole shook her head. "That's why he hired me, you know—to work on the project because, well, I'm the only expert you'll get to know on Algeria."

She slid around the bench toward him. "Are you quite sure?"

"Sure, I'm sure," he said.

She moved her lips as she scanned the lines. She nodded and said, "I like the style. What of Algeria do I need to know?"

"More than is on that piece of paper, but I can see you through the rough spots," he explained.

The rude waiter returned and took their order. Nicole continued to read, her lips moving occasionally as she went. "I like it," she said, looking up at him. "Did you say you were writing a book?"

"Yes. Nonfiction, something like Camus might have written had he not been killed in '62."

Nicole felt a sense of frustration welling up. "I would like to read it when you're done. For now, I need to be centered in this role. I need to know precisely where we are going. What is your theme?"

"You read the papers. I'm sure you know what happened in Algeria after France pulled out, and what has happened since the secularist junta took over in 1992."

Nicole stiffened. "My mother was blown to bits fighting for a free Algeria a long time before that."

Philippe raised his eyebrows. "Who did that?"

"The French Navy."

"Well, that's exactly what we're talking about. We've decided to use the Berbers' situation there to poignantly illustrate how religious oppression is as devastating as, say, Nazism. We'll do that by creating dynamic scenes recreating pillages, rapes, beheadings, and whatever else is necessary to keep the body count up; we need to crowd those blood-thirsty bastards with their fifteen-second attention spans into the cinemas to sate their taste for violence."

Nicole shrugged. "How antagonistic do you plan to get?"

"Whatever it takes to grab their attention and hold onto it. We're into guerrilla warfare now." He pulled out another sheet of paper and handed it to her.

† †

Reynard fumbled in his desk drawer and pulled out the can of lighter fluid. He pulled out his Zippo and pulled it apart, exposing the cotton-filled reservoir. He opened the can and inserted its nozzle into the cotton wadding and squeezed until he saw the fluid level nearing the top of the reservoir. He closed the nozzle and slid the two sections of the lighter together. He lit a cigarette and exhaled a smoke ring.

Reynard knew this was to be the final call to Claude before the company's departure for Algiers. He picked up a pencil and slid up his note pad. He tilted his head, inhaled some smoke, and exhaled it out toward the ceiling. He jotted down:

Reynard—Charles Gray
Nicole—Helen Demare (Hélène Demaurie in film)
Lamar—Jack Lum
Philippe—Phil Kam

Dropping the pencil to the desk, he looked down at the names, then nodded, muttering "Good." Now he was within the protocol. Now he was in range of the mission. Now he would run the gamut from false passports to bending French accents into American ones.

† †

Reynard met Claude at le Rayon de Lune. Claude seemed rather edgy as he gave him his final brief. "Do you have the name of your contact in Algiers?"

"Yes."

"What about your flight? Is that going to be a problem?"

"Not nearly as much getting out. Tunisia would be the best bet. Do we have contacts there?"

"We're getting some outside help. I'll confirm it as soon as I know."

"We'll take things as they come."

"Train your crew carefully; their lives depend on it."

"Mine too."

"Are you happy with the woman?"

"Yes."

"That's something."

"She and Philippe DuPont—old friends, you know?"

"Since when?" asked Claude.

"Tunisia. Grew up together during the Algerian conflict."

"Do you think their relationship will be a problem for you?"

Reynard thought a moment, then said, "No, it won't."

† †

In preparation for her role as Hélène Demaurie, Nicole cut her hair in a close crop, a mannish, pixie look. "I want the look of the American, Jean Seberg," she told the stylist. "The way she looked in her early movies, way before her tragic end." *Mon Dieu, that way. I should have sent a fan letter.*

To further prepare for the role, she spent hours boning up on documentaries. She read all she could find on cinema verité, finding it meant making up dialogue while the scene was being shot. *The way all famous French films are,* she thought.

Her research led her down many avenues: directness, method or system acting, French realism of character development, new wave directors, spontaneity of behavior, non-acting, intermediaries between the fictional character and the spectator, improvisation, rewriting scripts, and music.

In her case, she needed to metamorphose from strict acting to improvisation and from actor to activist. All the research brought her to one final question: *What significance in my acting style will help me in this role? I suppose all actors have to answer this one day.*

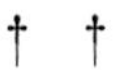

One afternoon as Malena cuddled with the man in his bed, he began to speak to her in a peculiar way. It was as if she could fully understand the ramifications of his life's journey, as if she had been beside him through all those years that had made him old, as if she had entered the same time-tunnel that had made him blasé about the political forays of heirs apparent and the half-truths of public speakers.

"I long to live in a country without flags or anthems," he told her, "a place soft-spoken of agendas. That would be true freedom." She formed an S with her body, scarfing his back with her front, her toes caressing his ankles, though her mind stood at the threshold of a time-tunnel of her own:

She sees the Djurdjura Mountains, the hovel, and her father coming home with the Victrola. She is six again. She watches the record spinning on the turntable. It's huge; she lies outstretched on her stomach, the centrifugal force stretching her out, but she hangs on, straining against the spin. She digs her fingernails into a groove to keep from flying off. When the record stops, she drops between the grooves. Vertigo. *She props herself up, hands on opposing walls with filigree panels. She wants to vomit, but chokes back the urge and stands up. She staggers amid eerie museum relics. Alcoved statues lean out—misshapen monsters from Ionia. She runs and she's in the folds of her mother's skirt, shivering.*

He brought her back by reaching to stroke her hair. "I know a song I could sing in Paris," Malena murmured.

"Caruthers?"

"Yes."

He began to speak of Caruthers, of France in the 1940s, and what he knew of the American jazz that had wafted across the Atlantic—he had made time for such things. "I saw her in Paris. She sang to us in English. Wonderful. Like nothing we had heard before. You had only a part of her, and you would think of her in another language."

"I don't think of her in any language," she mused.

"She was the ultimate lounge singer...never a large audience, but the joints she played were packed, even when she came straight from jail."

"She sang sadly."

"She said she never did a song the same way, always different."

"She sang what she remembered from the past."

Mallory rolled over and looked into Malena's eyes. "Your eyes just changed color," he said.

"How have they changed?"

"They're more grey than green now. Anyhow, she measured her life out with songs. When the Sun came up and they closed down the place, she would go to the hotel. At night, she'd be back again, singing out the memories. I heard Cinnamon talk about these things, what she remembered when she sang. Could you do that in Paris?"

Malena moistened her lips to kiss him, saying, "Memories must not be lost."

† †

"The Americans are coming!" the voice said.

"What is it you're saying?" Kelbeau was puzzled.

"The Americans are coming!" Kelbeau winced and pulled the receiver away from his ear. "Stop screaming, Piton, it's only the production company here to do a film on how we are spending American dollars the United States gave us. We've been hired to provide them security at that old hotel on the quay, the Fleur de l'Âge. No problem whatsoever; it's completely enclosed. Yes, I know it's open to the sea—are you expecting a naval siege? No connection with the DGSE. Shut up and listen: the woman, Malena, is another matter. I don't have time to explain it now; follow her and report back to me."

† †

Reynard received an encoded e-mail from Claude on his laptop. *Niagri,* meaning North Africa, was to be his code name.

Reynard pulled out his cipher wheel and turned it to the day of the month, lining up the alphanumeric substitute. The decoded e-mail specified when he was to meet with the Jeweler, through Sidu.

Sidu apparently employed a Berber woman as go-between for some of his more secret errands, including smuggling immigrants out of the country to Spain. The Berber girl sparked some interest in that she possessed some level of clairvoyance, or at least the DGSE seemed to think so. The Jeweler had signaled he was convinced of the validity of the information about her, as he came by it with a high level of confidence.

Reynard had a strong feeling of déjà vu from a previous project with the Agency, one which produced a report, *The Evocation of Consciousness,* exploring the techniques the mind uses, like self-hypnosis, to achieve survival. He thought mind tricks only seemed mysterious because of their obtuse treatment in medical journals only medical doctors could digest. He shook his head. *Authorship rests heavily on grounds of personal medical experience or pretense thereof.* Reynard remembered that after the research, academics with doctorate degrees were brought in to inject their thoughts on the matter. They in effect took the clairvoyance project out of his hands and he still had bitter thoughts on the subject.

† †

Disguised as the American film producer, Charles Gray, Reynard was the first to make the trip to Algiers. The production team, consisting of Talka, DuPont, and Soutane, would make their way there a day after Charles Gray made his entrance. They had been practicing their American dialects for a month, to the point of getting sore throats. Overcoming their French inflections when speaking English was hard enough without the difficulty inherent in assuming American ones.

† †

Anna Faberg and June Brae had been chums at their private school for girls in Lausanne, and had remained friends and business partners ever since. It was a complete coincidence that Brad Thomas had met June after he left the Mediterranean for Indochina. It was, however, no coincidence that their relationship had blossomed after June informed Anna of his presence there. Rather than seek revenge against Brad, she had recovered from her shock and supported their relationship, remaining through the years the silent in-love friend.

Anna adjourned to the great room and sat on the divan where Reynard had made love to her. She thought of June: *She holes up out in that damned house in the New Territories. I tried to coax her out of her lair, but she won't come. She tells me she hates to fly.* Anna wanted to connect just the same, and picked up the phone. "June, hello. How's it going?"

"Anna. Where are you?"

"Same old lake," Anna said. "I'm in a project—again. Why don't you come up?"

"Oh, no you don't; you know how I hate to fly."

"*Merde,* June, take the boat. Get a portside cabin and enjoy the trip."

"Takes too damned long."

"Well, here's the deal then." Anna told June about the upcoming documentary project in Algiers and to expect a call from Reynard. She told June she worried about the dangers, and of the escape contingency she would have to consider if things did not go well with security.

June understood. "Let's see what we can do about that contingency. And you believe the neutral zone would be best situated where—Spain? How about Ibiza?"

"Fine. I'll start the ball rolling at this end: people, hardware, and all...How's Brad? Don't tell him I asked."

"He's in a bit of pickle just at the moment. Hot water over the airline thing," June said.

"You must be more careful about whom you pick to run your affairs."

"Your affairs are my affairs, dear."

"You always had a penchant to pick up where I left off."

"Maybe we can arrange for a swap. Bye, love—my best to Lamar."

"I'll ignore that last remark for now. Love you." Anna angrily envisioned the upstairs flat across the lake, but shrugged it off. She chose instead to think back on Brad in Rome. She thought, *Life would be easier if everything could truly be resolved with such simple phone calls.*

† †

Malena was still stinging over Dack's death and Sidu's questioning. She was worried about the place she had hidden Dack's box. When Sidu summoned her upon his return to the Owl, she approached his office slowly, weighing her options. *Will the box be safe? What does it mean? I should just sell it, take the money, and get out of here once and for all. Why couldn't I simply get on a plane and fly to Paris, audition, and get a singing job? That would be the heaven the Church keeps talking about.*

When she got to his office, Sidu told her she was to be at Hôtel Fleur de l'Âge at three o'clock for the audition. She agreed to go.

Returning to her dressing room, she changed into her street clothes, including the hooded robe she wore during the day. She opened her dresser drawer and took out her father's rosary, sticking it in her pocket as she often did when facing uncertainty. She slipped out the back door into the street and made her way to the marketplace and 21 rue du Lobo.

As she drew near, she felt something at her back. She turned around but saw only the familiar street scene. She resumed her trek, pursued by a flood of memories. At every turn, through all these years, she would remember her original search for Kaarem.

She reached the marketplace, where everything from beggar

beads to melons was *à vendre*. She paused as if to browse at a fruit stand, surveying the area behind her from whence she had come. When she saw no one was following, she continued on. Halfway down the market, she came to a street sign saying rue du Lobo, partially hidden by a streetlamp. She had passed the rock-paved street many times, but because it looked narrow and unimportant, she had ignored it. She turned down the little road and started counting the numbers set into tiles beside the entryways.

She came to a two-story building that once was a condo for the well-to-do, and had now become an apartment where government officials and aides-de-camp might live. *Kaarem is inside,* she thought, and tried to open the door, but it was locked.

Examining a row of boxes beside the door, she found his name above a button, which she pushed. After a moment, a man's voice came through: "Who is it?"

"A friend," she said. "Malena."

"Malena?...Come up the stairs. It's the third door on the left." The door buzzed and opened slightly.

† †

June Brae had always hung out at her digs managing finances of great repute, then traipsed to town to accumulate men as she found them. Brad seemed to be the last, however—indeed they had lasted four decades, three past the morning on which her husband was found dead of a stroke in his hotel room in Singapore.

Brad's affair with Anna was over by the time he was ordered to Indochina to fly Navy gunships. In one horrible year, he saw many deaths on both sides. After meeting June in 1969, and fed up with military bureaucracy, he took the job the Braes had offered, heading up Hong Kong Helicopters, Ltd.

About the time June got Anna's call for help, Brad had discovered bank drafts of sizeable amounts were being transferred to banks in France and Switzerland. He confronted June over dinner, but she demurred, saying she simply had made the extra deposits to bolster the airline's cash reserve, just in case of a downturn or other economic setback. "I just didn't want you to worry, Brad."

In a thinly veiled attempt to distract him, June announced the Algiers project. The sudden turn caught him off-guard and he surrendered, becoming the willing listener. "You will need to establish two helicopters at Ibiza, to be able to fly under the cover of darkness across the Mediterranean to Algiers, land, and recover certain personnel to return them to Ibiza, where they will board a fixed-wing bound for Paris."

"I'm busier than a one-legged man in an ass-kicking contest, how can I get away?"

"I'll look after things while you're gone," she said.

"Look, that's what I'm afraid of. Besides, I haven't done that kind of flying for ages. And who are the other pilots?"

"You'll find someone," she said, and turned away.

How in the hell did I get myself in this mess anyway? He had put his trust in something that had come too easily. *Never believe in something that comes too easy— it'll bite you every time.* It had taken him a long time to realize that. Was it June who had gotten him into all of this? Then he remembered what she said when they met in the Kowloon Bistro: "*Roosters are mistrustful, short-sighted birds that pursue enterprises bound to expose them to the public eye.*" He didn't know if he loved or hated her; maybe it was both.

The Algiers project might be his best way out of being investigated now. He would tell her he would run the thing himself—no loose ends. She understood that kind of logic; she would let it go. He wouldn't tell her it would be a one-way trip.

† †

Malena entered Kaarem's building and climbed the stairs, which were carpeted in a navy blue heavy pile interwoven with palm leaves. Making no noise, she made her way down the hall to the third door on the left.

She knocked and a man in his thirties with black hair and piercing brown eyes opened the door. "Kaarem?" she gasped.

"My God, Malena, it is you. I recognize your face—and that hair." She found herself in his arms. "After all these years, how could you have—"

"Found you?" She looked up at him. "I wish I could tell you this was purely a personal visit, but that wouldn't be true. I was sent here by another, Chumie Radak—Dack." They walked together toward his sofa. "Did you know who he was?"

"Of course, I know him—I work for him. You said 'was.' Has something happened?"

"He was killed last night. I was with him."

Kaarem collapsed on the sofa. "My God, how did it happen? How did you meet him? I mean, I didn't know about you."

"We had just met. I only knew him briefly."

"But where did you meet?"

"At work."

"I don't understand. Dack worked in the Government Building, in the next office. Surely our paths would have crossed."

"It was at my 'office,' not his. I'm a singer, you see, and he came to listen to me. One night after the show, I sat with him and he told me he had something to tell me..."

"What could it have been that he felt he had to tell a stranger—you said you only knew him..."

"Briefly."

"Exactly—why would he do that?"

Malena moved slowly over to the sofa. "May I sit down?"

"Of course. Would you like something to drink, tea perhaps?"

"Tea, thank you." Kaarem went into the kitchen to put the water on. Malena turned her body toward the kitchen and raised her voice. "Dack was drinking that night. And well, you must know how it was with him—it made him talkative."

"You were drinking with him?"

"I drank tea."

Kaarem returned and sat on the opposite end of the sofa. He seemed to be mulling over the scene Malena had just described to him. "Did this happen at The Black Owl?"

Malena shifted uneasily; the cabaret's name echoed in the living room as if they had been transported to a dark cave. "I came here years ago, a young Berber running away, running to find you, but I couldn't read the street signs…"

Seeming to sense her hurt, Kaarem slid over to her. "It's all right, Malena."

"I couldn't read the street signs, and then I saw something happening on the street, and dodged into a recess in a building. It was dark and I couldn't tell what it was. I saw someone assaulted, and I screamed. The attackers were coming for me when the door in the recess opened, and someone pulled me in just in time.

"Inside I was safe, but trapped as well. I knew of no other way to survive, so there I stayed, in The Black Owl all these years." Malena's eyes began to smart. Reaching into the deep pocket of her robe, she clutched Fortola's rosary.

The teapot was whistling in the kitchen, and Kaarem got up to turn it off. Malena watched him through the doorway as he poured the water into a small teapot. "I understand what you are telling me, Malena and I am truly sorry for it." She watched him cover the teapot with white towel and place it beside two cups on a small wooden tray.

Returning to the room, Kaarem set the tray on the coffee table and sat beside Malena, taking her hand, which was still closed about the rosary. He turned her hand over and unfolded it to see what she was holding. "You're Christian."

She shook her head, saying, "It was Father's. He had it with him when he was killed. I keep it as a reminder of that time and of my father's killer."

"Yes, but why were you looking for me? I mean before today?"

"I was mad at you. You left without saying goodbye. You told me one day we would marry, and I didn't want you to…that is to say, I wanted it to happen, just as we dreamed when we were kids. Nothing works that way outside the tribe, I suppose." She looked at him. "We were always outside the tribe, weren't we?"

Kaarem uncovered the teapot, picked it up, and poured. Malena smelled a hint of cinnamon. Handing her the tea, he spoke: "We were just kids, Malena—you know—kids. Things were bad for us in the Kabylia. My aunt took us in here in Algiers, and I was able to get my schooling. I made a life for myself." Raising his eyebrows slightly, he said, "We were just children."

Slumping back, Malena sipped her tea, talking into her cup. "We loved each other. I believe that. I had to believe in that in that wretched place; there was nothing else."

"You had your family and your tribe. Your father was Christian, and your mother stuck to her tribal ways, cave-dreaming. We were Muslim; surely you must have known it was all just kid talk."

Malena picked up her cup and brought it to her mouth, but her lips were unable to sip the tea. She held it there, peering over it at Kaarem until her hand began to shake, then she quickly set the cup down. "Are you still Muslim?"

"*Comme si, comme ça*," he said, tilting his hand side to side, adding, "I believe in the Almighty."

She gazed at him for an eternity. He returned her gaze, his eyes full of wonder or something like wonder—full in any case. The years that had spanned between them seemed to dissolve beneath her feet. She felt as if she were falling.

She sees Samantha walking toward her, filling her mind's eye with her presence. She holds out her hands as if to clasp Malena's.

Malena shook her head and brushed back her forelock with her hand, renewing her stare into Kaarem's eyes. She took his hand again. "I don't know what I am. I'm not Christian—or cave-dreamer."

"What then?"

Malena put her arms around Kaarem's neck. "I am between my dreams." She held him tightly, but then eased her hold and pushed him back. "I have something to tell you about what happened at Dack's last night. I have to be someplace at three, so we haven't much time. And this thing between us—it was, as you said, kid talk, a long time ago."

Kaarem released her hand, which still clutched the rosary, and she returned it to her pocket. He said, "It's all right. Tell me what you have."

Malena told him about Sidu, and recounted how she became a singer, and how she got her name—Dark—in being a messenger and a go-between. She described Sidu's fits of temper and the beatings he gave her, and then recreated the scene at Dack's villa for him, and told him Dack had told her to seek him out for the truth, nothing more.

Kaarem asked, "Did Dack give you anything to bring to me?"

"I was given nothing."

He got up and went into the bedroom, returning with a wooden box. Malena was astonished to see it was identical to the one she had pulled from Dack's safe. Kaarem opened the box and showed her the contents: a twin to the dagger in Dack's box. "Now, do you still say he gave you nothing?" he asked.

Malena studied Kaarem's face. *He's showing me the truth,* she thought. "What if he did?"

"In that case, dear Malena, you are involved in something that goes even beyond your wildest dreams; something that would change everything for us, for the rest of our lives."

"How would it do that, Kaarem?"

"It begins with a password: Messouda."

"Messouda? I know the song!" Malena exclaimed.

"This is to be said to the proper contact—I think maybe an American."

"How will I know?"

"You have to pick a time to ask each one of them."

"How would it change our lives?" Malena asked.

"It would change it one hundred thousand euros' worth."

"I'm listening."

8

Hôtel Fleur de l'Âge

Nicole, Talka, and Philippe walked into the lobby, pulling their trolleys behind them precisely at 07h. Reynard had been up since five, and was on his sixth cup of coffee and second pack of cigarettes. "Glad you made it safely."

"The airport business is a crock these days," Talka muttered, shrugging his shoulders and rolling his head as if to shed the rigors of airport security.

"That leg is behind us now. Everybody ready?" asked Reynard.

"Fine. Ready to work," Talka said. Philippe forced a smile.

As they went to check in at the reception desk, Sidu and another man approached Reynard. Sidu said in a strained voice, "Good Morning, Mr. Gray. I trust you had a pleasant journey. I would like you to meet your head of security, Fezzan Kelbeau." Sidu stood stiffly, and gestured at Reynard. "Fezzan Kelbeau, Mr. Charles Gray, producer of Sun King Productions."

"Pleased to meet ya, Mr. Keelbow," said Reynard.

"Mr. Kelbeau has taken an office next to the reception desk. Either he or one of his assistants will be available day and night—and I'm sure you'll be quite safe here, but in any case, he—that is to say, he or one of his assistants—can answer any questions you may have about any peculiarities—that is to say, anything at all you may question—"

"I get the idea, and thanks for your assistance. There's some coffee; shall we have some, Mr. Keelbow, while we wait for my crew? They'll be here in a few."

"I prefer tea," Kelbeau said heavily, "and it's Kelbeau."

"Yes...of course we can have coffee and tea," said Sidu, pulling out a wad of papers he had stuffed in his coat pocket. "Uh, Mr. Gray, your memorandum says you would like to see some local talent this afternoon, and need some locals to interview. Of course we can get these; what you call 'talent' is at our disposal. Does three o'clock this afternoon still work for the audition?"

"Three will be fine."

"Here's the tea," Kelbeau reported.

"And my crew," Reynard said. "Let's sit in the lobby." They moved over to a large, round table with crooked legs, and Reynard made the introductions.

Kelbeau asked, "This is all the people you have?"

"We travel light—but I assure you everyone here has a job to do. Helen Demare is the talent, Jack Lum the cameraman, who will double on sound as well, and Phil Kam is the script man."

"Script man—what's that?" asks Kelbeau.

"He writes what the talent says in front of the camera."

"A book man then."

"Yes, a book man."

"You look familiar, Miss De-mare," said Kelbeau.

"This is my first time in North Africa," Nicole began.

"Care for some coffee, Helen?" asked Reynard.

"De-mare—sounds a bit French," Kelbeau said.

"Ahh, who knows where these American names come from? I guess we're all from someplace else, eh?" replied Reynard. "Just the same, Helen was born in Lake Champlain, near Canada. There's lots of French influence around those parts."

"I suppose," replied Kelbeau, sipping his tea while peering at Nicole over the rim of his cup. "What do you think, Miss De-mare?"

"I suppose, Mr. Kelp-bone, we just couldn't keep those French Canadians north of the border."

Fezzan Kelbeau carefully put down his teacup and stood up. "I must take leave of you; feel as safe here as you can. My men and I assure you of every convenience." Sidu squirmed out of his chair and left with Kelbeau.

"Christ, that didn't go very well," whispered Nicole.

"Do you think they suspect something?" asked Philippe.

"They probably think we're amateurs," Reynard said.

"Who gives a rat's ass?" said Talka. "Let's go out into the courtyard; I want to scope it out before the shoot."

"Right. Philippe—Phil—you have the script for Helen ready?"

"In my pocket." He pulled out the script and handed it to Nicole.

"Okay, let's go. We'll plan a shoot in one hour."

The courtyard of the hotel was open to the quay and the harbor leading to the Mediterranean beyond the breakwater. White wrought-iron tables with round glass tops tied into the symmetry of the flowering shrubs planted along a winding brick path. Central to the courtyard was a large opening, about one hundred fifty meters square, once a grass tennis court or bowling green. Since the hotel was devoid of its former French patronage, the square was simply a manicured lawn.

"This is great," exclaimed Reynard. "Good spot to begin our shoot, don't you think, Jack?

"Good spot for doing *The Great Gardens of North Africa.*"

From his office, Fezzan Kelbeau watched the group from his lobby window facing the inner courtyard, and said, "The sword also means death and purity."

9

Villagers line the streets and rooftops of the pragmatic Berber village with its angular eaves and thick mud walls. They ululate, wagging their tongues rapidly side-to-side, and clap as one bride after another makes her entry into the city. Twenty-seven bridal paths have beaten their way into the village. When each bridal group approaches the bridal house, vacated for the five-day ceremony, the girl sprinkles milk and butter on the doorway for luck.

† †

Piton watched through the window as Malena pulled her hair back and braided it into two braids, which she pinned to the top of her head. She poured some flesh-colored liquid into her hands and rubbed them together before rubbing the lotion into her face, starting with her high forehead and moving down over the long bridge of her nose. She smoothed the remainder in with circular movements, going back and forth over a firm chin.

She rinsed her hands in the sink and picked up a long shawl, draping it over her head. She snatched up her veil and hooked it to one side of the hood with a pin so it could hang or be brought across her face.

She took one last look into the mirror above her dressing table, squinting her eyes a little. Picking up her tote, she scurried out into the street and made her way across to the bridge spanning into Constantine and the Jewish sector. Piton followed.

Stopping, Malena peered down into the gorge. Piton thought, *Here lovers leap in acts of desperate faith while tourists take pictures all the while. Will she jump?*

He ran to the edge of the bridge, and amid the crowds crossing in opposite directions saw Malena lift her skirt, baring her legs above the thighs. He saw her stretch lithely over the protective rail. Then the space in the crowd closed up.

He raced to the place where she had been and scanned the gorge below, but saw no one lying there on the rocks. He looked back to the Constantine side, but only saw shoppers flowing toward him on their way to market. His shoulders dropped in defeat; Malena had vanished.

† †

Standing in front of Kelbeau's desk, Piton asked, "Could she be the agent?"

"That's what you going to find out," said Kelbeau. "We must get to the bottom of it or my head will roll—and so will yours, my friend. You must tail Malena, wherever she goes, and find out with whom she is meeting. Do that and we'll blow this thing wide open. Meanwhile, I will keep an eye on her from my end; she's coming to the hotel this afternoon."

"For what?"

"An audition; she's trying out for the American documentary."

Piton frowned. "There's something else."

"What?"

"I believe there's another working in the place of Dack and Hassan."

"Who?"

"Kaarem Khedda."

"What's his involvement?" asked Kelbeau.

"They say he was their aide, and so close to them they might have converted him into their secular fold."

"It seems we have not killed enough. If we stop short, we've gained nothing. But if we do away with this Kaarem, make it count for something—I want to find out if there's another agent out there."

Piton was puzzled. "Do you suspect there is another?"

"Maybe. Maybe something more—a plot." Kelbeau began pacing back and forth, as if stepping off the stages of the plot he was imagining.

"I can make Khedda talk." He gave Kelbeau a knowing look.

"I know you can, but wait for my signal." Piton got up and left.

Kelbeau glanced at the clock: it was two forty-five. He got up from his desk and went out into the courtyard where the Americans had set up.

Precisely at three, Malena showed up with Sidu for the audition. *So, not dead after all.*

The American, Gray, greeted Malena and took her over to the set erected in the courtyard. The cameraman, the book man, and the newscaster, Helen, all took their places around the camera.

Gray handed Malena some papers to look at. After scanning them, she handed them back, smoothed her hair, and stood ready in front of the camera.

Gray yelled, "Action!" and Malena began to speak. After she said a couple of lines, Gray yelled, "Cut!" He went over to Malena, and put his arm around her. Malena pulled back, like a cat not sure it wanted to be held. *Only an American would do that,* Kelbeau thought. Looking around, he thought, *All the infidels are happy on the set.*

Gray approached the cameraman, and together they looked into the camera's viewer, playing back what they had just filmed. Kelbeau marveled at how different the two men looked, considering they were both Americans. Gray was pale white with dark circles under his eyes. The cameraman, on the other hand, was tanned as if he had spent his idle summer days at All Souls Beach near town.

Kelbeau noticed Malena was a different kind of Berber. She

was ruddy-skinned, not the olive of the Arab. She came up to the Americans' chins, and from what Kelbeau could make out, had an ample figure, straight, with full breasts beneath her blouse. While they viewed the footage, Helen walked over to her, and appeared to be reassuring her. The two women seemed to get on with one another.

Gray approached the women and Kelbeau heard him say, "It looks good. Helen, Phil will make a script for your interview with Malena. Shooting restarts in one hour's time."

Not bad for a whore among thieves, Kelbeau thought. He bitterly noted everyone looked in good spirits, save the cameraman, who had been sullen since their arrival.

Kelbeau returned to his office. Something about Sidu was still bothering him. Unlocking his file cabinet, he pulled out the dossier labeled *Isaac Haroom aka Arago Sidu* and began to read.

AFTER HAROOM FINISHED SECONDARY SCHOOL, HE WITHDREW HIS MONEY AND MOVED TO ALGIERS, WHERE HE CREATED SHARMAN PRODUCTIONS. THE COMPANY FLOURISHED AND MADE HIM A WEALTHY MAN. HE CHANGED HIS NAME TO ARAGO SIDU AND MARRIED ESTER FRANÇOISE, A *PIED NOIR* IN GENERAL SALAN'S EMPLOY.

ABOUT THE TIME FRANÇOISE FLED THE COUNTRY, SIDU BORROWED FROM HIS COMPANY AND BOUGHT A CABARET, THE BLACK OWL.

Kelbeau had been a lieutenant in the FLN in those days, and he remembered bombing such places, lopping the heads off of couples he found in the rubble as they clutched each other to the climatic end.

Kelbeau's thoughts turned to Piton. *I must give Piton the tools he needs to help round up the conspirators. Maybe the DGSE itself is part of the act.* Whatever it was, Kelbeau vowed to stop it before it started. *Maybe Malena is seeing this Kaarem. He's stationary; it would be easier to make him talk than it is to chase the alley cat Malena all over the Kasbah.*

10

The bride's mother points to the ewe: "Give me more gold." Men force the ewe to the ground. The bride emerges from her house, goes over to it, and places her left foot on its neck. One man pulls out a knife and begins slicing its throat, cutting the jugular. He carefully wipes the knife blade clean on the ewe's cheek. It slowly dies, wagging its tail as it goes.

Through this sacrifice, the ewe symbolically becomes one with the bride. Its meat and skin will be delivered to the groom instead of her. They weave a rope made of the ewe's wool and give it to the girl. "I will keep this strand of life," she says, turning and walking back inside her house.

† †

Malena locked her door and removed the box from its hiding place. Opening it, she removed the jeweled poniard and examined the pattern of the jewels, in shades of blue-green, topaz, and aquamarine, arranged so subtly. She looked at one side, then the other; they were identical. She turned the dagger over and over. Suddenly she saw them, nearly unnoticeable: "Tifinagh!" Within the pattern of the stones she could make out three letters of the Berber alphabet. But what did they mean? They did not speak to her. *Maybe the password Kaarem gave me is connected to them.*

If the symbols on the daggers had anything to do with the mission Kaarem had told her about, the dagger could be the key to helping her escape to Paris. *In that case, Kaarem might be my best chance.*

She thought back to the photo shoot and the Americans. Kaarem had told her they were a front for the French, who wanted to help him. And among them, she thought, there was yet another person involved. She visualized each of them: Gray, Helen, Phil, and Jack. She could recite the password to each person—perhaps it would flush out the one who knew the riddle of the dagger. Now, she was Kaarem's ferret; she would find the contact.

And what of the man? He had told her his name was Lytton Mallory. She didn't believe it was his real name, but it didn't matter. Her relationship with him went beyond any casual acquaintanceship. She had grown close to him, sensing feelings beyond her usual fear and resentment, those constant companions in Algiers.

She and Kaarem had spoken of loyalties and love and honor. More than anything, she wanted to honor Mallory. Should she tell him about Kaarem, or Kaarem about Mallory?

Malena sighed and put the box back into its hiding place, put on the veil, and left, going straight to Mallory's apartment. Once out in the daylight, she kept the veil wrapped across her face so that only one eye was exposed. The eye is sex, as far as what Arab men see; she must keep them hidden to avoid suggestion regarding her other "eyes."

Berbers had no such tradition for body-wrapping, save the Tuareg tribesmen, who wore the veils in the family. *For what crime would I be punished if I wore this veil in their midst?* she wondered. But here she had to be cautious and avoid the streets where women had been killed by wanton men looking for their other "eyes."

She slipped into Mallory's room without knocking. He came out of the bathroom, rubbing his hair with a towel. Unruffled by her furtive entrance, he said, "I thought we could drive down to Tipaza today."

"Why there?"

"There's something there I want to show you."

She walked out onto the veranda. "They say some Berbers from the Kabylia came from there."

He walked over to her. "Your people were here before any of us. I want to show you this thing in Tipaza before it disappears and is forgotten."

"I will go with you." Stretching out her hand, she stroked his damp hair. His angular face had drops of water on it. As she watched, his wrinkles grew into deeper grooves as a smile crept into his eyes. He kissed her on the forehead and then on the lips before straightening his slim body and walking back to the bathroom.

† †

He had rented a small car for the day, and escorted her to it as if he were accompanied by royalty. She felt like a princess on this, their first outing.

They drove out of Algiers on the Avenue de Barbarossa, west toward Tipaza, which sat on the coast. When they passed the Square of Three Clocks, Malena felt a flush creep over her body, a foreboding. *Hurry past it, Lytton.* They came next to the Bologhine sector, where back in the distance they could see the Byzantine structure of Notre-Dame d'Afrique above the box-like apartments.

Mallory gestured to the basilica, saying, "It has a counterpart across the Mediterranean—did you know that?" Malena shook her head. "It's Notre-Dame de la Garde, in Marseilles. They stood guarding the sea separating Africa and old France for two hundred years."

Malena turned around and looked at the domed structure with massive fort-like sides. "Whom are they guarding against?" Mallory only laughed.

They veered north to the coast, then headed west again, speeding above the Cornice of Algiers. In less than a mile, they came to an abandoned three-story *château* with a parapet. When Malena saw it, she brought both hands to her temples, "Oh, but could we move that to Paris and live in it?" she mused.

The highway opened up and they could see the blue of the Mediterranean as they came to Zeralda. "Here," Mallory said, "it snowed in 2005. Did you know that?" Malena shook her head again, watching the coastal scene speeding by; she remembered the snowy peaks of the Djurdjura and the feel of cold snow against her face. Passing through the coastal villages of Bou Ismail and Tagaurait, they arrived at Tipaza.

Heaving a sigh, Malena asked, "What are we looking for?"

"Ahead, just there, see?" Mallory pointed with his free hand.

"That rubble?"

"It's Roman—an open-air arena." He pulled over. "Let's walk the rest of the way." After they got out, he locked the car.

They strode over to the ruin, and Mallory led Malena through a narrow entrance and out onto an open area surrounded by fallen rocks. "This is what you brought me to see?" she asked.

"This is where people—mostly Christians—came face-to-face with a circus of carnage, their destiny."

They stood at the edge of the promenade. Even in its crumpled state, the edifice exuded the prelude to a Roman holiday. Malena moved a stone with her foot. "What happened here?" she asked.

"Here your ancestors were thrown to the lions for refusing to renounce the Christian faith."

"I don't understand."

"The Romans used people for their entertainment, you see. Final entertainment. Those who did not favor Roman gods were favored by the Romans for this deadly sport."

"And these—Berbers—died for what? Being Christian?"

"And not paying homage to the Roman gods—to Rome itself. The Romans demanded allegiance to the state, even for the Berbers who lived and loved on their own soil. It was your people who died Christian that day."

Malena pushed her hair back with her right hand. "I can't imagine anyone dying for a church."

"Oh, it wasn't for a church, it was for belief. Do you believe, Malena?"

"I believe the Church taught me about fear—I remember grotesque statues leaning out of the church walls."

"When you remember only bad things that happened to you, it erases your faith."

"Fear of the Church became my faith." She squeezed her shoulders up and held them there, then let them drop, looking at Mallory and pushing her hair back again. "I don't want the Church legislating my fears." Bending down, she picked up a concrete shard and examined it.

"But faith is a pact you make with yourself; it's *what* you believe, not how others treat you."

"How I'm treated *is* what I believe. If the Romans had asked, I would have gladly gone over to their side; one leaning-out statue is as good as another." She threw down the concrete and it shattered in two.

"In time, you'll recall things that left you feeling good—not bad."

"My father wanted me to accept the Catholic faith. My mother wanted me to be a cave-dreamer. When neither worked, they tried to marry me off to get me out of the family. That's not what faith is about."

"Your father probably had too many mouths to feed."

"He was murdered."

Mallory put his arm around her. "So it fell to your mother, then?"

They wheeled around together and slipped back through the arched portal to the arena. "Not for long," she said, "I wasn't to be one of them."

"No, I guess you weren't to be one of them, but you are—shall I say—one of us." When they reached the car, Mallory unlocked it and opened the door for her before going around to the driver's side.

She looked at him inquisitively after he got in and slammed the door. "How do you mean?"

"I mean we are together in this thing."

Malena eyed him suspiciously, not knowing which intrigue in her life he was talking about. She took in a breath. "What thing?"

"Meaning we both want to get out of this place. You have your ambition, and I want it for you also. Malena, I'm tired of the game I've been playing for so long. I just want to be with you—to love you and watch you accomplish that for which you have a talent, that for which you've waited so long. That thing."

"Oh..."

Mallory maneuvered the car back onto the road and drove a short distance before parking again. "Where are we going now?" she asked.

"Out to the end of this path here. There's something else I want to show you." They got out and walked on a dirt trail worn into a groove by others who had come to the spot to stare and wonder and take photographs. The trail was lined with stubby trees that grew despite the salt seeping beneath the soil.

They came to a solitary rectangular stone. Mallory took Malena by the shoulders, faced her toward the stele, and stood behind her. "Stand here," he said, and rested his chin on top of her head. "Do you see what it says?"

Malena's lips moved as her eyes scanned the chipped inscription. She turned around to face him, and grabbed the front of his shirt, burying her head in his chest. "Oh, Lytton—do you really love me?"

He put his hand on her chin, and tilted her head up to his face to kiss her. "Read it aloud to me; I want to hear you say it."

Malena turned around again and stared at the stele. She rubbed her nose and recited:

> *Je comprends ici ce qu'on appelle gloire:*
> *Le droit d'aimer sans mesure.*
> —Albert Camus

She turned to Mallory again, saying, "Love me without limit, Lytton," and kissed him hard on the mouth.

Mallory held her and they stood in front of the stele for a long time before walking back to the car. It took the better part of an hour to retreat to town with the Mediterranean off to their left, and they didn't speak. By the time they passed the abandoned *château*, Malena had decided that Lytton Mallory was her best chance for glory after all.

† †

The following night, as Mallory looked on, Malena finished her song, walked to the stage's side staircase, and slid into the darkness of the room. Then she practically ran to his table, overflowing with excitement. She slid into the chair next to his, and leaned over and kissed him. "I got the job—it's some speaking, but mostly to help the American, the one who calls herself Helen!"

He took a sip of his anisette. "You got a job?"

"With the Americans. They called today. I'll be doing some sort of movie."

"What sort?" he asked.

"They call it a documentary."

"How did you find out about the Americans?"

"Sidu, the man who owns this place, told me. He arranges things. He found the company a place to stay and someone to guard them so they don't get killed straightaway."

"You seem to have been in the right place at the right time. Are you going to sing?"

"Not until Messouda does."

"What?"

"When Messouda sings, I will sing."

"I don't know what that means."

Malena wrinkled up her long nose; her green eyes shining, she kissed him again. "Funny, I thought you might; you knew about the Romans."

† †

Lamar Talka had been labeled as a "slow student" in school. The stigma made him a laughingstock, and dismayed his parents.

Nevertheless, he persevered and finished his secondary education. He had never liked going into the classroom, and hated reading. In fact, he could barely read at all. It wasn't that he didn't know the words or their meanings; it had something to do with his lack of concentration when it came to books. It seemed that every time he opened a book, something in his brain shut down.

Talka had always liked the out-of-doors and looking at things. Precise examination of things became a pastime; it was the one thing he could do. So it was, one Christmas, his father gave him an inexpensive still camera. He took to it at once, and began looking through the lens at things all around him.

He was one of the Lumières, reincarnate. He astounded everyone with his quality photographs, and his father said, "The boy has some kind of hidden talent; that's what makes him so damned good with the camera." The following Christmas, he received a more expensive single-lens reflex.

The 135 mm solidified Talka's predilection for camera work, and his parents paid the expensive tuition for a technical school in Paris, famous for turning out superb cinematographers.

Talka's stellar performance earned him honors at graduation, and Reynard, already known for his superb documentaries, hired him immediately. Talka traveled with him to Africa to film the impoverished tribes, to Asia to film the teeming population, and to Yellowstone to document the decline of forest wildlife. Talka's list of awards grew larger than available shelf space upon which to set the trophies. One film earned him recognition at Cannes, and an Oscar for "best documentary."

Reynard and he went to Indochina under contract with a front organization for the SDECE, and shot *Film for France,* a pseudo-documentary with hired actors portraying the French *légionnaires* who fought and died there. They won commercial acclaim, but Talka was never happy about the production.

† †

SUN KING PRODUCTIONS
RETURN TO ALGIERS

Produced and Directed by Jean Reynard

Based on the book,
Freedom in North Africa:
A Hope for Independence

By Philippe DuPont

FADE IN:

EXTERIOR. Courtyard of Hôtel Fleur de l'Âge, Algiers

JEAN REYNARD, a tall salt-and-pepper-haired man, walks out of the arches of the colonnades of the French-style hotel and steps in front of the camera. LAMAR TALKA stands by the camera. JEAN carries several pages of production notes. JEAN points to the camera. "Roll it! Okay guys, gather 'round; let's go over a couple of things before the shoot."

PHILIPPE DUPONT, NICOLE SOUTANE and MALENA CARTOBE step into camera view. MALENA (who knows the talent PHILIPPE and NICOLE as 'Phil Kam' and 'Helen Demare,' JEAN REYNARD and LAMAR TALKA as 'Charles Gray' and 'Jack Lum') hangs back, but NICOLE grabs her hand and pulls her into the light beside her. "Stand right here, Malena."

JEAN REYNARD looks out at the four people standing in front of him. "Before we get started, I want to introduce Malena, who just came onboard as talent." JEAN extends his hand toward her. PHILIPPE, NICOLE, and LAMAR each take a turn shaking her hand.

LAMAR goes back to the camera. He shuffles through the papers, pulls out a page, and looks at it. "Okay, listen up. I wrote some stuff when I was back home. I want to go over it now. First thing: the script. We want this to be true documentary and that means no editing of what happens in front of the camera. Therefore, the script has to be void of opinion. I talked to Phil, and told him to come up with some questions we will ask when we get on scene. Helen, it's your job to keep it that way, Okay?" NICOLE nods. "Great. Helen, it's also your job to coach Malena so she has a handle on what we're trying to do here, all right?"

NICOLE nods again and puts her arm around MALENA's shoulder. "She'll do fine, Jean." MALENA smiles shyly.

"Great. I know I can count on you girls to get the response we need when we get out on the streets," REYNARD concludes, looking at the crew severely.

"Does she speak our language?" asks TALKA.

MALENA nods. «Oui, Monsieur. Je parle bien français, j'espère.»

REYNARD jumps in. "That's fine, Malena. I hope so too; thank you." They all laugh. "The next thing is dress. We want to blend in as much as possible, so we went out and took a look on the streets to come up with costumes for the girls—a combination of a shawl, veil, and street clothes. We call the getups 'Fun Arab.' Wear these and you'll be real troopers." Laughter.

NICOLE leans over and whispers to MALENA. "I'll bet they itch."

LAMAR peeks out from behind the camera. "Charles, I'm not wearing any damned robe," he laughs, and squints back into the viewfinder.

"That's all right, Jack—we'll let you wear your usual evening dress." They all laugh.

"Enough with the levity. Phil, did you give Helen the scripts?"

PHILIPPE gestures to NICOLE and MALENA. "Yes, I did. Helen has them."

"Helen, you and Malena come up center camera here, and go over the questions." NICOLE pulls two folded scripts from her bag and lays it aside. She hands one to MALENA. The two walk to center camera and stand by JEAN.

Jean turns to his script. "Okay, just start out and read through it. Be natural. Helen, you read first. Malena, I want you to imagine you have just witnessed an explosion. You narrowly escaped, but a friend of your is dead because of it. Position yourself just there to the left, out of camera range. When I point to you, run past Helen like the devil himself is after you."

Malena walks ten feet left, off camera range.

Nicole is center. Jean walks out of camera view and cues Malena, who runs to center, where Nicole is standing. "Excuse me, excuse me —Madame! What happened down there?" Malena stops. "What happened down the street?"

"A bomb exploded?" Malena says tentatively.

"Cut!" Jean walks over to Malena. "Great movement, Malena. Remember, you just saw one of your friends killed. Act scared and mad at the same time."

Malena, abashed, glances at Nicole. "I am scared."

Jean joins Lamar behind the camera. "Let's try it from there, and action!"

Malena regains her composure. Nicole starts her line. "What was your immediate reaction?"

"A bomb—a bomb! My friend was killed back there; my friend is dead!"

"Cut!" Jean yells. He comes over to Malena and kisses her cheek.

"Great job. You're going to do just fine," he says. "You're on your way to being a real trooper."

Not used to the attention, Malena recoils from his French gesture. "Merci, monsieur." She looks around at Nicole, who is smiling. "Did I do fine?" Malena asks.

"You did." Nicole replies.

"I'd like being a 'real trooper.'"

† †

Jack, the cameraman, turned off his equipment and caught up to Mr. Gray. Jack leaned over to him and said in a loud whisper, "Jean, the truth is on the streets, not in hotel gardens."

Mr. Gray frowned and said, "You're right."

Malena was startled but tried not show it. *Why did Jack call him "Jean"? Who are these people?*

† †

The next couple of weeks were hectic. Malena would finish her last gig around midnight, and have to get up and find her way to the hotel by six a.m. Sometimes she would have to walk when no taxis or pedicabs were in sight.

When she fell asleep on Helen's sofa after the last shoot of the week, she missed her gigs altogether. The next day she crept back to The Black Owl in the early morning and collapsed onto her bed.

Sidu came into her room without knocking, and stood over her. "You missed your performance last night—where were you?"

She rolled over and looked at him sleepily. "I'm exhausted. Get out."

Sidu bristled. "Since you're spending so much time with the Americans at the hotel, why don't you take a room there and get some rest before work?"

Her eyes widened. "Maybe I should." She got up and began packing, filling two bags and her tote. She grabbed the cheap record player she had bought with her first paycheck. Balancing the record player on top of her bags, she pushed past Sidu, saying, "I like this idea."

Stunned by her rapid recovery, he exclaimed, "When are you going to work?"

"I am going to work," she said, and slammed the door.

She walked out to the Kasbah and hailed a cab across from le Palais du Dey. "Take me to Hôtel Fleur de l'Âge," she yelled over the traffic noise, and they sped away.

While she was checking in, Helen came up to her at the desk. "Malena—hi. Are you checking in?"

"Yes, I'm fed up with that damned place," Malena said.

"What place—oh never mind. I'm glad you're here. What room did you get?"

Malena checked her key. "Number four-twelve."

"Hey, we're on the same floor. You're just down the hall from me."

Malena gave a half smile, saying, "That's good. I need to practice with you." She picked up her bags and struggled with the record player.

"Let me help you with that," Helen said, taking the record player. Malena grabbed it back from her and set it on top of her bags. "I can manage."

"Well, let me carry something."

Malena juggled a bag out. "Take this one." The bag tumbled but Helen caught it. Malena stomped off for the elevator. Once they were inside, she eyed Helen suspiciously. "Maybe we can be friends, is it 'Helen'?"

† †

Talka met Philippe and Nicole at the hotel's long bar. The massive mahogany structure was bound on either side by potted indoor palms; their fronds waved in a downwash from the ceiling where a black fan swirled. Bottles fitted with pouring spouts lined the shelf behind the bar. A mirror running the full length of the shelf showed grey spots where the silver on the back had peeled away from the glass.

Nicole described Malena's check-in for the two men. "At first I was amused," she said. "You should have seen her; she walked into the hotel lobby as if she had been out on safari. I mean, long, striped dress, exotic jewelry clanking from her neck and arms, carrying a stack of bags with a record player teetering on top of the whole mess—and a tote slung over her shoulder to boot...God knows what else she brought. What a balancing act!"

"She's been through a lot," Philippe observed. "Those things she balanced were probably the sum total of her worldly possessions."

"Ah hell," Talka said, "at least she's free to come and go as she pleases—that's more that I can say for the rest of us." He shot Nicole a sly glance.

Philippe caught his look. "I guess we all need to get out more..."

"You'll get your chance, Philippe, I promise you that." Talka asserted.

"What do you know?" Philippe asked.

"Just that we're going deeper into the city, where bombs are likely to explode."

"I wouldn't mind seeing a little action," Philippe said.

"Like I told you, you'll get your chance, and you won't need to bring your pen with you."

"You'd like that." Philippe snapped back.

"No, *ami*, I'm just saying the bombs have a voice of their own."

Nicole slugged back her drink and stood up. "We'll know it when we hear it," she said, and walked out of the long bar.

"What's eating her?" asked Philippe.

Talka stood up, finished his drink and smiled. "Too much excitement, I guess."

"Lamar, can we talk about the next couple of days?"

"Not now Philippe; I'm tired. I'm turning in. How 'bout tomorrow morning?"

"Sure, anytime."

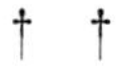

Nicole was lying down in her hotel room when a knock came at the door. Getting up, she went to the door and opened it to Talka. "Hi. I was resting—what?" When he just stood there, she asked, "Do you want to come in?"

He walked in, toting a bottle of bourbon, and held it out to her. "I saw you drinking bourbon, and thought we could get better acquainted over a couple of glasses of the stuff."

Nicole shrugged. "Sure, why not? Have a seat." She took the bottle over to the dresser and poured two fingers of liquid into each glass. "I have some water."

"No water. Just neat for me." She poured water from a bottle into her glass and walked back to the sofa, handing him his glass and sitting beside him. "Cheers," she said, sipping her drink.

"*Tchin-tchin,*" he replied and gulped down the entire glass.

"You've had practice," Nicole mused.

"Long and hard," he said.

Nicole raised her eyebrows and takes another sip.

"So…"

"So…?" She put down her glass.

"So, how do you like working with Jean?" Talka asked.

"Pretty straightforward guy," she said, nodding slowly. "I always know where I stand. I kinda like him."

Talka stretched his arms out on the back of the sofa. "You do always know where you stand with Jean. How do you find Algiers?"

Nicole shifted a little away from him and sipped her drink. "Haven't seen much of it, but what I have seen is okay."

"The coast is beautiful. We should make time to see it."

"I'd like that. Do you really think we could?"

"Sure. No problem. We can rent a car and make a day of it."

"Maybe we can. Your glass is empty; would you like another drink?"

"Yeah. One for the road." She went to the dresser and poured another drink, not quite two fingers. Talka held up her glass, saying "Here, pour one for yourself."

She shook her head. "No, I'm still working on that one," she said, then added, "Pretty good whisky, though." She brought back his drink, sat down, and picked up her glass. "Here's how."

They clinked their glasses together. Talka smirked, "I know how; I'd like to know who." They laughed.

Nicole put down her glass and turned toward him. "How do *you* find Algiers?" She softened her gaze a little and crossed her right leg over her left so that it pointed toward Talka. She looked at his copper-colored hair, closely cropped above his high forehead. His eyes were friendly and his smile genuine.

"I've been here before. It's a beautiful place, if you know where to look—and I do. I would like to show you around, if you'd let me."

"Why not? If you think it's safe," she said.

"No worries." Talka dropped his right arm so that it rested lightly on her left shoulder. "I can take the right precautions."

Nicole stiffened and narrowed her eyes slightly. *I'll bet you can.* "Maybe we can get away after the shoot."

He fidgeted with the sleeve of her blouse, doubling the cloth between his fingers and sliding them one way, then the other. "We'd need at least a half a day."

"Half a day's a long time," she replied.

"Half a day's long enough." Talka turned his body toward her, moving his fingers to her collar. "There never seems to be enough time, does there?"

"Depends on what you need to do," she said, and leaned back against his arm, pinning it between the sofa and her back. The offending fingers stopped, and Talka put his hand back on the sofa. He took a sip of whiskey, rolled it slowly around in his mouth, then swallowed it.

"What do we need to do?" he asked, leaning close to her.

"That remains to be seen."

"How's the girl working out?"

Nicole relaxed a bit. "She's a hoot. She's so unusual, but I like her. I think she suspects something though."

"Who we are?"

"She's concerned about it." Nicole felt the pitch of her voice go up. "Once in a while, she comes by after her last show at that cabaret where she sings. Just to let down, I suppose. She's been asking questions about where we come from in America."

"Just stay in character; you'll be okay."

"I don't know—it's a little stressful. When she shows up at my door, I always feel like I need to put on my bra or something."

Talka laughed, repeating, "Put on your bra?"

"A figure of speech."

He looked down at her chest. "And a pretty figure it is too."

"Oh stop." Nicole waved her hand at him.

"Did you feel that way when I showed up?"

"Nooo..."

"You're not wearing your bra, then?"

"I'm wearing one."

"I wouldn't want you to feel stressed out or anything like that."

"What—you want me to take it off?"

"Why not? We're friends."

"Not *that* friendly."

"Okay, don't get your panties in a bunch; you don't have to do anything you don't want to."

"Excuse me—get my panties in a bunch?" she laughs.

"A figure of speech."

Nicole searched his eyes. *What's this guy really about?* She took his hand in hers. "Lamar, I don't know...maybe we shouldn't get involved."

"Hey, who's involved? I just stopped by for a drink. Come on, Nicole, lighten up."

"You're right; I'm just on edge, that's all." She gave his hand a squeeze, and tried to let go, but Talka had a grip on it. He brought her hand up to his neck, and leaned over to kiss her on the lips. Nicole didn't pull back. She scooted closer to him and put her other arm around his neck. She felt his hand slip inside her blouse. "What are you doing, Lamar?"

"Just making sure you have your bra on," he chuckled.

"Just a minute." She let go of him and unbuttoned her blouse.

"I'll be damned! You are wearing one."

"Told you...," she whispered, kissing him. "And you're not tearing my clothes."

"I won't do that."

"I know," she said, taking his other hand and placing it on her knee.

† †

In the following days, Sun King Productions would venture out onto the street, to get the lay of the land, as Reynard put it.

Talka leaned around the camera, chuckling, "I'm glad someone's getting laid, Charles." Nicole burst out laughing.

"What's so funny, Helen?" Reynard asked.

"Sorry, private joke." She looked in the direction of Talka's camera, and then quickly ducked her head, covering her mouth with her hand to hide the smile.

Nicole marveled at how quickly Malena had fallen into the routine and how rested she seemed. She would dash off after the last shoot and head out to the Kasbah, disappearing into the labyrinth of winding streets and alleys to God knows where. She returned to the hotel in the evenings, carrying a dress or other clothing.

Malena often came into her room to unwind or to ask her questions about acting. "You'd better get to bed, Malena," Nicole always told her. Despite Malena's unique behavior, Nicole grew fond of her, describing her to the others as "sweet, if a bit unusual." Sometimes Nicole had the nagging urge to confess her real identity to Malena, but thought the better of it. *What she doesn't know won't hurt her—and what she does know may hurt me.*

† †

Despite the early calls, Malena did get more rest. After her last performance each evening, she would grab some clothes and sneak out before Sidu or Nuluna could corner her, knowing sooner or later a confrontation would happen, if for no other reason than that she would have to demand her pay. Malena liked her new employers much better; she was delighted by Reynard's quips, his describing as her "Miss Grit," and dubbing her "Real Trooper."

After the shoot, Malena would hike over to Mallory's before going to The Black Owl. One day she showed earlier than usual, disguised as a Tuareg man. It was early afternoon and he was not at home, so she stretched out on his bed.

She was asleep when Mallory came over to the bed and kissed her. She woke up and said, "Oh hello, Lytton. What time is it?"

"Five. Would you like some espresso?"

"I have time," she said. She got up and went to watch him prepare a small pot, admiring his agile hands. Everything was a matter of precision with Mallory. "I'm not 'Dark' anymore," she declared.

"Who are you then?"

"Miscrit—Real Trooper."

"What? Who calls you that?" he said with half a laugh. He poured out two demitasses and brought them over to where she sat on the sofa.

"Mr. Gray. He says that I'm 'Miscrit Real Trooper,' especially after a long shoot, when he calls it a 'take.' I don't understand why he says 'take.' We haven't, you know."

"What?"

"Taken anything. The first part of the name, 'Miscrit,' he says, must mean like—misplace. You must know."

Mallory let out a laugh, "More like Miss Take—you've been taken."

"Where?"

"Inside the camera."

Sensing a joke, Malena laughed, "But we're outside."

"Just your image goes inside."

She put her arms around him. "And what, my dear Lytton, does it do there?"

He pulled her to him. "Waits to be seen again."

† †

Philippe caught up with Reynard at the long bar. "Jean, we need to talk." He was out of breath as if he had just run the marathon.

Reynard looked at Philippe's red face, radiating from beneath his dark hair. His brown eyes were bloodshot, like he had tried to read in the dim light of the bar. "What's up, Philippe?"

"Why didn't you tell me we were changing our venue?"

"It's true. So far we've haven't had much action here."

"I like the idea of more action," Philippe tapped his index finger on the bar's counter "But why didn't you talk to me about it?"

"Philippe, I depend on you as the expert here. That hasn't changed. The truth is, I was going to do one shoot and then discuss it with you tomorrow night."

"I just think I ought to be in on these changes—ahead of time. It's unfair for you and Talka to keep me out of the picture."

"I'm sorry, Philippe. I didn't mean to offend you. It's just that I've been so busy; I thought you would understand what kind of pressure I'm under."

Philippe softened a little. "I know, Jean, we're all a little stressed. Okay, tomorrow then. We'll talk." He got up from the barstool to walk out, then turned around and asked, "Is something going on between Nicole and Talka?"

Reynard was caught off-guard. "I haven't any idea. What makes you think that?""Just a look she gave him the other day; I thought you might know something."

Reynard turned around and faced the huge mirror. "Is that something that's bothering you?"

"I just don't think she should get involved with a guy like that. But I guess I should mind my own business." Reynard started to reply, but Philippe continued, "Never mind, Jean—forget I said anything. We'll talk tomorrow." Philippe turned and left.

Reynard looked at himself in the mirror; the grey spots were superimposed on his reflection. *God, I'm getting old.* He finished his drink.

When Reynard returned to his room, he slumped into his desk chair. *This isn't going well. I have no one to blame but myself. Talka is right—we're not getting what we're after in the courtyard, nor on the streets where we're shooting. We have to get down where the action is, or at least where we think it is. Nothing ventured, nothing gained.*

Reynard's thoughts turned to Philippe. *When I met Philippe's dad, and we talked about his experience flying combat over Indochina and Algeria, what did he say? "If you want action, you must go where the action is; if you want glory, you must go within."* Then Reynard laughed, remembering his paraphrase aloud: "No guts, no Croix de Guerre."

He got out his briefcase and pulled out his production notes he had jotted down back in Paris. It felt as if he were reading them for the first time. *Have I gotten so wrapped up in the nuts and bolts of production that I have forgotten why we are filming in the first place?* He reread them again. *No cross-purposes for the film; we must film only what is true,* he thought. *We came to film about freedom—the precious freedom Philippe goes on about; freedom to believe as you choose, without fear of being blown up by the guy sitting next to you because he disagrees. And people are being executed right on the street. Old men killed for believing, women killed for not wearing the veil.*

Reynard felt torn by Philippe's insistence on casting the meaning of all of it through dialogue, not just questions. *Talka wants the film to tell its own story: "Let the truth unfold." That's a lot of takes. Great idea if we don't run out of film. Dump Philippe's dialogue into it, and it's no longer a documentary. I want Philippe's ideas but not his words—they are true, but they'll destroy the documentary. I have to find a way to get him out of the picture without hurting him.*

Reynard wrote:

Focus on the woman; she's the sympathetic character. Use Nicole and the Berber girl Malena to this advantage, by showing destruction of their freedom. Nicole through the translations becomes Malena on the screen. Let Philippe write a script that makes Nicole the algérienne with whom the audience will sympathize.

Nicole will have a look at it, then show it to Malena. They'll have the idea; they can extemporize at the scene. Malena can back Nicole up on the street.

He put down the paper. *I must get to Sidu tonight. We need to take to the streets. It's dangerous, but as Robert DuPont said, "No guts..."*

First he called Philippe to tell him they needed to talk. Philippe showed up at his door *tout de suite.* As he let him in, Reynard asked, "Philippe, that book you're writing—who is it, Camus? *Theatre of the Absurd* thing? Anyway, I want you to frame Nicole's questions to center around the absurdity of the killing in the street.

Philippe thought for a minute. "It's the absurdity of the street that's the cause of the problem. Camus, as you said, put it succinctly in *The Rebel:* in our generation, the logical conclusion is that suicide and murder are the same thing, the final shutting out of things."

"Take as many with you as you can, so to speak.

"Exactly. As this logic teaches us, since nothing makes sense, then anything is possible—and acceptable. Murder has become a science."

"Fine. Go with that line. Question people on how they feel about it."

Philippe nodded. "As the Americans say, 'See ya.'" He went out the door and closed it behind him.

Reynard picked up the phone to call Sidu. He told him they needed to get out on the street, and they needed proper attire and some measure of security—a perimeter around the area where they would be filming. When they moved, the perimeter must move. "I don't want my people becoming the victims while they're filming the victims," he said.

Philippe returned to his room flushed with excitement; he could finally inject something of the reality of the situation into the documentary. *What is Algeria really saying to me?* He sat down and opened his laptop. He looked at the ceiling while it booted up, as if the answer to the riddle of the universe was displayed there. *Independence.* He called up his word processor and typed:

In its search for freedom, it found confinement; in its search for God, it found death.

He looked at the line he had just typed, and pursed his lips. *Good concluding line—I'll keep it.* He spent the better part of an hour reworking his idea. After saving it, he hooked up a portable printer and printed out Nicole's introduction. He grabbed up the pages one by one as they came out of the printer, rereading them for errors and for content. The words excited him.

He got up and went to the window, rereading what he had snapped up from the printer. Philippe nodded with approval and clipped the papers together, opened the door, and ran down the hall to Nicole's room.

Nicole opened the door, saying, "La, la. Onward Christian Soldiers. You're here." She took the script and sat down. "This is Hélène Demaurie speaking to you from Algiers. Today we document what's been happening here in the streets. Just moments ago, a bomb exploded, just there." She pointed to the imaginary scene. Then she looked up at Philippe. "How are we going to arrange that?"

"It's being arranged; the terrorists are perfecting their skills for somewhere else."

"Where?"

"I don't know—Spain, maybe."

"Oh, good God." Nicole continued with the script: "People were killed." She pages down to the closing comments. "I love this ending, Philippe; you really do understand things the way they are, don't you?"

"Yes…yes I do, but remember, the first step doesn't tell the whole story."

"Maybe the first step is asking the four questions in Arabic. Malena won't have to be there."

"How will you do that?"

"She and I can get together and practice." Nicole tried saying something to him in Arabic. "See, we've been at it already."

Philippe held his hands up to his ears and shook his head. "Never mind, never mind, you sound great. *I* believe you, but will they?"

"They'll get it all right; don't you worry your shaking little head about that."

"Get me a piece of paper, won't you?"

Nicole went over to the desk and got a piece from the drawer, bringing it to him. Philippe scribbled something and handed it to her. She continued, "After the French colony fell in 1962, a new regime took over the government. Now there are bombings in the streets and murder in the marketplace. We'll witness what's happening to them in a country that has reportedly been a spawning ground for terrorism. Perhaps this is a prelude—a dress rehearsal for the rest of the world. We'll see the atrocities firsthand, unedited—" She threw down the paper and glared at Philippe. "Oh brother, I don't need this. I'm supposed to what? Say this with bullets and bodies flying by? How *are* we going to get all these shots?"

"Lamar and Jean are pretty good at getting to the heart of the matter. Don't worry; they'll get the live shots. All you have to worry about it is reporting what you see."

"I haven't seen anything yet."

"You will."

"At least I won't be a talking head—" Nicole flounced down on the couch. "Might lose it though."

† †

SITREP #1

WE ARE IN PLACE NOW. I AM ORGANIZING THE SHOOT. WE HAVE A LOCAL BERBER WOMAN NAMED MALENA. SPEAKS HER NATIVE TONGUE, ARABIC, FRENCH, AND SOME ENGLISH. NOT BAD-LOOKING IN A ROUGH-CUT SORT OF WAY. SHE MAY BE OF USE TO US IN THE LONG RUN. NIAGRI.

† †

Nicole was having trouble with the script and the memory of Talka's touch. She picked up her blouse and dress she had heaped on the sofa, and put them up to her nose. They smelled of sex and sour mash. Taking them to the bathroom, she tossed them in the hamper.

She took a bath and put on fresh underwear under her terry cloth robe. Wandering over to the dresser, she pulled out some jeans and a white linen blouse.

Once dressed, she sat down on the sofa. Talka had connected with her in a way she hadn't expected, and they had made love. Now she wanted him again, yet she knew better than to get involved. *Was she just a conquest?* Her desire, rising to the base of her diaphragm, pushed upward against her lungs. She gulped air down to quell the feeling. *It's more a prelude to human addiction than to the whiskey-water,* she thought. Getting up from the sofa, she went to the dresser and poured herself a drink.

Sitting back down, she picked up the script Philippe had given her. Looking at it, she thought, *Poor Philippe, what's to become of him? He seems too sensitive for this sort of work.* From the moment they reunited back in Paris, she had known he wanted her. Somehow with her it didn't click, and she could only remember him from their childhood in Bizerte, when he had loved Catherine Pozzi's poems and known them by heart.

Nicole shook her head in reverence, thinking, *How he loved poetry.* They would lie on the grass at the edge of the field, and Philippe would recite while his brother, Michael, played soccer. Nicole would ask him to say the poems again, and he would. They did this for the entire game. Whenever Michael scored, Philippe immediately suspended his recitation and jumped up, and she did along with him; they'd cheer like mad, then flop back down. Philippe would continue as if there had been no break at all.

Philippe and Michael had had a pet chameleon, *DeGaulle*, with a reptilian personality, who would bite Nicole whenever she tried to pick him up. *Whatever happened to that damned lizard?* She picked up her glass, said, "*Merde!* Too long ago," and swigged down the rest of the whiskey-water.

Picking up the phone, she rang Malena to ask if she would come and help her with the translations, then poured another drink.

Malena knocked. "Door's open," Nicole said. Malena swirled

in, wearing a sea-green dress that accentuated the *vert glauque* of her eyes. She was bare-legged and wore brown leather sandals.

"This," Nicole said, "is our test," handing Malena the questions Philippe had written down in French. She took a quick swig of her drink. "I'm in deep trouble here. I told Philippe I could do this—ask these questions in Arabic," she said.

She and Malena stood close to each other, face-to-face for a moment. Malena blinked and said, "Your eyes and mine are nearly the same color—have you noticed?"

"Yes, I'm half-Berber on my mother's side."

Malena smiled, said, "Maybe we're related, way back," and began reading the script, her lips moving as she went over the questions. She looked intently at Nicole. "You're going into the dangerous part of the street, aren't you?"

Nicole nodded. "You're going with me."

Malena frowned. "We could be killed," she said, then sighed, "We had better get started, before Messouda sings."

"Who's Mess-uda?"

† †

Malena worked on the difficult Arabic with Helen for six hours, until they were exhausted. Helen gave Malena a hug and said, "Let's rest —lie down for a while." Malena nodded. "You can take the sofa, and I'll lie down on the bed." Helen finished her drink, and crossing over to the bed, rolled into it, pulling the bedspread over her.

Malena swung her legs up on the sofa cushions. She put her hands beneath her head and closed her eyes. Then she sniffed the cushion where her head was, wrinkled her nose, and sat up. She slipped down onto the Oriental rug, curled up, and fell asleep.

A boy walks on the beach; a girl appears beside him. At first, the girl is Malena and the boy looks like Kaarem. They are on the road in the Djurdjura Mountains leading to the Marabout Tashoda's house. When they get closer, they're different children, not themselves.

"Oh, isn't it beautiful?" the girl says. Under his arm, the boy carries a scroll, which he hands to her. She takes it and unrolls the paper as if it were a flag, or Holy Scripture. She reads.

What words vibrate in her head so? Where they are taking her? To the Kabylia, to the cave?

The boy and girl are watching a soccer match. Another boy runs for the goal, kicking the ball ahead of him. The girl admires the boy who is running for his prowess, but loves the boy next to her for his words.

Malena turns around and sees the scroll awash in the surf. It begins to unfurl, and from it, a girl emerges.

There's someone at the cave entrance. Malena runs toward it, but a large stone rolls over it, and she's in the dark.

Malena awoke in a cold sweat. The dream was still at the corner of her lips as if she'd been talking in her sleep. She got up and went over to Helen's sink to wash her face. She looked into the mirror; her green eyes stared back, knowing the reality of the dream's meaning. She looked down at Helen, still asleep with her forearm over her eyes. Malena wiped her face with a towel and left the room.

Waiting for the elevator, she rubbed her hands together to wring out the rest of the dampness. When the door opened, she got in and pressed 5.

Getting out of the elevator, Malena rushed to Mr. Gray's door and knocked. When he opened the door, Malena walked past him. "Helen has learned her lines in Arabic, so there's no need for my presence on the street."

"What's wrong Malena?" Mr. Gray asked. "You sound like you don't want to go."

"It's not safe."

"It's not safe for any of us, Malena."

"It's especially not safe for me. I'm a Berber who hates the veil, living in an Arab nation."

"That's the story we are telling the world. We need you, Malena. I'd like you and Helen to take turns, so the camera can find out what works best. And in case anything unexpected arises, like

Helen forgetting her Arabic lines. In the end, we may help your cause."

Malena raised her dark eyebrows. "It's too late, Mr. Gray. I only want out."

"Stay with us Malena, and maybe we can see to your escape, if that's what you really want."

That was not what Malena had expected. She really wanted to get to the man. She had been bursting with the knowledge that Kaarem had passed along to her. However, the documentary was not the only reason she had come to Gray's room—she was looking for the agent Kaarem had told her about. Biding her time, she simply told him, "I really don't want to be seen on the street during daylight."

"This shouldn't take more than a week," he insisted.

Malena searched his face for assurance. He smiled and placed his hands on her shoulders. "Okay," she said. "I'll be there."

"You're a real trooper."

Malena took the chance. "We may be there too long to sing."

"Sing what?" he asked.

"When Messouda sings."

"What?"

"When Messouda sings," she said again.

Sitrep #2

Connected with Malena this afternoon. She says it isn't safe on the streets for her. I told her I decided to ask questions in Arabic on the street. Don't know how it will work out yet, we'll see.

Malena said something to me that sounded like code: "When Messouda sings." Wasn't that the name of the first front company here? Advise. Niagri.

† †

Malena was waiting with the others in the lobby the next day when Sidu showed up with some Arab-looking robes and a plan.

He told the group he knew of a place in town that was a favorite spot for the suicide bombers to blow themselves up, taking as many shoppers with them as they could.

"Where?" Malena asked.

"In Bab-el-Oued—in la Place des Trois Horloges," Mr. Gray said

Malena blanched. She knew the area well. "Many have died there," she said. "But they never seem to blow up the clocks."

"What's that about the clocks?" asked Jack.

"It's a traffic circle with a tall standard at its center. At the top of pole are three clocks facing in different directions, so no matter where you are when the bomb goes off, you'll know what time it is when you die," she explained.

Jack laughed at her description and Helen said, "I don't see what's so damned funny."

"I can't help it," he said, "it *is* funny." He looked happy about going into danger, and Malena hated him for it.

Mr. Gray said, "Let's go," and the company wrapped themselves in the robes that Sidu had brought, picked up their gear, and followed Sidu to a pickup he had brought with him.

The drive from the hotel led along a wide street filled with pedestrians, pedicabs, and cars. There was the familiar din of horns and shouts as people vied for their pieces of the street. Gulls flew in huge circles above them, echoing frantic calls as they dove and banked, snapping away at each others' food.

The pickup inched to the northwest beneath the aerial combat, crossing several more clogged streets. Finally they cleared the traffic jam, and Gray accelerated onto the Cornice of Algiers, speeding past the same view Mallory and Malena had enjoyed on their trip to Tipaza. Veering to the left up into a narrower street, they could see the basilica standing above them in the distance.

When they came to the wedge-shaped Square of Three Clocks, Mr. Gray swerved into an empty parking spot with such violence that they had to grab onto the sides of the bed to keep from tumbling out. Gray ratcheted on the parking brake and killed the engine, and they all piled out.

Malena looked around at the claustrophobic square; shoppers flowed in from narrow streets, crowded shops, and stands where vendors touted their wares.

Jack had been the first out, and he pointed to a likely spot. Helen positioned herself in front of him, and he began to adjust the camera lens.

"You're too close—you must be photographing my tonsils," she said in a stage whisper.

"Yes, and I see you've had them out, and you're wearing the blue bra."

"Smart-ass, I'm wearing a robe; you can't see my bra."

Jack peered through the lens, zooming in to Helen's chest. "Still, it gives one pause..."

"Keep your dirty paws off me."

He looked up and smiled. "You're just fine; stay there on the street and quit acting like a pair of boobs. Now shut up and say the lines, and let me worry about the camera angle."

"That's harassment; I'm telling..."

Mr. Gray chimed in. "Okay you two, remember what we're trying to do here: street scene, factual reporting. Helen, I'll cue you to start the questions. Just pull in the first person who runs past."

Malena stood on one foot, then the other. Minutes went by and... nothing. People swirled around them as if they did not exist. Then suddenly, almost as if Mr. Gray had cued an explosives man, they heard a dull thud down the street. A swirl of dust rose.

"That's it!" Mr. Gray cried. "Action!"

A woman carrying a tote full of vegetables tried to hurry past Helen, who hooked her open arm. Jack squinted into the viewer, and pressed the record button as Helen held onto the squirming woman. But the woman wrenched free and continued running down the street. Another woman ran by, and Helen held up the mike, but the woman pushed it out of the way and continued on her way. Next, a man tried to pass. Helen stopped him and began the questioning in Arabic. "Zut alors!" he cried, and fled down the street.

Helen looked into the camera. "Jeez, I forgot most of these people speak French."

"Keep shooting," yelled Mr. Gray. "Here comes another."

Helen stopped another man. This time she yelled the questions in French: "Sir! Excuse me, you're running. Did you hear an explosion?"

The startled man stopped dead in his tracks, and began to answer the questions. "Of course I heard the explosion, I was only a few meters away—and of course I'm running, wouldn't you? The man was a maniac...who knows what he was thinking?" The man looked at her for a moment. "What in the hell are you doing here? Why aren't you running? Did you people start this thing? Who are you anyway?"

Helen, looking startled, said, "Well...thank you for your time..."

Mr. Gray yelled, "Cut! Now Malena."

Another woman came running. Mr. Gray yelled, "Rolling!"

Malena successfully stopped the woman and asked, "Did you know the man who blew himself up?"

"*Non, l'étranger*—not from here. I saw him browsing suspiciously, sneaking looks this way and that. I didn't like the way he was looking at me, so I moved away; a good thing I did, eh? No, I didn't know him."

"Has this been going on down here a long time?" asked Malena.

"Too long; many people have died."

"Have you personally known any of those killed?"

"No one."

"What do you think was going on in the bomber's mind?"

"Someone told me that these extremists think they are committing acts of martyrdom to go straight to heaven."

"You say they kill to be saved?"

"I'm saying someone told them they could have all the virgins they wanted once they got there—who knows, maybe they're sex-starved."

After that interview, Malena had broken the ice. She stuck to the general line of questions Phil had written down, but she found she could improve on them. After sizing up each passerby, she would launch into the questions. By the end of the shoot, Helen had caught onto Malena's tactic, and she was getting good footage too. By four o'clock, they had ten solid interviews.

"A couple more days of this, and we'll have enough for the final cut," Mr. Gray said.

Jack didn't sound so sure. "We need more action if we're to get to the heart of the matter. A shocker, something that will grab the audience."

Mr. Gray said he would talk to Sidu again and see what he could come up with. "We can't exactly create massacres on command," he said.

"With all the stuff going on in the streets, I think we should be able to come up with something," replied Jack.

"I don't know if I want to get that close," Helen said. Malena nodded in agreement.

"Yeah, pretty soon I won't have to write any script, but just keep my head down," said Phil.

"Pipe down now, here comes Sidu." Mr. Gray said.

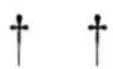

Over the next two days, an ugly man Malena had seen around the hotel drove up in his car with Sidu. They came in the mornings and watched from the car. They observed the takes, keeping their distance, but toward the end of the day he drove his car within meters of the actual shoot.

Jack said he wanted to get shots closer to the explosions, but they stayed near the pickup. Then on the second day, just down the block from the three clocks, a bomber detonated the belt of explosives wrapped about his waist. Jack and Helen jumped into the back of the pickup, and Helen grabbed Malena and pulled her up as well. Mr. Gray jumped behind the wheel, and they dashed into the middle of the carnage before anyone could think better of it. Sidu and his companion remained behind.

When they stopped, Malena jumped off, pulled the veil over her face and trotted to the source of the explosion, from which smoke was still rising. Jack followed her, then Helen, Mr. Gray, and Phil. *Where are the people? There's no one coming.*

† †

Malena sat in Mallory's apartment, gulping her anguish down like bad food. She knew Mallory sensed something was wrong; she couldn't stop fidgeting and her body was tense in his embrace.

"Tell me—what's the matter?"

"We've been shooting scenes downtown."

"Dangerous?"

"Yes; I told them I didn't want to be there, but Mr. Gray insisted." She described the vivid scene to Mallory. "Now I have been trying to stop people who are running from explosions and ask questions while Jack films me. If I can get someone to talk, he stores it. I didn't like taking to the streets in daylight. As far back as I can remember, insurgents have been killing people in the name of Allah, and for no other reason.

"Gray insisted that I snag people running and ask, 'What happened, and who did it?' Most people would just keep going; a few stopped and screamed a few words in Arabic or French. Some would curse me for somehow being the cause: 'You and those bastards you're dealing with have caused this. Allah is angry with you and taking it out on us for allowing you to be here in the first place. Death to all of you; death to the Jews of the world.'

"Today we were near the Trois Horloges—you know the place?" Mallory nodded. "We sat there, waiting for something to happen. Then a bomber exploded just meters away. The street was packed and most of the impact was absorbed by people between the bomber and the crew. They simply fell over like bales of straw. Men made of straw. Then Mr. Gray yelled, 'We're rolling,' and down the street I went. That time there was no one to grab or talk to.

"I began to see the full effect of the explosion: a severed arm here, a leg there. The street was covered in red, as if someone had dropped a vat of red paint from a roof.

"Mr. Gray yelled at me to let Jack through. I jumped out of the way, and Jack walked past me in a crouch, holding the camera up to his eye. He went to the spot where the explosion happened, and stood upright, still holding the camera, focusing on the spot. Then he stopped filming.

"No one said a thing. I saw dead people and those who were still dying. Some were moving, badly injured. I was thinking, *They awake only to die again.* I heard someone crying softly. I remember what she said: 'My poor daughter…'"

† †

After that last day of shooting, Malena went missing. Reynard had been to her room several times, but decided to try one last time. He knocked, but there was no answer. He wanted to ask her about what she had said to him. He was convinced it was a code, meant to be answered with the proper reply, but he didn't have a clue as to what that response might be. Maybe she had been in contact with a person who knew of or had one of the daggers. Reynard had to assume that whoever had killed Hassan was looking for the other envoy. *Where in the hell is Miss Grit?*

When Reynard got back to his room, Sidu was waiting in front of his door. His plump face was dotted with beads of sweat on his forehead and his upper lip. As Reynard let him in, Sidu asked, "Have you seen Malena? I've been looking for her."

"So have I. I want to discuss the shoot tomorrow. But I'm glad you came. The shoot today went well, but we need…mmm…an incident, something that we're right in the middle of. Is there a boiling pot where something like that might happen?"

"I'll snoop around a bit and see what I can come up with," replied Sidu.

"One more thing," Reynard handed him an envelope inside a sandwich bag. "Get this to our man, won't you? It's urgent."

Taking the package, Sidu said, "As soon as I get back to the cabaret."

Someone knocked on the door. Reynard opened it to find Malena standing there. Her hair was disheveled, and her eyes looked as if she hadn't slept in days. "Helen says you have been looking for me, Mr. Gray."

"Yes, I want to discuss your role in the shoot tomorrow—come in. Mr. Sidu and I were just finishing our business, weren't we?"

"Correct. However, before I leave, I want to speak with Malena."

† †

Sidu pulled Malena out of Reynard's room, and closed the door behind them. Still grasping her, he said, "Be at the cabaret in an hour."

Malena wrenched her hand free and said, "I don't work for you anymore. Find someone else!" He grabbed her by the shoulder, but she kicked him in the groin and he doubled over. She reached back, fumbled for the doorknob, and twisting it open, fell back into Reynard's room.

"Malena, you *fatma*," Sidu hissed, "I'll make you disappear."

When he got back to The Black Owl, Sidu removed the envelope from the sandwich bag, and discovered Reynard had forgotten to seal it. Smiling, he gingerly opened it and removed the single page, which read:

Established at Hôtel Fleur de l'Âge. Urgent we make contact with diplomat who has the goods, or knows where they are. Do you know meaning and/or response to code "When Messouda Sings?" said to me by Malena, a singer who is working for us as an extra. Advise soonest. Niagri.

Sidu returned the message to the envelope, and put it back in the bag. He thought, *Perhaps it's time to take stock as to where my true allegiance lies: with France or with Algeria.* He thought of Malena and said, "Messouda."

† †

Talka was daydreaming about Nicole, about the scent of her body. He wanted to make love to her again. He was enjoying his *saveur* when Philippe walked up to him at the long bar, saying, "I hear you're still not satisfied with the way the shoot is going."

Talka slugged back his sour mash and swung his legs around the barstool. "Just like the old days, Philippe."

Philippe took Talka's bottle and poured a drink for himself. He took half of it, turned to Talka and raised his glass. "Here's to silent filming, then," he croaked, and choked the rest of it down.

Talka put his glass down behind him, looked up at the churning ceiling fan, and chuckled, "He's going to whistle up an incident, like we did in Indochina when we filmed the Foreign Legion."

"What sort of incident?"

"No dialogue, no preplanning, just raw footage."

"How raw?"

"Don't know yet, but if it's what we talked about, he and I, then the documentary might as well be a silent film like *Nanook of the North.*"

"That's great, just great." Philippe slammed his glass down onto the bar and stomped out.

Talka stared after him. "What the hell did I say?"

† †

SitRep # 3:

Claude:

We went to town today, and shot live footage of a real suicide bombing. Philippe came up with some great questions and Malena helped "Helen" learn them in Arabic. After six hours of practice, I have to say Helen had them down.

Before Malena left, she said something to me that sounded like code: "When Messouda sings." Perhaps you have some intelligence on her.

After I rested, I went downstairs and we all piled into a pickup and left for a likely spot for a bombing. It took an hour or so, but almost on cue, there was an explosion. People were running everywhere. We tried snagging a couple of women at first, but they were simply too terrified to talk. We changed tactics, and after a while we were able to get ten or eleven to respond. You'll like this part: we did it all in French, so the Arabic lesson wasn't necessary. Totally forgot that most of the Algerians speak French.

Actually, we were all pretty proud of our shoot. Not too sure about Sidu, and Kelbeau's behavior is quite suspicious. Have to keep an eye on them both. Nicole.

She was proofreading what she had written when the door to her room burst open and Philippe rushed in. He was so enraged that he took no notice of what she had on her laptop. She scrolled up to *Send* and clicked it, then closed the laptop. "Well, this is a surprise—what's happening?"

"Lamar tells me they are going to do a shoot without the benefit of a script—did you know anything about that?"

She breathed a sigh of relief, saying, "Not a thing. When did this come to pass?"

"Jean promised me I would have complete literary freedom."

"So how has he taken that away from you?"

"Lamar told me that what they are planning doesn't require words, that the scene will be so traumatic, no words could express it."

"Yeah, but that's not the whole film. If the scene cuts, let the facts speak for themselves."

"I am the facts," he screamed.

"Calm down, Philippe, I can hear you."

"I tell the people what they want to hear. What do they know of the truth?"

"Know the truth and it will—"

"I know the rest of that, thank you. But let me tell you, in the words of Simone Weil: 'History is written by the survivors.'"

"Whose history?" she asked, then added, "Which survivors?"

† †

The long dark hours after her last gig found Malena slipping into Mallory's room, disrobing, and crawling into his bed.

"I understand Cinnamon's song," she whispered in his ear. He grunted some sort of acknowledgement and shifted his body, and the bed shook. Malena rolled onto her back and stared up at the ceiling fan. She could faintly see its rotation as it pushed the air downward.

"How do you know?" he murmured, more awake now.

"I know by the sound."

"By the sound..."

"Just when it's serious, the voice becomes quiet, and the word is barely uttered. Sometimes you can't hear the last part of it...almost as if the person singing were afraid to utter it...almost as if she were unsure the word's meaning said what she wanted it to."

† †

When Claude received Sitrep #2 from Algiers, he immediately began an interoffice search for "When Messouda sings." His aides gathered up what had been salvaged from the hacker's break-in, and pored through a ream of research on what had happened to the Faberg Account since 1962. The only thing they came up with was the company name.

In part, the aides' report suggested that old Gustav must have had a hand in the name of the company, and "When Messouda sings" must be the code to identify the envoys to the company; now it had carried over into the new mission. It seemed to require some sort of answer. As the aides understood it, the envoys would have told Messouda Drilling where the valve was located. The report suggested that Reynard or Nicole should give Malena a response that alluded to a secret hiding place, so she might open up.

Claude went to his computer and wrote his response to Reynard:

YOU'RE RIGHT IN THINKING IT HAS SOMETHING TO DO WITH THE FIRST COMPANY WE HAD IN PLACE. SUGGEST YOU REPEAT THE WORDS, "WHEN MESSOUDA SINGS," TO MALENA. IF SHE RESPONDS, FOLLOW UP WITH SOMETHING LIKE, "SHE SINGS IN SECRET." SEE WHAT SHE SAYS.

† †

Malena didn't return to her room, but went out into the courtyard to plan her strategy. She needed help, and didn't know anyone else to turn to except Kaarem. What could she really tell him? She had gotten no response from Mallory or Reynard. When she said the code phrase to Helen, she too had been unresponsive.

She retreated to the shade of the colonnades and looked out onto the courtyard where they had first begun shooting. She wanted to see the crew out there again, preparing the shot, but they had left, gone inside or wherever they went when not filming. Then she heard someone behind her and wheeled around to a face distorted by something almost unearthly. "*Bonjour, pute.*"

She ignored the insult. "*Bonjour, Monsieur.* Do I know you?" She remembered the ugly man had come to the shoots with Sidu.

"You may or may not; I'm Fezzan Kelbeau, the security chief of the hotel."

"Kelbeau..." The name stirred something inside her. Something that had been repressed for years. Suddenly she realized who he was. His image came over her body like a rush of fear. She saw her father's headless torso lying beside the road, his arms outstretched as if searching for that missing part of his body. No one had seen Kelbeau swing the sword across her father's neck. But Sol had pointed him out to her as the man who had slaughtered Fortola. That was years ago, when she had first heard the name. Her eyes widened.

"Oh, so you do know me."

Malena shook out her hair as if she had snagged it in something. "I know you, monsieur. You're in the government's security as well."

"Perhaps you know more than you should..." Malena turned to leave, but he grabbed her arm with a strong hand. "Maybe we should have a little chat." She wriggled free and ran away, through the colonnades and into the lobby.

I'll go to Helen, she thought. *I will tell her the sordid story of my life in Algiers, of my childhood and Kaarem, and of my exodus from the Kabylia to the city when I was fourteen—how the years have vanished. Of my love for Lytton, the only man other than Father who has treated me with kindness and dignity.*

Malena deftly slipped in and out of the colonnades, and made her way over to the elevator, but she saw Kelbeau had followed and spotted her, and she bolted out of the hotel.

She kept running all the way to Lytton Mallory's apartment, this time without looking back or taking the usual precautions she had trained herself to take in the city's streets.

She rapped on his door insistently. When he opened it, she rushed past. "Shut the door," she exclaimed.

"Why—what?"

"Just shut the door, won't you!" Mallory closed the door and Malena ran back to him. "Just hold me, Lytton—I'm frightened. For the first time in my life, I don't know where to run. Please help me."

"I'm here. No one's going to hurt you."

"I saw the man who killed my father."

"Where?"

"At the hotel. He's been there all along. Security. He's followed us to the streets. He's behind everything—I've got to get out."

Mallory held her closely. "What's the man's name?"

"Fezzan Kelbeau."

"Did he follow you here?"

Malena was startled by the suggestion, realizing she hadn't been as careful as usual. She looked up into Mallory's face, pleadingly. "No—no, I don't think he's here."

"It's behind you now…"

"There's something else."

"Get it off your chest."

"Remember the other day, when we were at Tipaza, and I said something to you?"

"You said many things. Tell me again."

"When Messouda Sings."

"Yes, I remember—but it doesn't mean anything."

"It's a song I sang as a child:

'Twas on her wedding night
She saw her plight.
Oh, country!

Oh, lovers!
Come back, come back to fight.
Upon the quay she points the way.
Oh country! In thirty days
We wait for three nights.
This is our fight.
This is our night.

Now it's the fortieth day;
What a price to pay.
Oh, country!
Oh, lovers!
It was her night,
It was her night.

"It's an introduction."

"To whom?"

"To the one who will bear witness."

"I still don't get it."

"There's a place in the desert, just beyond the city limits. Go there with me."

"What's there?"

"It's a place where something is buried."

"What's buried?"

Malena hesitated, then told him about her encounter with Dack, the dagger, and finding Kaarem.

"Is that what you buried in the desert?"

"Yes. I took it from its hiding place in The Black Owl to my hotel room. I was afraid someone might find it, so I took it to the wadi and buried it."

"From what you tell me, we should get the dagger and see Kaarem. Carry through with the plan, and we can all get out of this place."

"I want to get some things at my hotel room."

"There isn't time."

"I'm sorry..." Somehow, Mallory's room seemed strange to her, almost as if she were there for the first time. She had just lifted a giant load from her shoulders, and the dingy little apartment seemed brighter.

"Okay, go to the room, but don't let Kelbeau see you. Get what you need, and I'll go get the dagger. Tell me where it's buried."

"There are three stones. I buried it next to the one closest to the oil machine, the one they call 'Assia.'"

"We'll meet at the wadi. I think I'll get us out of here tomorrow morning, but you may have been followed, so I will arrange another place to meet. "

† †

Piton bounded into Kelbeau's downtown office. "I've got the goods on that little Berber tramp."

Kelbeau looked up from his desk and gave Piton his toothy grin that looked more like a grimace. "I tried to corner her at the hotel, but the little bitch slipped out of my grasp."

"I know whom she is seeing," Piton yelped, expecting a reward.

Kelbeau remained unexcited. "I was going to question her, but the others were watching me at the hotel, so I had to let her go."

"She's seeing a man by the name of Lytton Mallory; she went to his apartment."

"Never heard of him or that name. It could be an alias. How did you get near enough to hear what they said?"

"I got around to the open window on the veranda, and heard every word." Piton related their conversation almost verbatim.

Kelbeau frowned. "Messouda...where have I heard that before?" He raised his eyebrows and went to his file cabinet. Thumbing through the myriad of files, he came to one labeled *Saladin,* pulled it out, and opened it. "Here it is. Messouda Drilling, the company set up by the SDECE. They were shut down because of ties to France. I wonder what they're up to now."

"Maybe it has to do with the wadi place she kept talking about. She said she wanted to meet with someone else and then go there."

"But for what? What could possibly be out there in a wadi that's so important?"She said something is buried there," said Piton, "at the Wadi of the Three Stones."

"What's buried?

"A dagger, near the production platform 'Assia.'"

Kelbeau frowned again. Then it hit him like a bolt. "That's it!"

"What?"

"Don't you see, Piton, that wadi is next to the production rig that stands over the main oil line. This whole thing must be in regards to that; the damned French must want to tap into it. I don't get the dagger's connection, however. One thing is for sure; the little Berber bitch is mixed up in it. Stay with her and she'll lead us to the ones behind this intrigue."

"We can follow them and see what they do."

"Better yet, dig up the dagger and put something else in its place."

"What?"

"You know what I'm talking about."

"The wire?"

"Precisely. One less infidel."

11

An hour passed before he saw the tool pusher leave the shack standing forlornly next to the massive oil rig. Tonight he was Lytton Mallory, the geologist who had been charting endlessly. He put down his pencil and walked stiffly over to the door. Swinging it open, he peered out into the night.

Mallory looked about to make sure the tool pusher was gone for the evening. He was always careful about these things. He stepped down on to the fine sand below the entry. The heat radiating off the pipelines felt good in contrast to the cold Algerian night. Mallory was not that old, but pain had replaced lost tissue from a bullet he took in the shoulder during the French-Algerian War. Long after the scar had faded, the ache reminded him of an awful time, especially when it was cold.

Lifting periodically, poppet valves released steam that welled up from the bowels of the desert. Mallory noted how the floods' yellow light penetrated the inversion layer of smoke and steam as the stench of crude oil stung the corners of his nostrils.

He moved beyond the vapid atmosphere toward the wadi, where Malena had buried the dagger. *Last out the year—last out this one night,* he thought. Then he saw a shadow that moved; it was a man.

"Hey Lytton, you need to go over to Pump Station Four and confirm the reading," the tool pusher said.

"Okay, give me a minute." *What the hell,* he thought, *it's right on the way to the spot—perfect!*

"You have your minute, but we need the reading for the evening closeout report."

"Okay, I'm after it." The way was unlit; he draped his jacket over his shoulders and moved out into the darkness, stepping cautiously to avoid an encounter with a scorpion or snake. He was in company with the incessant noise from the rig, always at a hundred decibels as it squeezed the natural gas down to four thousand pounds per square inch through a four-foot opening of stainless steel pipe.

This had been the prime pumping station from Algeria to France, last of the old colon to connect the pipes between North Africa and the Western World. In better times, these pipes were buried beneath the Mediterranean to turn fossil fuel into francs. That had ended in 1971.

Ahead was Station Four. Mallory looked back at the rig one last time. In its superstructure, men moved like tree ants amid the vibrating pipes and girders, touching valves, jotting numbers. They became figures shuffling from station to station in a ritual oil bath, basked in the ghost of French Algiers, Muslim nomads who had pushed the *pieds noirs* away from the oasis of the oil field.

Something scurried ahead of him. *I've got to be careful.* He came to a pile of black rocks that marked the way to the wadi. He edged toward the triad of stones, stopping at the one closest to Assia.

Removing his jacket, spreading it at the foot of the stone, and then kneeling on it, the man began to dig. As he cleared out around the hole, something slid between his fingers. *A wire!*

All he heard was the beginning of the sound, sudden, blatant, and final. He felt a stinging below the waist, then silence.

The low rumble turned to a loud roar and the sound of glass shattering from windows, blown inward. Piercing shards tore through coveralls, sticking to something more solid.

Halfway out to Station Four, Lytton Mallory lay faceup, looking at the stars, his legs amputated from his torso. His body still hummed from the explosion. He forced his elbows beneath him to where he could sit up on them. He stared at the hole in the sand by the stone, then looked down to see the red flow in the sand. "*Mon Dieu,*" he uttered, and began to shake uncontrollably. "*Mon Dieu,*" he said again, falling back. He thought he heard Malena calling to him. "I'm here," he whispered.

† †

Back at the rig, the red rush of air blasting from behind knocked several workers to the iron deck plates; one fell from his three-story perch. A momentary glow created a bright light on the horizon of the desert.

The tool pusher heard the noise. "An explosion!"

"A line must have given out," the men were yelling. The tool pusher nodded and began to run toward Station Four. Just as he reached the edge of the rig lights, he stopped, took out his cell phone, and began to dial.

At that moment, a man with a scarred face stepped in and moved a knife across his throat. The tool pusher gurgled and let out a stifled scream. The scarred man took his cell and dialed, and the last thing the tool pusher heard was his whisper: "It's done."

12

THE WEDDING RITE: DAY THREE

When the grooms' fathers throw away dates and wheat to the wedding crowd, it signifies the engagement period is at an end. The crowd sings to ensure the grooms will sire many children. Women retrieve the wheat and grind it into flour to be baked into loaves and devoured by the grooms to ensure fertility.

The grooms wear red shawls as a sign of their status in the ceremony, and are forbidden entry into the bridal house; only women and children are allowed to enter. Old men stand guard to keep the young grooms at bay.

† †

Kelbeau was more than helpful when Sidu asked him if he had heard of any upcoming Berber massacres. He told Sidu, "There's a small village ten miles out, toward the Kabylia, which might just be a target. I have heard it will be hit tomorrow night."

Sidu went to Reynard and told him, "I found what you've been looking for. You and the crew should be ready about teatime tomorrow; the pickup will be in front of the hotel. Reynard raced off to get the news to his crew.

† †

Malena slipped into the hotel lobby and saw no one. Kelbeau's office door was shut. She went to her room and packed everything, including her Cinnamon Caruthers records. Once again she left her old phonograph. She filled two bags with her things, and left the room.

She slid along the back street that led to a corner of the city she knew. She was still a half a kilometer from the place when she saw the sky light up ahead and heard a low rumble.

Dropping her bags, she broke into a run. Smoke rose from the explosion, and she smelled charred flesh. She reached the wadi, but could barely make out the three stones ahead of her.

Then from out of the smoke and darkness a figure appeared, and Malena dropped. Lying flat, she turned her face toward him. He stopped and said something into a cell phone; then he came closer but still did not see her. The light from the rig illuminated his face, and his scar, the one belonging to a face she had seen on one following her, the man in a shabby coat she had seen in Kelbeau's office at the hotel.

When he was out of sight, she rose and brushed the sand off her dress. The soot mixed with the sand remained on her sea-green dress in black streaks.

She reached the triangle of three stones. The black lines radiating out from the stone nearest Assia had turned to one solid black mark on the desert floor. She could make out a crater at the base of the stone. A few meters away, she saw the man's body. She ran to him, and saw he was moving. Dropping to her knees beside him, she cried "My God! You're okay, you're okay."

"I was getting the dagger for you," Mallory said in a whisper.

Malena looked down to where his legs should have been, and threw her arms about him. "Dear love...I'm so sorry."

"I saw him; he got the dagger."

Malena held him close so his head was on her chest. "Who, darling? Who got it?"

"No name, scar on his face. Lousy dresser. Maybe you will find the dagger." The man relaxed. "Sorry about Paris."

She kissed him, murmuring, "Rest now."

† †

In the late morning, the crew crept up to the Berber village. Talka had said he was hoping for an early morning shot, but nothing was happening down in the village and the sky was overcast, making the light bad. As the day wore on, the sky cleared.

Talka had set up the camera and adjusted his zoom lens to appear as if they were on the main street, although they were a hundred meters away. Just as he and Reynard finished anchoring it, two lorries carrying squads of security forces dressed in cammies entered the main street and stopped.

"Nicole, I want you to get the flavor of this for tomorrow's commentary," Reynard said.

The soldiers spread out and called out, firing their AK-47s into the air. When the people came out, the soldiers singled out all the pregnant women and their children, pulled out their bayonets, and slit the women's abdomens open, pulling the fetuses from them as the children watched.

"My God, who are these people?" Talka whispered.

"Maniacs and fools—keep shooting." Reynard replied, choking back a sob.

"You bastards, you utter bastards," muttered Nicole. Philippe began to vomit.

Then the soldiers began beheading the children, stuffing their little bodies into the screaming mothers' open bellies. Others were doused with gasoline, set afire, and left to run screaming down the street. Some were merely shot. For ten minutes, the soldiers shot people as they scurried to their houses or any hiding place they could find. When there was no one left, the shooting stopped.

With tears streaming, Talka kept rolling, and zoomed through the smoke to the middle of the street, where a child's severed head lay. It stared back at them, eyes fixed in horror. Reynard put his hand over the lens, and Talka stopped the camera.

Nicole grabbed Talka. "Did you get your shot? Is this truthful enough for you?" They crept away to their place of refuge, the hotel, where Talka would prepare the film.

† †

Nicole, stung into numbness over the bloodbath she had witnessed, listened to the chang-chang country music over the one radio station in Algiers that played it. A sudden announcement interrupted the old favorite with a crackle, as if some hapless beetle had electrocuted himself inside the small radio: *"A woman was on her way to Tipaza when she happened upon a roadblock, run by armed men posing as Security. As she rolled to a stop, one man approached her car, raised his gun, and shot her in the face. Malena Cårtobé, it is said, died instantly, bringing the total number of Berbers killed to over twelve thousand since the assassinations began in 1992.*

"Responsibility is being attributed to the Armed Islamic Group, the most prodigious insurgents identified to date. This new outrage has sparked protests around the country. When word of this latest killing of a Berber reached the regional capital of Tizi Ouzou, violence erupted as thousands of protesters sacked public buildings. Government troops have been called out to the disturbance, and it is undetermined what the outcome of this latest development will be. The insurgency has claimed 75,000 lives so far..."

Nicole collapsed onto her bed. "The world's gone mad. Well, if it's *vérité* they want, I'll give it to them." She got back up and stomped out of the room, muttering, "I need a stiff drink."

She found the rest of the crew in the dark, air-conditioned bar. Looking around at the bamboo walls, she thought, *For all you'd know, we're in Zanzibar with tropical birds. All we need is rifle bearers and a Land Rover.* She dismissed the delirious thought, and walked behind the bar, grabbing a bottle of bourbon and a glass. She dipped out some ice from the ice chest and went back to the barstool, sat down, and poured out two fingers of bourbon.

Philippe walked over to where Nicole perched at the bar and handed her a script. "Here's tomorrow's shoot. Reynard wants to start at five tomorrow." He pointed across the room at Reynard, who raised his hand.

Nicole lifted her glass and tipped it up, hissing through the clinking ice cubes, "You know what you can do with that."

"Nicole, we're nearly through this thing; don't get that way now."

"Then you tell me what this shit is all about." She swung around to face him. "Tell me."

"Sshh, not so loud—do you want Reynard to hear?"

"Don't shush me; you were the one throwing up back there. I don't give a rat's butt, not anymore."

"Look, later we'll talk. Meanwhile, for me, get this done."

Nicole swung back around to the bar, tears coming "I really don't care anyway, Philippe, about that drivel you write, or whatever axe Reynard wants to grind."

"Be patient."

"We can afford to be—we're not the ones getting our heads lopped off."

"These things take time; it isn't easy to write such a book you know. There is much research to be done. Why don't you try it yourself if you don't believe me?"

"What the hell are you talking about? Do you even know what's happening? You were there."

"Let me explain—"

"No, let me. There was a bloodbath today, and I saw things I cannot believe. Oh, don't be too overwhelmed by what I say... I thought we depended on each other, you and I; well, there's no need for that now."

"What? What's wrong? What's happened to you?"

"I need another drink."

"This thing will work, Nicole, I promise."

"In the meantime, what about them? What? What good is a book for those poor bastard Berbers lying out there in the dirt, drowning in their own blood?" She motioned toward the door as Malena came through it, carrying her totes. She walked up to them, set the bags down, and faced Nicole. Her dress was covered with smears of soot and blood.

Nicole stared at her in disbelief. "You're dead; they said you were dead."

"*I'm* not, but there has been death." Malena's knees buckled slightly and she grabbed the back of a bar chair to hold herself up.

She reached out toward Nicole. "I'm alive…" Tears rolled down her cheeks; she retrieved one and watched it spread out on her finger. She shook her head. "I'm alive!"

Nicole grabbed her and held her for a long time. "The radio, you see, it said you were ambushed in your car, killed."

"I don't drive…someone…maybe one of Sidu's others…I don't know."

"Oh God, but you are alive. Come to my room."

13

THE WEDDING RITE: DAY FOUR

Men beat open-ended drums outside the bridal house, and the brides dance in their seated positions, while assistants prepare a feast within. Women swarm about the brides, decorating the brides' faces with henna designs, bringing cleanliness.

† †

When they got to Nicole's room, Malena collapsed onto the Oriental rug beside the sofa. Nicole crouched and took Malena's hand. "I think it's time you know who we really are."

Malena looked blankly at Nicole. "Yes, it's time."

"First of all, we are not Americans—we're French. My true name is Nicole Soutane, Mr. Gray is Jean Reynard, Phil is Philippe DuPont, and that...cameraman...is Lamar Talka."

Malena stared out into space for a time, feeling nothing, and not looking at Nicole. Then she squeezed Nicole's hand. "Thank you for telling me."

Nicole cleared her throat. "There's more. We're here on cross-purposes. I don't want to say everything now, but I think you are in it deeper than any of us would have wished."

"How do you mean?"

"We think you know a piece of the puzzle we're trying to solve."

"I don't know anything."

"We'll talk about it later," Nicole said, sliding down on the Oriental beside Malena. "Tell me when you were really free."

"Before I came to Algiers, when I was fourteen."

"Yes, on the road—you told me before."

"On the road—that was when I left the family and walked to Algiers. I spent five days with little to eat or drink, but it was there that I was free for the last time." Malena thought of the family and childhood that had begun to fade from her memory like an old friend who had died. She felt her voice wither from song and her features grow pale, paler than her own skin.

Nicole said, "I lost my mother to the war. It's terrible to lose your parents when you're so young."

Malena looked up at Nicole, and wondered if she could know the kind of losing someone where you could still feel their touch on your cheek. *Everyone has a special touch, just as everyone stares out onto the desert with their own special wonder.* "I'm not sure it's the same."

"What isn't?"

"Losing freedom. When you lose someone, only a part of you remembers. When you lose freedom, all of you remembers." Malena remembered the Cinnamon Caruthers records she had brought with her. She remembered cradling them so carefully in her bag. The singer's picture was on the jacket; inside was her voice. "*Caruthers sounds molded into songs,*" she had told her father once. Malena had sung those songs to keep her company on her trek to Algiers. "I sing her songs," she told Nicole.

Nicole registered surprise. "Whose songs?"

"Caruthers's. I have her records I brought from home."

"Do you have them here?"

"They're downstairs in the bar; would you like to hear them?"

"I would like to very much."

Malena looks around Nicole's room. "Do you have a record player here?"

"Gosh, I don't."

"Tomorrow, then."

"Then."

"I remember what Cinnamon Caruthers looked like."

"Describe her for me."

"I have not seen her in person, mind you, but from the picture on the album, I remember."

"Go on, Malena, tell me anyway."

"I remember the beauty of her skin, and her dark shining eyes and black hair. I admired her for those things. I can remember that last walk into Algiers, wishing I looked like her. Not my pale skin, and I hate this reddish hair."

"Malena, there's nothing wrong with your looks, believe me. In some parts of the world, you would be a raving beauty."

"What do you mean, 'raving'?"

"Exceptional."

"Where would they say such things?"

"France."

Malena was caught up in the image of Cinnamon Caruthers. "Her skin, it was the color of coffee, just as you pour in *la crème* and it reaches the bottom of the cup, making the turn to come upward. It rises because of the heat, you know." Nicole nodded. "It becomes warmer as it rises amid the hotter coffee around it, reluctant to change its color at first. But as it nears the top, slowly swirling little by little, it yields the whiteness and begins to tan." Malena looked at Nicole and smiled. She meshed her fingers together and inverted her hands, bringing them up past her face, moving them toward Nicole's. "By the time it reaches the surface, it has already changed to golden brown. That is the way I shall always remember her looks—golden tan. The day I walked into the streets of Algiers, I remembered her. The last day of my freedom, I remembered her."

"You wish you could be her color, don't you?"

"Yes. And my hair, black."

Nicole reached out and touched Malena's face, turning her hand, comparing the color. "You and I are almost the same color, did you know that?"

"We are. There was another who is light in color, a man-friend.

He was white like us, but grayer. I would like to be in the Sun more."

"You don't get out in the day."

"Only here, since we began the film. Before, I only went out after dark. In fact, they called me 'Dark,' because I went out into the night."

"Why did you do that?"

"Many reasons—different reasons. It's not safe for women on the streets of Algiers in daylight, you know."

"I've heard. I'm sorry."

"Not your fault."

"I know, but I'm sorry anyway."

"I became the Dark. I earned that name at The Black Owl."

"The Black Owl. Is that a bar?"

"Bar and more. I didn't know at first. The night they pulled me in from the street." Malena looked at longingly. "You want me to tell you?"

"Yes, tell me."

"I could not read the street signs, you see. It was getting dark. Then I heard gunfire, and then came the screams. It frightened me and I ran wildly, like a scared goat, down a street where I came upon them. Three men and a girl. They were doing ugly things to her and I was horrified by what I saw, and I shrank into a recess, a door. One of them raped her, and her shrieks brought a shriek out of me.

"They saw me cowering in that crevice, and came for me. Behind me, a door opened, and I was pulled in before they could touch me. Later I heard the girl was dead, her belly slit open from one side to the other. Some men came and dragged the corpse to the side of the road. No one else came for her. The street cleaners picked up the body and threw it in a truck.

"Behind the door was total blackness. Outside was that sad scene, and the last freedom I knew. Inside, a voice asked me what my name was. I told them it was Malena. Why are you out after dark; are you Dark? I told them I didn't know what that meant.

"After I was there awhile, they still didn't call me by my name. I asked why. They told me I would get a name after I had earned it. Later, when Sidu had me going out on his various errands, I got my name. And that, Nicole, is how I became Dark."

"All the same, I will call you Malena. Malena the fair. Malena the beautiful. Malena." Nicole pulled Malena to her and held her close.

When Malena lifted her head again, Nicole's blouse was wet from Malena's tears. "I've got to go to Kaarem and tell him what has happened."

"Stay with me tonight, Malena; it's not safe to go out. Sing to me."

"I know a song."

"What song?"

"When Messouda Sings."

"You told me that before." Nicole remembered.

"Do you know it?"

"My aunt knew it. She sang it to me when I was young."

"Do you remember it?" Malena wondered.

Nicole seemed to ponder the ancient words: "Let's see, 'When Messouda sings…she sings of a secret place—when Messouda sang, she called back her tribe.'"

"A long time ago," Malena said.

"Yes, a long time ago; we're talking about the here and now."

"Should I lie here on the rug?"

"No. Come to bed and I'll tell you who we really are."

Reynard turned on his laptop, hoping desperately for an email from Claude. He typed in his password and the Agency's logo appeared center-screen. *Great! Here it is.*

NIAGRI, WE RECEIVED A *COMMUNIQUÉ* FROM THE AMERICAN EMBASSY IN TUNISIA TO THE EFFECT THAT ONE OF THEIR OPERATIVES HAS REPORTED THE DEATH OF OUR OPERATIVE THERE IN ALGIERS. HE WAS NOT POSITIVELY

IDED; HE WAS A FOREIGNER WORKING FOR THE OIL COMPANY. THE AGENCY HAS TAKEN THE POSITION WITH GOOD CERTAINTY THAT THE MAN KILLED WAS THE JEWELER.

Reynard's shoulders dropped and he closed the lid on his laptop.

He's the one who uncovered the OAS plot to kill de Gaulle in '61. The Jeweler, with his delicate touch with munitions. The idealist who became bitter waiting for the Service to show some kind of morality in its motivation. Looking for some hint of humanity behind its actions. But it was more than that. *He was a comrade-in-arms,* my *comrade-in-arms, whom I trusted beyond myself, whom I called friend.*

Reynard thought of him blown to bits. *Dying alone. For what—money? Certainly the patriotic motivations have long since been swept away. Certainly the concern for humanitarian affairs had long ago dried up—by expediency, by agenda, by political innuendo and quick eyes.*

Anger swept through Reynard's body. Anger he had not felt since the last time someone had shot at him, the anger he had felt while killing one who had killed his comrades. Anger he had felt when he sat down in the middle of a war and wept for the dead men around him. *Who in the hell am I anyway? A farce-seeker,* Theatre of the Absurd *turned topsy-turvy!* Merde!

Aren't most of us avant-garde people expressionistic, exploring beyond the surface of this material world? We tweak the public's noses for the grins of false cheer beneath them. We tweak the public's noses, for they are afraid to poke them around in the less attractive aspects of life. We sober the face from glibness. We've created living hell out of abstraction. Now we will create abstraction out of living hell!

He began to write furiously. *This time we'll turn the tide.* He remembered that in the beginning he had come up with a backup, in case things did not go well. Now, as fate would have it, his backup had evaporated.

14

Avoiding the lights of Assia, Piton made his way back to his car and drove to town and Hôtel Fleur de l'Âge. Finding Kelbeau at his desk, Piton dropped the box he had recovered in front of him. Kelbeau looked at it curiously, picked it up, and dusted the sand off the elephants inlaid into its cover.

Piton rubbed the scar on his face, which had started to itch. "It's all right; I checked it," he assured Kelbeau.

Kelbeau grimaced a forced half-grin and carefully opened the box, removing the dagger. "It must be worth a fortune. Look at this on its handle; it's Tifinagh—spells something out."

"What does it say? Maybe the Berber girl can tell us."

"She's dead. But there's another who can tell us. Get over to that Kaarem's apartment and make him talk. Do you have your gun?"

Piton nodded, saying, "I have it. The Berber girl, how did she die?"

"Some friends of ours. Now get going—there's no time to lose."

Piton put the dagger back into the box, and stood. As he began to leave the office, Kelbeau picked up the phone and dialed. "Security Headquarters...this is Kelbeau. Roll out thirty of my attack team. Have them fully equipped and here at the hotel in one hour."

15

Piton had no trouble unlocking Kaarem's apartment door. When he had just begun searching for the box containing the dagger, he heard a key slip into the door's lock. He glided across the living room, slipped through the bedroom door, and crouched down into the corner behind it. The lock rattled open, and Piton peered through the crack as Kaarem turned on the living room light and walked in, followed by the Berber slut and the ones who called themselves Helen and Gray. *Kelbeau said she was dead,* Piton thought in confusion.

Kaarem went toward the window and pushed an end table to one side, then switched on a table lamp sitting on top of it. Where the table had been was a floor safe. Reaching down, he opened it and plucked out the box. "I've been saving this for you for a long time. I'm glad you are here."

Joining Kaarem by the window, Gray took the box and opened it. He lifted the dagger out and turned it over, running his finger over the engraved symbols. "You say it's like the other?

Kaarem shrugged. "I haven't seen the other, but that is what Hassan said in his letter."

Gray held out the dagger to Malena. "Do you know what it means, Malena?" he asked.

Malena walked over and took the dagger to have a closer look."It's Berber Tifinagh." She began reciting the letters aloud:

"*Tar'erit, ies,* and *ïet;* the symbol on the blade looks like a three on its side."

Piton had been scribbling the phonetic spellings when his pen slipped from his fingers and clattered to the tile floor. "*Merde!*" he muttered. He saw Reynard bolt up and catch sight of him. "*Alors!*" In a panic, he drew his automatic and fired it at Kaarem, who fell to the floor.

The two women sprawled to the floor and Piton wheeled on Gray just in time to see a muzzle flash; then he felt the beginning of a sting below his nose and a sensation of great pressure inside his head. Next thing he knew, he was on the floor, feeling cold tile against his left cheek. His right eye could make out a dim flow of red onto the stone.

† †

Rising from the floor, Malena rushed to Kaarem, who lay motionless. "Kaarem," she whispered.

He rolled over and looked up at her. "I'm okay—is it safe to move?"

Bewildered, she grabbed him and held him close to her. "Oh God, you're alive."

Reynard went over to Piton and kicked the pistol away from his hand. Then he pointed at Piton's body. "Look!" he said, crouching down and pulling another box out of the dead man's coat. Opening it, he exclaimed, "It's the second dagger!"

After slowly rising, Kaarem helped Malena to her feet, and they crossed the room to see. "We have them both," Kaarem said triumphantly. Nicole joined Reynard, who was still holding the other box. They all stood in silence over Piton's body. Kaarem looked at Malena and began to smile. "Now, God willing, we can solve the riddle."

Malena gazed at the expanding pool of blood beneath her feet, then grasped Kaarem's hand, squeezing it harder than she had ever done before. "Kaarem, fetch me a towel; you have blood on your floor."

Reynard picked up the box and handed it to Malena. "It's up to you," he said.

Malena took the box and ran her finger over the engraved symbols. "It's Berber Tifinagh," she repeated. She stopped for a moment, examining the blades.

Nicole stepped closer to her. "Sit down and tell us about the daggers." They walked over to the sofa and sat down.

Malena held the daggers, staring intently at the inscriptions, and said, "Maybe we can help our people after all."

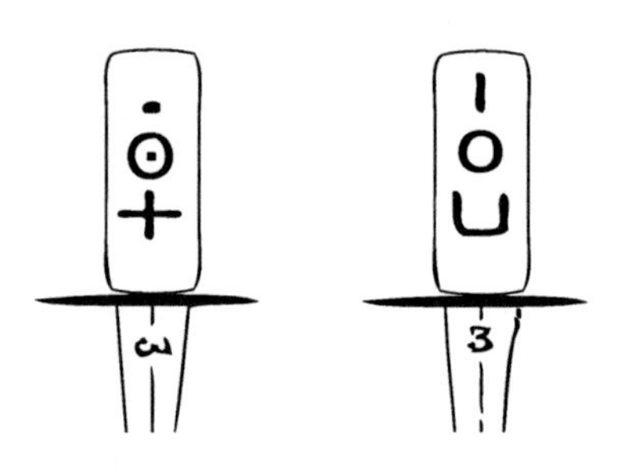

Reynard came to look, followed by Kaarem. "Let's put the code together and get on with it," Reynard urged.

Malena wiped her nose and began again, "*Tar'erit, ies,* and *ïet,* and the sideways three. The second dagger: *ïen, ier,* and the last is...looks like a fragment...perhaps of *ied.* And on its blade, the number three."

"Do they have French equivalents?" asked Reynard.

"Let me see. *Tar'erit* sounds like *eu* in *Est. Ies* sounds like *ess* in silencieux, and ïet sounds like *tay* in *temps.*"

"*Eu-Ess-Tay*—right so far?" Reynard repeated.

"So far. As for the second dagger, *ïen*—*enne* as in *Cannes*...*ier* is *err* as in *erreur*...and the last, *ied*—*de* as in *danger.*"

"*Enne-Err-De*—right?"

"Right."

Reynard picked up the daggers and stared at the ceiling, then pulled out a cigarette and lit it with his Zippo. He took in a drag, held it for a moment, and exhaled. He suddenly looked down at the daggers and clanked the blades together into the shape of a cross, saying, "*Est,* and *nord*...*nord,* and *est*—*nord-est.* Northeast! The rest, threes. Look! As I lay the first dagger over the second, thus, so the three is upright; it points ninety degrees from the second dagger, which is *nord*, or north, then it's *est*—east—and we get a three and another three—Could it be thirty-three? Thirty-three what?"

"Maybe thirty-three steps," said Nicole, peering at the daggers.

"Thirty-three steps from where?"

Kaarem pointed, saying, "Everything on the daggers is in threes. Maybe something's hidden thirty-three steps from the center of a place. If you hold the daggers crisscross as you have there, you read 'thirty-three,' then have one blade pointing out from your body pointing north, the other will point to the east. I would say pace off thirty-three paces to the east first, then dig. If you find nothing, go to the north. Do you know of a place we should start, Malena?"

"I know of such a place," she said.

Reynard put the daggers back in their boxes. "Can you take us there?" he asked.

Malena squirmed, searching Kaarem's eyes, arching her eyebrows into a question. *Do we tell?* Kaarem stared back at her, then gave a slight nod.

Reynard frowned at them. "You two okay?"

Malena gave him a quick glance, then looked back at Kaarem, saying, "Yes, we're quite okay."

"Where is this place?" Reynard asked, mashing his cigarette into the ashtray on the coffee table.

"It's called the Wadi of Three Stones; it's at the edge of town."

"Remember, Kelbeau and his men will be looking for us. Do you think he knows about the place?"

"He knows; he had my friend Mallory killed there—he did the killing," she said, pointing to Piton.

Reynard straightened up a little. "We'll have to be careful then. The next few hours are critical. All of us must be on our toes and you two must do exactly as I say if we are to survive this. Do you understand?" Malena and Kaarem nodded obediently. "Malena, I want you to take me to the wadi. Kaarem you come with us. Together we can put this thing together and find what we're looking for."

"The valve?" Kaarem asked.

"Yes, the valve. That's what this is all about. But there's another thing," Reynard said.

"What?" Malena asked.

"Our escape from this place." Reynard turned to Nicole. "Can you do something?"

Nicole smiled. "Something."

16

Young girls who have worn their hair loose for three days now have their hair braided with a ring and two distinct pigtails. As an attendant pulls her hair tight, a girl winces as she might in the ensuing nights in the groom's apartment.

† †

Malena and her mother walk down the dusty road. "I will bring you to the cave, Malena, and I will show you what you must do. Learn to respect this holy place, for the saints dwell here."

They reached the Cave of Dreams, two miles south of Azouza. Malena is six years old and given to daydreaming, which is something much different than the incubation her mother is talking about.

"When you sleep atop a saint's tomb, wisdom will pass through into your body. You must ask the question."

"What question?"

"Whatever needs to be answered. Sometimes you must be a marabout. Today, I've asked the question, so all you must do is dream. In the morning, when I come for you, tell me what you've seen in your dream.

Malena will do this as generations of Cårtobé women have done. But not Tamia. Malena can see her thoughts, can see she resents this injustice, for although she would deny it, she can dream with the best of them. She plots to seal Malena up in the cave the first chance she gets.

"Did you dream Malena?"

"I've been dreaming in caves." She still feels the coldness of the rock.

"Will Tamia's marriage last?"

"I saw something."

"What?"

"A black woman, singing strange music. Music I never heard at the fires or the weddings. I could understand what she was singing, but not the words. She sings in a dark room where people sit at tables, and she stands on a platform above them. Some men have horns and other men play instruments I don't recognize, but the instruments sound like her voice. Drums keep time. When she ends her song, the people are unable to ululate and have to clap their hands together.

"It's a song of death, about someone she loves; it's about someone I love.

"That powerful feeling, it leaps over language; it reaches me. It's beyond all the women in my dreams, the Supreme."

Malena, Kaarem, and Reynard took a cab to the outskirts of the city, where Malena had gone so many times. This would be her second time that night, in her last act of locating the valve and turning it on. Having broken the Tifinagh code on the dagger hilts, she flew to the indicated place, driven by Mallory's dying voice to where he was blasted to bits in front of the third stone. She would start once again next to the crater where she had pushed his dead body into the earth, covering it with charred sand.

They spotted Kelbeau's men around the three stones in the wadi, so dropped into a swale. Malena and Kaarem huddled close together.

"Wait here," Reynard whispered, and stole off into the darkness toward Assia. There, at the edge of the light from the oil rig, they waited, Malena clutching the boxes close to her. Minutes seemed like hours before they saw the fire come alive. It glowed slowly at first, then lit up the sky, shooting flames fifty feet into the air. Malena could see men shouting and pointing at it.

Someone called to Kelbeau's guards at the three stones to help them fight the fire. They left their post, and ran toward the oil rig.

Reynard came back out of the darkness and whispered, "Let's

go," and they all ran. When they reached the center stone, Reynard pulled a small device from his coat pocket, along with two thin metal flashlights. He gave one flashlight to Kaarem and turned the other on, holding the beam on the small device. He turned one way, then the other.

"What's he doing?" Malena whispered to Kaarem.

"He's finding north."

Reynard stopped and put the device back into his pocket. "Give me the daggers, Malena," he said, holding out one hand. She dropped down onto the sand and put the boxes in front of her, opened them, and pulled out the daggers, giving them to Reynard.

Holding the daggers in a cross, Reynard shone the flashlight beam out toward the east. "Go!" he said, and Malena and Kaarem stepped off the thirty-three paces in the direction of the light.

At the thirty-third step, Kaarem turned on his flashlight and pointed it to the ground. Malena dropped to her knees, and washed by pangs of grief for Mallory, dug furiously, clawing the sand with hands still bearing scars from her frantic dig in the Cave of Dreams.

Reynard came up behind her and stood beside Kaarem, adding his light to the spot where she was digging. *God knows,* she thought, *how much sand has moved over this place, and how far down we must dig. Maybe we'll be lucky. Maybe we'll find what we're looking for.*

Kaarem walked away and came back with a large stick. "Mind your hands," he said, and began scraping as Malena leaned back, wiping the sweat from her forehead with the back of her hand. He scooped out more sand from the deepening hole. Then he struck something solid, something metallic. He threw the stick aside and dropped to his knees, clearing away the spot. "There's something here," he said. "Help me." Reynard crouched too, and they all began digging together, soon baring a strange bronze gadget with a square hole in the middle.

"That's it!" exclaimed Reynard, slapping Kaarem on the back, "You did it!" They finished clearing away the sand, exposing two small round windows on either side of the square hole. The window on the right showed a small flag reading *Arrêt,* and the other was blank.

Malena saw something else sticking out; she kept digging and uncovered a crank lying beside the valve. Kaarem picked it up and inserted it into the square opening between the windows. "It fits," he said, and tried to pull the crank counterclockwise. "It won't move." He kept struggling with the crank handle.

Malena took the crank from him. "Let me try, Kaarem." She twisted the crank clockwise, the same direction in which she had wound her record player, and after a little while, turned it. The *Arrêt* flag disappeared from the window. As she continued to crank, each stroke became more difficult. She felt a surge feed up through the valve and crank into the palm of her hand. She looked up, smiling. "I can feel it—a vibration—something's moving." She brought her other hand up, using both to get the crank to rotate. With one last turn, she heard a click and *Marche* appeared in the window on the left.

Stretching her arms over her head, Malena sank back onto the sand and took in a deep breath. She covered her eyes with a forearm, exhaling, "Lytton."

Reynard reached down and touched the valve. The flag said it was open, and he could feel the powerful surge of liquid flow through the pipe. "That's it. Let's get out of here."

Malena got up and brushed the sand off her striped dress. "What about Sidu?"

"What about him?" asked Reynard.

"Kelbeau will hunt him down."

Reynard heaved in a deep breath and then released it. "I don't know..."

Malena grabbed one of the daggers and bolted back from the men. "I'll meet you at the hotel," she said. Reynard reached out, but she evaded his grasp.

She heard Kaarem yell, "Wait!" and then bark to Reynard, "Be back in thirty!" but she kept running into the darkness toward Algiers.

† †

Sidu was scared; he feared the worst for himself and the Jeweler. He knew it wouldn't be long before Kelbeau's Security would be upon him. He had packed two suitcases in anticipation of his departure. He looked around the office that had been his domain ever since Ester left him.

He picked up a picture on his desk: Malena's face with its straight nose, auburn hair surmounted by two white gardenias, and green eyes looked back at him. The mouth mustered as much of a smile as the eighteen-year-old could manage. "I did it for you," he said aloud.

His gaze moved up to the Picasso print on the wall. The nude. *She struggles to free herself of her apartment,* he thought, *just as I struggle to free myself of this place.* His plans were hazy, but he knew he had to get out of Algiers. He might make his way to Cherchell, to his family there. Then he would follow the immigrants into Morocco and across the Strait into Spain. He would become Isaac Haroom again, a respectable Jew. Maybe open a theatre, or even a cabaret.

Malena ran into his office, carrying a box, and out of breath. "What the hell have you done? Everyone thinks I am dead!"

Sidu was startled by her appearance, but then relaxed, and with a half-smile said, "I did it for you." He looked at her dirty, blood-soaked dress. "What have you been doing? You're a mess!"

"Digging. Who was it in the car?"

"Nuluna. I told her to gather your possessions, and go to the Wadi of Three Stones and scatter them around to make you look guilty. Then I made a call to someone linked to an extremist group and told them she was on her way to tell Security about them. That was all it took."

"You had her killed?"

"I had you killed—she had your identification, posing as you as she went. You're free Malena; get out while you still can."

Malena gave him a bewildered look. "But I came to warn you: Kelbeau is a murderer—he killed my father and Mallory; he'll be coming for you, coming for all of us. I'm here to get you. Reynard has arranged an escape."

"It's no use, Malena. I'm going my own way, back to my roots."

She slammed her tote down on the desk. "No! There's still time. Reynard told me to come for you," she demanded.

"I'm not going with you, Malena. Now go sing in Paris—it's my gift to you."

"It's not safe in Algeria for you," she yelled, pulling on his sleeve.

Sidu took her hand and held it for a moment. "You've had enough of me and this place, now go; *I* am." He gave her hand a squeeze, then dropped it. He picked up his suitcases and walked out of the office.

† †

Malena stood in Sidu's office, the silence closing in around her. She looked up at the nude print and then back to the open office door through which Sidu had just disappeared.

She went and took the picture down, gazing at it closely. She wiped her nose, and curled her arm around the picture, bringing it to her chest. She picked her tote up from the desk and shoved the dagger box inside; then she turned and walked out the door.

Men I've known are dead. Men I've seen have tried to kill me. Men I've known are going to die. I turn the corner and escape. How many more times must I turn?

† †

While Malena, Kaarem, and Reynard were at the wadi, Nicole caught a cab from Kaarem's apartment back to Hotel Fleur de l'Âge. She had the cabby stop a block away, and she slipped in the servant's entrance.

Going straight to her room, she phoned Philippe. "Get ready to leave," she said. She called Talka too, then opened her laptop and sent a terse signal to Claude that they were planning their escape, then sent another requesting the helicopter. The arranged meeting place, she knew, was the large concrete pad in the hotel garden.

Nicole gathered Malena's clothes and records that she had moved into Nicole's room, and loaded them into her suitcase.

She picked up the portable AM/FM radio and turned it on. Twirling the tuning knob, she found a local pop music station, then turned the radio off and stuck it in her pants pocket. She placed her laptop in the pocket of her canvas suitcase, and slung its strap onto her shoulder. Going out into the hallway, she met up with Philippe and Talka.

"What's happening?" asked Talka.

"We're getting out of here, that's what," she said.

Philippe was jostling around, trying to hold his manuscript and his tote at the same time. "How are we getting out of here?" he asked.

"By helicopter in the courtyard." Nicole replied.

"How in the hell do you know so much?" asked Talka.

"I know high people in low places," she quipped, and gave him a dirty look. "Look, we gotta be careful; Kelbeau's men are all over the place."

"Where's Reynard?" Talka asked.

"He's coming." Nicole said.

"Alone?"

"No, he's with the girl and her friend, Kaarem."

"If things are as bad as you say they are, we don't need extra baggage," Talka said, picking up his camera and the bag containing the shots for the documentary.

"Look, Lamar," Nicole said facing him, "You have no say in this. He has to come."

"Who is it?" he insisted.

"His name is Kaarem Khedda; he's a diplomat and friend to all of us."

Philippe had started trying to stuff his manuscript into the side pocket of his tote, which was too small, and he ended up just holding them. "How do we know we can trust him?"

Nicole wheeled toward Philippe. "I trust him. Look, we've got to create some sort of diversion to distract Kelbeau's men. Lamar, do you have those portable lights you use for filming?"

"Yeah, what about them?"

She took out the AM/FM radio and handed it to Talka. "I want you to set them up at the end of the courtyard, just by the colonnade. Have your cell phone handy, but put it on vibrate. Philippe and I will wait for Reynard and the others to get here. When we're all in position, I'll signal the helicopter to come for us, then I will call your phone. When you feel it vibrate, turn the radio full volume to the station I have tuned in. Then turn on your lights, and get the hell out of there. Don't let his men see you. Can you do that?"

"Yes, I can do that." This time, Talka softened.

17

When I turned eighty, I got a chance to visit Algiers. There, on the outskirts of the Kasbah, I met a lady older than me, who told me an unforgettable story about a Berber girl who hiked out of the mountains. I can tell you, this lady, despite her age, had the mind of a twenty-year-old.

This was, I believe, her story. She talked about her sister who had inflicted terror by closing her up in the cave, causing her nightmares, an aversion to Catholicism and closed-in places, and her inability to cry. After the cave terror, she could not sleep inside, but curled up on the floor of the desert, listening to its many voices, carried up from caravans trekking up from the South, and the voices of the winds that swept down from the Djurdjura Mountains. They filled her eyes with sand and her mind with wonder.

She told me she was the warrior Fatima charging into battle, and Messouda coaxing the tribesmen back with song. She said, confidentially, that she was Cinnamon Caruthers come back for her records, and that that was her raison d'être *in Algiers in the first place. Here, in terror and sadness, she sang for the things she could not see, and she angered when they called out,* "Malena de la noir!"

She knew a man who promised her Paris, but he was killed. That was when she worked for a film crew, filming the atrocities taking place in Algiers in those days. But she found the love of her youth, Kaarem, who had promised to marry her one day.

† †

Malena cornered him in his office, the one who had killed the men in her life. He tried to push her into the closet, while she raged, "You bastard—you killed my father, you killed Mallory—and what of Kaarem?"

She pulled a jeweled dagger from its box and slashed at him, her tears flowing quicker than the speed of light "This time I will not be shut up in a dark space. My dreams of the Dark are enough." She flailed out with the instrument again, and it found its place deep within his chest.

Fezzan Kelbeau gasped and fell to his knees at Malena's feet, and then onto his back. Malena reached for the dagger and withdrew it from his chest, which made a gurgling sound from deep within. Next she placed her foot on his neck, aimed, and plunged the blade just below his sternum with an upward thrust. His body quivered, and then was still.

She pulled hard on the hilt, and the blade slid back out. She wiped it clean with the hem of her dress, and carefully replaced it in the box. *I have learned the two purposes of the poniard,* she thought, tucking it safely into its box and returning it to its place in the tote next to the Caruthers records and the painting.

She opened the window and slipped out into the hotel courtyard, joining the others who were running in panic. Gunshots rang out from the colonnades.

Malena saw Nicole, Talka, and Philippe crouching behind the metal lawn furniture, where patrons had once enjoyed cool drinks in the sultry Algerian afternoons. Now it was the night, and there were no drinks, only sounds, strange and droning, which she didn't recognize.

Malena scurried across the lawn to join the crew, and they huddled behind the furniture for what seemed like an eternity. "It worked!" said Nicole, "They're firing at your lights, Lamar."

Malena asked Nicole, "Where's Kaarem?"

Nicole looked surprised. "He must be with Reynard." Malena

looked wildly around the courtyard, and spotting Reynard hiding behind an overturned table, crawled over to him.

A bright pencil-thin light winked on from the sky, circumscribing an oval of daylight that moved along the ground toward them. A blast of air and sand stung Malena's face. Shots rang out, but the bullets no longer kicked up the dirt around her; the gunners were firing at the light above them.

The light centered in the courtyard. A sirocco rose up as the metal furniture tumbled away and Malena's clothes flailed about in the shriek of wind. Suddenly something struck her on the head, and she fell. Wetness streamed down her face.

She got up, clutching her head with one hand, and grabbed Reynard's arm with the other. "Where's Kaarem?" she yelled over the noise. Reynard shrugged, and ducked behind the table, pulling her down with him. "Get down!"

Bright pinpoints of orange flashed from the colonnades, but she could only hear the howling. As a helicopter descended, the light grew smaller and brighter, and the rattle of the rotor echoed through the hollows of the colonnades.

Malena grabbed Reynard's arm again and yelled, "Where's Kaarem?"

"He went with you."

"No, I haven't seen him."

Reynard's mouth dropped open. "Then I don't know..." The gun blasts were more frequent now, and closer—Kelbeau's men were moving out of the colonnades into the table area. The helicopter's own guns flashed at the shooters on the edge of the courtyard.

Reynard stood up, shouting, "Come on, then!"

They all stood and ran toward the helicopter. Philippe, caught by a burst of gunfire, stumbled, spilling the manuscript he was holding. The rotor tore at the bundle of papers; they slid from his hands and swirled into a miniature tornado.

Running to Philippe, Nicole and Malena dropped to his side,

and covered him with their bodies. Holding his face, Nicole cried, "Philippe!"

Reynard ran up and squatted beside them, feeling for a pulse. "There's nothing to be done. Go! I'll cover you!"

Nicole grabbed what she could of the manuscript, and they stumbled away to the helicopter while Reynard fired back toward the hostile muzzle flashes with his automatic. As Nicole and Malena drew closer to the helicopter, Malena could make out the crew as they raked the colonnades with machine guns.

When they reached the helo, they leaped into the back, then turned to watch the scene outside. Standing, Reynard broke into a run for the helicopter. Ten feet from the rear door, he arched his back and fell, as though a giant fist had pounded him and sent him sprawling. He struggled to his feet and turned around. Malena could see the bewilderment on his face as he pulled himself into the helicopter. "Made it, Malena!"

Malena leaned out and yelled, "Kaarem!"

Nicole grabbed her. "For God's sake, Malena, stay down." She looked back at Reynard. "My God," she said, "you're bleeding."

Reynard looked down at his abdomen. His shirt was turning deep red. "Oh God, that was it; I thought someone hit me in the back," he said. He sat on the deck of the helicopter, propping himself against the rear bulkhead of the cabin. "Shouldn't I feel bad?"

"Move back." Nicole shoved Malena toward him, adding, "Find something—cover his wound with your hand. Hold it tightly."

Malena could hear the dull thud of bullets hitting the side of the helicopter. She slid back to Reynard and tore off a part of her underskirt, folding the cloth into a square. "Do you see Kaarem?" she yelled up to Nicole; Nicole shook her head. Malena reached over with the compress and pushed it up against Reynard's back. He winced and cried out. "I'm sorry, Jean," she yelled.

Swiveling around, she peered out the side window and saw a figure—hoping it was Kaarem, she squinted. It was Talka, camera in hand, framed against a flurry of muzzle-flashes behind him. *My God! He's filming!*

As he started to climb into the helicopter, he lurched as a round caught him, and he sprawled onto the ground, his arm holding the minicam draping over onto the metal floor. He slid the minicam back toward Nicole, then pulled the bag of film off his shoulder, throwing it to her. The door gunner stopped firing for a moment and tried to pull him the rest of the way, but Talka's arm slipped out of his hand as he slumped over and fell prone beneath the helicopter. Nicole, clutching the bag, watched him in horror, then screamed, "Lamar!" when he fell.

Malena went to the door. "There's one more guy!" she heard the door gunner yell into the intercom. She saw sparks fly up around the door, accompanied by sharp cracking sounds. The gunner grabbed his arm and jerked back in his seat, writhing in pain.

Nicole joined Malena, looking down at Talka. "I can't tell…is he dead?" she yelled, then jumped out onto the ground, hiding behind his body. Malena heard more sharp cracks, and dust flew up around Nicole.

Nicole threw her leg over Talka's body and straddled his torso, then lay prone against him, cradling his head in her hands, looking for signs of life. "Lamar!" she cried, placing her hand on his carotid artery. Her face wrinkled up in a soundless sob, and she laid his head back down on the ground. In one motion, she got up and leaped back in. "He's gone," she yelled, and shut the door. She grabbed the headset from the wounded crewman and yelled, "Let's go!" into the mike.

Revving up, the helicopter blotted out the courtyard in a swirl of dust. Malena felt it tilt backward and scuff the ground, as if it were fighting to remain earthbound. The pitch of its whine reached a shrill crescendo as they lifted free. Malena experienced no elation, no feelings of relief, just an awareness that they were out of the conflict, throbbing through the sky.

Nicole grabbed the gunner, who began to slump over. Rooting around, she discovered a cleaning towel and wrapped the gunner's arm with it, laying him down across the front bench seat. As the helicopter gained altitude, the light on the ground below winked out as suddenly as it had come on. A peace settled into the cabin once the wind was gone.

Nicole slid over to Reynard. Malena was still pressing against his wound with one hand, holding his body with the other. Reynard held out his box to Nicole, grunting, "See that Anna gets this." He winced, then muttered, "Damn." The pool of blood around him spread as he slumped down and lapsed into the deepest sleep. Malena thought that he dreamed of Cannes and of what he had accomplished. Nicole felt his wrist, and then slouched back, holding her face in her hands.

Malena slid over to the wounded crewman. "Can I do anything?" she asked. He shook his head. "Where are we going?" she asked.

"Ibiza."

† †

An hour later, the helo settled gracefully to the ground, and the engine's whining began to subside. Three vans pulled up alongside as the rotor stopped turning.

Nicole still clutched Philippe's papers in one hand, and held the blood-caked box Reynard had given her in the other. Malena clutched the second box to her chest. They struggled out through the cabin door as four EMTs approached, carrying two stretchers.

Standing out of the way, Nicole watched as two of them crawled into the cabin and checked Reynard, then scooted him out to the others, who laid him on a stretcher. They checked the crewman as well, then lifted him down and onto the other stretcher. The EMTs carried the stretchers to the vans, loading Reynard into one and the crewman into another. Malena and Nicole stood a few yards away as the vans sped off. They walked a ways and turned back to view the helicopter as if to offer silent homage for their flight to safety.

Nicole held up a page of Philippe's manuscript—the last page, torn down the middle. With trembling fingers, she tried to piece it together. "I can't do it," she said. Malena grabbed her hand and Nicole heaved a sob, wiping her eyes with the back of her hand.

One of the men from the front of the helicopter stepped out and approached them. "Are you okay?" he asked.

Nicole folded the torn paper in with the rest of Philippe's manuscript. "Who are you?" she asked.

"I'm Brad. Are you two okay?" Nicole and Malena nodded absently.

"Where are we?"

"Ibiza," he replied. He scratched his head, then moved his hand back and forth over his grey hair. "I landed at the hospital helo pad. We're about halfway between the Ibiza International Airport and the hotel where you'll be staying."

Nicole looked at him and decided he looked younger than he really was. She wiped her forehead with the back of her hand, which was still sticky with Reynard's blood. Her nose was stopped up with dirt, and her mouth tasted of ashes. She felt almost too weary to ask, "Is there an emergency room here?"

"Yes. Sorry. Look, you're safe now. That van will take you to the hotel; you can clean up and get a good night's sleep."

"Where's that?"

"In town—the Hotel Rústico; We'll be here overnight."

"Where next?"

"Paris."

† †

Anna was late in getting to the Hotel Rústico in Ibiza. She had brought only a carry-on bag, and tossed it onto the bed while kicking off her shoes. She was about to get into the shower when there was a knock at the door.

She opened it, and found Brad framed in the doorway. "My God, here you are," she said, throwing her arms around him.

Brad held her closely. "Barely," he whispered, and kissed her cheek.

"How was it?" She moved back.

"Deadly. We lost three people, including your husband, I understand. The producer Jean Reynard died in the helo."

Anna stiffened for a moment, recalling her comment to Reynard when she had dropped him at the train station in Lausanne in April. That was the last day she saw him alive. She shook it off.

Brad took her hand. "Your husband kept filming their escape; that cost him his life. I'm so sorry, Anna."

"We knew it might be a one-way trip. Truthfully Brad..." she said, moving closer, "We weren't getting on." She stepped back and sighed, "*Quel dommage*...there was another who didn't make it to the helicopter."

"I heard someone yell 'Kaarem'—is that whom you mean?"

"Yes, we wanted him out..."

"What happened to him?" Brad asked.

Realizing he still held her hand, she led Brad over to the sofa. "Come and sit down—we've got to discuss something. I heard the French got a signal from an operative in Algeria. He was kidnapped, and is being held there."

"Who got him?"

"Some splinter group of the GIA."

Brad shakes his head. "What a mess," he said.

"There's more. They said if we want him, we have to pay."

"How much?"

"Fifty thousand euros."

"Who pays for that?"

"We'll have to come up with it privately," Anna sighed.

"How are we to get him out?" asked Brad.

"They said to send a helicopter to the same place, the hotel courtyard. They said no one will fire a shot, unless we want to start something."

"Why don't the French send in the helo?"

"It's not official, you know. From what I understand, Kaarem helped the agency all he could, but they can't acknowledge that; it might blow the lid off the operation."

"The oil flow?" asked Brad.

"Yes." Anna got up and went to the window. "Damned oil; it'll ruin all of us one day. Brad, do you still have contact with your helicopter crew?"

"The copilot is staying right here in the hotel. The crewman's in the hospital."

"Should we get another crewman?"

Brad got up and joined Anna at the window. They look out onto Ibiza, where a myriad of cars crammed the streets, their tin voices adding to the din of the city. "The bird is pretty well shot up; we may need a replacement and we'll need a second crew. I want another armed ship as a backup."

"That may take a few days, Brad dear."

"It's okay; I've got time if this guy Kaarem does."

"If the second aircraft is that important, he'll have to have time."

"It *is* that important. Do you need to make a call?"

"I can contact the French, and then Hong Kong." Anna gave Brad a straight look.

Brad frowned and looked the other way, "Okay then."

"Sorry, I hoped to get you to France." Brad gave her a slight smile.

† †

Anna felt terrible about asking Brad, but she had no else to whom she could turn, and she couldn't think of anyone more qualified to get Kaarem out alive. She threw her keys on the bed and took out her cell phone. "Hello, June, how's tricks?"

"From the look of things, that's your department."

"Low blow, but I'll accept it."

"Well, when are you going to send him back?"

"He's a big boy; he can decide for himself."

"He still doesn't like poetry." June paused. "How many got out?"

"The copilot, the newscaster, Nicole something—Hélène Demaurie was her stage name—and a Berber girl."

"What's the Berber got to do with it?"

"Everything."

"I don't like the tone of your voice; what are you driving at?" asked June.

"We left someone behind, had given him up for dead, but he's been found."

June's voice hardened. "You want something, don't you?"

"Yes, love, another helicopter."

"And Brad to fly the damned thing…"

"Yes, Brad to fly the damned thing. There's more. He needs a replacement crewman plus another crew—and he wants to arm the second helicopter."

"This is all costing a great deal of money, darling." June said. "What's wrong with the French—don't they have any helicopters?"

"Can't touch it," Anna said.

"Crap! They need some *rancheros con huevos* in their political corps."

"Ha, ha—*Bueno.* I'm afraid you won't get *that* kind of breakfast in France." Anna retorted.

"How much will you put up?"

"Can I put it on my tab?" Anna laughed.

"Stop laughing! He could be killed," June chided. "Besides, I'm fresh out of helicopters."

"Brad's indestructible—you know that." Anna said. "Anyway dear, it's not the money; it's the resources, and you're the one with all the helicopters."

"All right, all right, I get it. Look, if you're so sure it's safe, why don't you go in with him?"

"I just might." Anna concluded.

"Oh *merde,* I was only kidding—don't do it. I might have to come to your memorial, and you know how I hate to fly. Well… better make some calls. When do we need to do this?"

"The sooner, the better—they might get tired of waiting."

"Well, if it's as long as all that, I think I'll do my shopping." June replied, then with a note of resignation added, "That's that, then."

Anna mimicked June's serious tone. "That's that, then."

"Talk to you soon, love." June said.

† †

Once they reached the hotel, Malena and Nicole showered, then fell into the king-size bed. They were still asleep when the phone rang ten hours later. Nicole answered groggily, "Hello?"

"It's Brad Thomas. I went by the hospital."

"Jean?" she asked.

"I'm sorry, but no," he replied in a lower voice. Nicole didn't speak for a long time. Eventually he said, "…Uh, look, I'll see you at the airport, okay?"

"Okay," she whispered, and dropped back onto her pillow, eventually falling back asleep.

The alarm went off at eight in the morning, and Nicole struggled out of bed, kissing Malena on the forehead. "Time to wake up." She went into the bathroom, disrobed, and stepped into the shower.

When Nicole came out, Malena was sitting on the edge of the bed, and she ruffled Malena's hair with the towel. "Your turn."

When Malena went into the bathroom, Nicole picked up the phone and called Aunt Lalla to ask about her father. "All I know is that he is living on the waterfront, and has one old crony named Pipon. Your father's dying Nicole," Lalla said sadly.

Malena came out of the bathroom wearing a bath towel and stood in front of her. Looking inquisitively at her, Nicole said, "Aunt Lalla, I'll call you back." She put the phone down.

Malena put her arms around her. "Just hold me for a moment. I think that's the only way I can forget last night. I forget my dreams when I'm with you."

† †

Nicole held Malena tightly. "We need to forget last night, don't we?"

"You're my introduction to the new reality."

Nicole released her grip on Malena. "Believe me, there's much, much more."

"We have to forget."

"Lie down and rest for a while."

"For a while." Malena said, and then asked, "When will you show me the rest?" Nicole didn't answer. She sat at the edge of the bed for a few minutes, then got up, took the phone into the bathroom, dialing as she went, and shut the door behind her.

† †

Malena scooted up on one elbow and stared at the telephone cord feeding under the closed bathroom door. She slumped onto her back and covered her eyes with her left forearm. Tears flowed freely down her cheeks. The deaths last night, bidding farewell to Sidu, and Kaarem's disappearance all seemed unreal. Now Nicole was disappearing. Malena was at the juncture of the singing career she had so wanted for so long—why now such sadness?

She put down her arm and looked over at the bathroom door, which was still shut. *Will she join me in Paris? And once there, how do I begin?*

After some time, Nicole came back into the room and put down the phone, sitting once again on the edge of the bed. Malena held out her hand, and Nicole gave her a thin smile, stroking her forehead. "We'd better be getting ready," she said before getting up and beginning to put on her clothes. Malena got up too, and without saying a word, found some clean clothes and dressed alongside Nicole.

After she finished putting on her makeup and combing her short hairdo, Nicole came over to Malena, who was sitting at the desk, and pulled her to her midriff. "Time to go," she said.

Malena felt something deep within, surging up like a muffled cry, "You're not coming to Paris, are you?"

"No, I can't."

"But why?" Malena was crying openly now. "My father is dying." Nicole hugged her more tightly. "Go ahead, let it out."

"I didn't cry for thirty years, and now I can't seem to stop!"

† †

Gathering up their things, they went down to the lobby. Its square marble tiles were obscured by dust seeping up from the grout, which had lost its seal. Between two Doric pillars sat a large wooden desk, occupied by a small man with slicked-back grey hair.

Brad was standing by the desk with an attractive blonde Nicole hadn't seen before. "We have a car outside," he said. Then, as an afterthought, he motioned to the woman beside him and said, "Excuse me, this is Anna." Nicole stepped forward and took her hand. "You're ready to go then?" Brad asked Nicole.

Malena stepped toward them. "She's not coming; her father is ill."

Nicole looked at Anna. "Anna," she said, realizing she was still holding her hand, and shook it gently. "Thank you." She dropped Anna's hand and removed a box from her bag. "Jean wanted you to have this."

Anna took the box, opened it, then closed the lid, recoiling. "Whose blood is this?"

"All of ours," Malena said. She removed the other box from her tote and handed it to Anna as well. Looking into her eyes, she said, "I see kindness in you." Turning to Nicole, Malena tugged on her arm and whispered, "Come with us, won't you?"

"He's my father, you see?"

Malena released her arm. "I had a father."

"You remember him."

"He told me he liked the way I sang." Malena looked at Nicole, then pulled her close.

"Go on for a little while. Go to Paris, Malena, and sing. I must do what I must do. I'll catch up with you, I promise."

Malena whispered back in Nicole's ear, "Please don't promise."

18

A lambda-shaped horn is placed atop the bride's head, symbolic of the ewes' golden horns. The women circle the bride with care. A few spangles are from the girl's trove; the rest of her coif is bejeweled with borrowed gems.

† †

Malena lay awake on the plane, stirred up about seeing Paris, being on an airliner, and her trauma in Algiers. Anna slept beside her, facing her and the small window, through which light poured in onto Anna's fair skin. Malena reached out and touched Anna's blonde hair, and couldn't remember if she had seen hair so light.

The poniards had started with Anna and her father, or so she had said. *That was when she was young, and her father old. Now he's dead and she's old. What makes people old?* Her thoughts drifted back to Lytton Mallory, who was old, but she had felt the youth in him before they were torn apart by the explosion.

Anna felt Malena's hand on her and awoke. "Was I sleeping?"

"Yes, Anna, you were sleeping."

The fasten-seat-belt light came on with an accompanying chime. "We're starting down; you'd better fasten your seat belt and bring your seat up," Anna instructed.

Malena registered surprise. "Bring my seat up?"

"Yes, the back part."

"I don't think I can do that."

"Of course, you can. Pull on the lever, just there." Malena

searched, but could not find the lever. Anna reached over and pulled it up, moving Malena's seat back forward.

"Oh."

After the airliner landed at Charles DeGaulle International Airport in the early afternoon, Anna and Malena disembarked and were met by Charles, who had already picked up their luggage. "Welcome back, Madame," he said stiffly, and escorted them to her old Rolls opera coupe throbbing in front of the main terminal, where a man stood guarding it.

"How did you manage that, Charles?" asked Anna, pointing at the security guard.

He shrugged. "A small expenditure, I assure you, Madame." He dropped their things in the continental trunk at the rear of the car. When he opened the door, Anna got into the back seat.

Malena hesitated. *What's wrong with the front seat? Should I take it?* Charles extended his hand, indicating she should accompany Anna. Malena felt strange, but followed Anna into the rear of the car. Charles went back to the front and got into the right side, behind the steering wheel. Malena continued to stare at him in amazement. Then she gave Anna a quizzical look.

"He's sort of an assistant," Anna said.

As they rode, Malena peered out the opera window beside her, watching the street scenes whir past and thousands of people crowding into her senses. *I should* feel *this miracle,* she thought. *I'm here. Everything is working out.* She choked back the lump in her throat.

"What are you thinking?" Anna asked.

"How everything has seemed to work out—we're here."

Anna squeezed Malena's hand and smiled, saying, "And here you'll stay."

It took them the better part of an hour to reach the Hôtel Grand Palais, where they were already checked in. The hotel was a miracle of marble. The ground floor was a pink hue, like the cliffs along the river Malena had seen on her trip to Algiers years earlier. Several massive columns rose from the floor to a coffered ceiling, upon which blue angels flew. A staircase circled up to a brasserie, where a flow of patrons climbed into an aroma of croissants and espresso. There they found seats at wrought iron tables, while waiters in white shirts moved among them, speaking Parisian French and whisking white towels into *plein aire* as if snapping at flies.

The City of Lights became Malena's cosmos. Anna saw to it that she got a new wardrobe and hairdo. Equally remarkable were the facials and manicures, and all the things Anna called her routine. After they returned to Anna's hotel suite from their pampering, Malena asked, "But all of this requires a great deal of money, no?"

"Yes, but there's more where that came from dear, I assure you. Besides, you have the beginning of a nest egg of your own, don't you?"

"Nest egg…I don't what that means. This has all happened so quickly, I don't know what to think."

"You will dear, believe me, you will. Now, we must consider what you need to do with yourself."

"I want to sing."

"I know. I've got some ideas on that count as well. Sing for me," said Anna.

"Now?"

"Why not? We have a piano in the salon; come on, I'll accompany you."

"Am I trying out?" asked Malena.

"No dear, you're singing." Malena nodded and told her what song to play, and Anna began the vamp. Malena swung into character, swelled inches above her height, and imagining her hair was piled up and adorned with white gardenias, she spread her arms, opened her mouth wide, and let the soft jazz simply come out.

When she had finished her song, Malena slumped a little and smoothed her hair. Anna got up from the piano bench and hugged her. "Thank you for your lovely song; what a marvelous, wonderfully unique voice you have," she said. "We'll have no trouble finding a place for you." She added, "Leave it to me."

Malena wasn't sure she wanted Anna's help. More than anything now, she wanted her independence. If she accepted help, would she trap herself as she had at The Black Owl? Malena had made up her mind her last day in Ibiza that she would never be beholden to anyone again. If there were a singing job out there, she wanted to find it on her own. Now was the time. "Anna," she began—"What's become of Kaarem?"

† †

Anna showed Malena to her car that evening, where Charles waited. "At least, Malena, I can help you settle into a decent part of town."

"I'll be all right, Anna; remember where I've been."

"So you will, and so right you are, but let's start out in the right direction, *d'accord?*"

"*D'accord.*" Malena replied, and they got into the car.

They decided to drive to each *arrondissement.* Anna would point out the advantages of one apartment, the disadvantages of another. "When you find your place, I will help open a bank account for you. You can transfer your funds into it; do you know how to do that, Malena?" Malena shook her head. "Do you know how to write a bank draft?" she asked, and again Malena shook her head; she had always dealt with money on a cash-and-carry basis. "You see, you do need my help. Paris is unforgiving of those who don't know these basics. I will help you with these things, and leave it to you to find your work, okay?"

"I learn."

Charles double-clutched and occasionally missed a gear while negotiating traffic and juggling real estate ads. The Rolls bucked its way through Parisian streets to Montmarte, the Quais de Seine, and the Marais and Latin Quarters, while Anna and the car's motor hissed with annoyance. When the engine sputtered and stalled at an intersection and the horns started blaring, Anna screamed, "Damn it, Charles, that's enough! Do you want me to drive?"

Charles plopped the ads down on the seat next to him, mashed his foot on the floor starter, slammed the gear lever into first, and tromped on the gas pedal; the old opera coupe roared ahead in defiance with an assertive cough. Reeking of gasoline fumes, they trundled across town to the next location.

Each time they parked, Malena got out to have a look. At first, nothing caught her eye. But then they came to an apartment complex on rue du Faubourg-Saint-Denis. "Strasbourg-Saint-Denis," Anna said, "is a place where artists come to live. Charles, stop the damn car!" Charles immediately swerved, running the front wheel up on the curb.

Malena peered out of the car's side window with interest. She got out and walked slowly into the courtyard with her hands clasped behind her back, looking like a real-estate executive looking to purchase. The courtyard was lined with a beige brick planter and ficus trees surrounded by low-lying shrubs. She sat on the planter beneath one of the ficus, and just sat for several minutes. *Here,* she thought, *is the scene of artists and passion*—a place she would want to live.

She hurried back to the car and looked in. "Anna, come quickly; I want to see inside." Anna told Charles to phone the agent. Within fifteen minutes, a woman wearing a business suit arrived, and they went up.

The apartment was filled with light afforded by ample windows and glass bricks that were inset in the walls near the ceiling. The kitchen was charming and quite efficient, with a washer-dryer and a dishwasher, side-by-side. Malena ran her hand along the appliances, murmuring, "Anna, you'll have to show me how to run these things."

"Of course—let's have a look at the bedroom and bath." The agent escorted them to a charming bedroom, where more glass bricks allowed the light to filter into the room. The adjoining bath had a sink made of green transparent material resembling marble. The shower had a backsplash of the same material. Multiple water jets jutted out from the backsplash.

Malena was taken by the place and began, "Anna..."

Anna put up her hand and turned to the agent, politely saying,

"Thank you very much; we'll let you know." They went back out into the courtyard and the agent left her card with them and left.

"This is *mon Algérie nouvelle,"* Malena said to Anna.

"Well, your *'Algérie nouvelle'* is a vacation rental that will cost thirteen hundred euros a month."

"Do I have enough?"

"You do, but you must consider the expense."

When Nicole returned to Paris, she didn't go to her apartment, but checked in at a modest hotel on the rue de Richelieu, not far from the Palais Royale and the Louvre. She couldn't face Arnold after all she had been through. *Anyway, he's such donkey's butt.*

After checking in, she unpacked and dialed their number. Unsurprisingly, Arnold was out. She caught a cab and went to the apartment to pack her things. She left a short note for Arnold to the effect that she thought it best that she left, and didn't feel the worse for it, especially after smelling a strange perfume lingering there.

She returned to the hotel room, and phoned Anna to check in. After emailing the Agency, Nicole caught a cab and went to Sun King Productions with the film and audio and videocassettes Talka had collected, knowing she would spend the next several weeks at the studio piecing together the documentary.

"What will you call it?" asked the costume designer, Henri, surveying the pile of media on the table.

"I dunno—*Return to Algiers*—what do you think?" Nicole asked.

Henri eyed the group of editors. One shrugged, but after a moment's thought, most murmured or nodded approval.

"So be it—*Return to Algiers* it is," said Nicole, and gesturing to the pile, added, "It's a mess; we'll have to get to work."

The next day, while Nicole was viewing some rushes, Henri called her into his sewing room. "I've got something for you," he said, removing a letter from his desk drawer. "Reynard sent this a week before you left Algiers..." He handed it to her.

Nicole held the letter delicately, turning it over a couple of times. "It's still sealed," she said softly, and opened it.

Dear Nicole,

If you are reading this, it's because I didn't make it back, and you are at Sun King trying to put together the final cut of the documentary, n'est pas? In any case, Lamar and I talked it over, and we did a lot of editing because we feared the worst. If he's there, you won't find it much trouble to finish. It's a good film, and I hope it does well.

I want you to know, on a personal note, I admire you greatly. You draw no quarter for your convictions and you do an honest acting job. No producer could have asked for more. Your courage is truly admirable. You're a real trooper!

One last thing I need to tell you: call Bank Swiss, Zurich, and give them this account number: 302733. The account holds one million euros, made out in a trust to you. Since there's a vacant seat at Sun King Productions now, I would very much like you to fill it. Keep up the company's tradition of creating quality documentaries—there's nothing more stunning than the truth. Lamar may be right about one thing: to get at it, you don't always have to have dialogue or actors. But there are few scenarios in life in which you can control such truths. The audiences will either run out of the theatre en masse or fall asleep.

Take some of the money and get yourself a nice apartment uptown; Montparnasse is washed-up. Tell any of the others who made it back to work well with you, or I'll make it hard on them later on. Be sure to pass this on to Claude when you submit your final sitrep. By the way, I had you figured for a plant on Claude's part. He was always fond of insurance, and it's SOP, as you must know.

Adieu,
Jean

My God, Nicole thought, *right from the start he must have guessed who I was, but didn't say a word. Claude sent me because Reynard had been away from the service too long—it* was *standard operating procedure. He also thought Jean might need my help—which he did when we broke the code and found the valve. And then there was the documentary. We filmed our way to the truth, and it cost him his life, as well as Lamar's, Philippe's, and God knows, maybe Kaarem's. What a non sequitur. Maybe Camus had it right the first time, before he repented of* Theatre of the Absurd.

When Nicole turned in her final report, neither she nor Claude spoke of the trust in Zurich. Nicole told herself she would keep Sun King Productions open, though she would need to find a director, a cinematographer, and maybe a good writer, when a script was called for.

She and the editors cobbled the media together and planned for a private showing for Anna before canning the film. Nicole phoned Anna and apologized for the long delay, explaining that the rigors of film editing had taken longer than she had anticipated, and invited her to watch the documentary the following day. Anna agreed to come to the studio in the morning.

† †

When Anna walked in, Nicole hugged her and escorted her to the viewing room. They sat down in loge-style seats, and Nicole signaled the operator to roll the film.

What appeared on the screen was at once remarkable and terrifying.

After the last frame had flickered past, the house lights came up and Anna wiped the perspiration from her forehead. Then she leaned forward, burying her head in her lap and sobbed, "I have never been in the heat of battle."

After a bit, she sat up and dabbed at her eyes. "The street bombings and the village massacre were horrifying. I was moved to tears at the sight of Philippe's death. But in an odd, permanent arrangement, through the lens of his camera, when at last I saw his work, I cried for Lamar."

Nicole put her arm around her. "It was horrible for everybody. Maybe this will help you close this chapter of your life's book."

Anna put her head next to Nicole's. "It does, thank you. Come to my hotel, the Grand Palais, later." She got up, straightened her dress, picked up her purse, and left.

Two hours later, Nicole had changed into a t-shirt with *Return to Algiers, the Documentary* emblazoned on the chest, worn over her jeans. She caught a cab to the Hôtel Grand Palais and wasted no time in getting to Anna's suite. She had remembered to bring a bottle of French wine and Philippe's papers, including the last torn page, which she had finally mended.

Anna greeted her at the door in her robe. "Oh, wine," she said, and fetched a corkscrew from the dresser, sitting on the sofa with Nicole. After negotiating the stubborn cork, she poured two glasses and they toasted the manuscript.

They sipped the wine, then Anna put down her glass and said, "Let's see what you have, dear." Nicole took another swig of wine and handed her Philippe's papers. Anna put her feet up on the coffee table, and began turning the pages, examining them as if they contained ancient text. Nicole finished her first glass, then poured herself another and drank while Anna read.

By the time she had flipped through the manuscript, Anna had finished her second glass of wine as well. She looked up and said, "Well, it's not *Theatre of the Absurd.* He's like a corsair in pursuit of Camus on the high seas of existentialism."

"I hope he found the shore. I hope for that most of all," Nicole said, finishing her glass.

"And this title, *Freedom in North Africa: A Hope for Independence,* it's—it's wonderful," Anna said.

"I'd like to find someone who will publish it for those killed in the streets in Algiers, for everyone killed by the Kelbeaus of the world," Nicole growled.

Anna fanned the pages of the manuscript. "Maybe we can get *Le Monde* to run it as a series. But after all, Jean Reynard deserves most of the credit. What a film he has made."

Nicole leaned toward her. "Yes, you're right of course; I was so involved with Philippe, I had forgotten who the real player in this was. I intend to get that film to Cannes."

Anna reached out and took Nicole's hand, asking, "Do you really think all of this will make a difference?"

"I asked my father what he thought before he died, and he said, 'We can trade one tyranny for another.'"

Anna tilted her head back and laughed. Straightening up, she gave Nicole a hug. "Sorry, I find that amusing. About your dad—did you have much time with him?"

"Too little, too late."

Anna nodded consolingly, then said, "Nicole, not to change the subject, but do you feel like helping me on another matter?"

Nicole snapped back to the moment. "Sure, anything."

"It's Malena. I put her up over at Saint Denis, but she won't let me help her find a singing job; she insists on going it alone. I don't need to tell you she'll pound the pavement until the cows come home. After everything that girl's gone through and done, it's the least I can do."

Nicole straightened up, pulled a Kleenex from her purse, and wiped her nose. "Oh trust me, I can relate to that. In some ways, Malena is as tough as nails, but here," Nicole shook her head, "she's completely vulnerable. How can I help?"

"I'll arrange a little charade. All you have to do is to show up at a restaurant and make like it's a surprise reunion for you and Malena. Can you do that?"

"Sure, it'll be fun, seeing Malena…is she, I mean, is she still wearing that striped dress?" Nicole giggled.

"No dear—we did an entire makeover. You may not recognize her."

"I will when she speaks."

"Of course, you will, dear. Now there's another player."

† †

Malena strode around her apartment at rue du Faubourg-Saint-Denis. Despite Malena's reluctance to accept help, Anna had furnished her with a dozen places in the city to try out. Malena told Anna she couldn't accept her help finding a job, and she would pay her back for helping find the apartment. Anna said, "Fine. Pay me back by getting a job."

But Malena had been adamant that Anna would not interfere with her job search. "It's my destiny to seek out my place here," she said. "I don't want to spend the rest of my life afraid to do things on my own."

Malena cradled the Picasso print in her arms. She searched her new place, examining each wall. She strolled into the bedroom, then stopped in front of the wall separating the closet from the bathroom. And there she hung the print on an expectant nail. *Here you can struggle indefinitely.* The figure in the painting reminded her of herself and then of yet another girl, Little Egypt.

After the explosion in the Square of Three Clocks, she runs. Panic twists in her gut. Frantically she searches for a refuge, any refuge, and rushes headlong into the dismal recesses of the area, coming face-to-face with Little Egypt just beyond the square. Her eyes are wide and she smells of cordite and has an AK-47 slung beneath her arm.

"Why have you sought me out?" she asks, as a dozen children, each of them armed, surround Malena and her as they stand facing each other.

"It's an accident I found you. Who are these children?" Malena asks.

"My army of carnage," Little Egypt replies, shifting the weight of her weapon to the other shoulder. "They bind themselves to me for a cause."

"What cause?" Malena inquires in confusion.

"The cause of survival." She looks at their dirty faces and seems to try to smile, but only grimaces, saying, "Most of them have been sexually abused. That's why we understand one another."

"I need a place to hide for a day or two," Malena says to Little Egypt. She tries to take Little Egypt's hand, but Little Egypt pulls away.

"It's too dangerous here for you; you must leave."

"It's too dangerous anywhere for me," Malena begs. "Please. Don't you have a place for me?"

Little Egypt surveys her face suspiciously. "You still have a pointed nose."

"And yours is flat."

She smiles. "Come with me then; at least I can get you something to eat."

Later in her apartment, Malena asks Little Egypt why she didn't return to Tizi Ouzou. Little Egypt says she was halfway there when she was captured by rebels. "So why are you still doing this?" Malena asks.

"They gave me a choice: join them or die. I chose the former," she shrugs, and bites into an apple, then offers one to Malena.

Then a teenage boy, whose face is smeared with soot, comes in. His mouth forms a grotesque sneer. "Get goin', slut,"

Little Egypt touches Malena's arm, saying, "I have to go."

Malena hugs her. "Me too—I..."

"It's okay, Malena, stay here the night and then leave while you can..." She shifts her eyes to the male youth. "It's not safe here."

Malena lets her go, whispering, "Till sometime."

"Sometime."

† †

Two days later, Malena was still opening boxes containing the myriad of dresses and the accoutrements she and Anna had liberated from the exclusive shops Anna frequented. In the afternoon, two more cartons showed up at her door. She brought them in and sighed. One contained an array of CDs that overwhelmed her; its collection of artists would only pass muster with the jazz greats: Billie Holiday, Josephine Baker, Ella Fitzgerald. Malena gasped out a tear when she realized Anna had also included Cinnamon Caruthers's complete repertoire.

She found a note included in the carton: "Malena, these are for your appreciation and training. Love, Anna." When Malena opened the second carton, she found a Bose CD player with speakers of sufficient strength to broadcast jazz hot all the way to Djurdjura. She picked up the phone and called Anna to thank her.

"You're welcome, Malena. While I have you on the phone, I want to give you an address."

"Is this an audition somewhere?" Malena asked.

"No, it's a surprise. Not to worry, dear; it's quite safe."

"I'm sure you wouldn't lead me into danger, Anna. What's the address?"

"The Blue Elephant, at 43 rue de la Roquette; tomorrow evening at seven-thirty you have reservations."

"Should I take a cab?"

"No, I'll send Charles around, at say, seven?

"What should I wear?"

"The red dress with the brocade top—wear that one."

"Anna, what's this all about?" Malena asked uneasily.

"I told you, it's a surprise. Now be ready, go, and enjoy yourself."

"I'll have to trust you. Oh and Anna, I wanted to thank you again for all that you've done."

"You're welcome, Malena. Now I have to run. Ta ta."

Anna had bought her ensembles for galas, premieres, guest appearances, jam sessions, business meetings, and just knocking about town. And Anna avowed that the money came from Malena's Swiss bank account. Later, when Malena was able to comprehend the monthly bank statements appearing in the letter drop, she recalled her aching suspicion that Anna had financed her wardrobe all along. Nevertheless, she was very proud of it and hung all the dresses up with care. When she found the red dress, she put it at the end, ahead of the other dresses.

It was now October, and the Paris evenings were becoming cool. She had several overcoats to keep her warm through the winter months, and hung them in the bedroom closet. Anna had said, "After all, you're not in Algiers or the Djurdjura anymore."

Malena had just finished hanging up her clothes when a knock came at the door. She opened it and was confronted by a rotund man with dark eyes and a handlebar moustache, wearing jeans and a black t-shirt. "Who are you?" she asked.

"My name is Yves, what's yours?"

"Malena."

"You're the one."

"Why are you here?" she asked, bewildered.

"A friend of yours sent me; she said you need an accompanist."

"Anna?"

"Didn't give a name."

"Anna," Malena affirmed.

"Well?"

"Well what?"

"I think we should get started." Yves picked up his guitar case and pushed past her, saying, "May I come in?"

Malena eyed him as he walked into the living room. Yves put down his guitar case and pulled out a piece of paper. Cocking her head, she peered down at it and saw a list of names. "What is that?"

"A list of prospective employers, but first I need to hear your repertoire to see which joint is the best for us." He grabbed the list back and stuffed it into his pants pocket, then sat down, opened his guitar case, and asked, "Shall we get started?"

Still bewildered, Malena tried to make sense of it. "Started?"

"Yeah, started. Whenever you're ready." Scooping up his guitar and holding it carefully like a baby, he tuned it. Satisfied, he nodded. "Okay, sweetheart, start belting them out. I'll pick up on your lead."

Malena had had enough. "Damn it, whom do you think you are?"

"Just like you, love, a jazz musician."

"I'm a singer, not a musician."

"Have it your own way. Just the same," he said, softening, "I'd like to hear you sing."

Malena regarded him suspiciously for a moment, but said, "Well, I guess there's no harm..." and shrugged. She took in a big breath, and sang.

Yves picked up on her song, and said, "Making beautiful music," shaking his head and strumming the guitar, and then added, "ha-cha."

Within an hour and a half, they had put together ten songs. Despite her misgivings, Malena enjoyed the session.

"Well, I know a couple of places on the list that would be good bets for us," he said.

"Good bets?"

"Yeah, you know, places where we would have the best chance to get a job, sounding like we do—sabby?"

Malena nodded. "Sabby, whatever that means. Say, what's your name again?"

"Yves Cardin…and pleased to meet ya…hmm, Cårtobé and Cardin, Cardin and Cårtobé, Malena and Yves…"

"Why are you saying our names?"

"Seeing what sounds better…Yves and Malena…"

"Just say them."

"What?"

"Just say them naturally: Malena Cårtobé and Yves Cardin."

"Yeah…hey! How about Malena Cårtobé and Yves?"

Malena sighed and shook her head. "Whatever…"

He put his guitar back into its case. "Okay, here's the squeeze."

"The what?"

"Plan—we'll go to this joint first, La Danse Jazz, in Montmartre, then we'll buzz over to the J'ai Bleu over by Noisey de Sec, okay?"

Malena relaxed her shoulders, nodded, and offered him a smile. "Okay, but I have an engagement tomorrow night."

"What time?"

"Seven."

"Great. We'll be done by then. I gotta go; I'll be by at seven in the morning." Yves picked up his guitar case and went to the door. "Well, nice meeting you. See you tomorrow." He opened the door and Malena stood up to reply, but he was gone.

The next morning, Malena was up at six a.m. She showered and dressed in the bloodred off-the-shoulder dress Anna had said would be the knockout punch for any audition. She checked herself in the full-length mirror hung outside the bathroom door. She repeated the names of the places Yves had selected over and over: "La Danse Jazz and J'ai Bleu." Malena wasn't sure what J'ai Bleu meant, but thought it was some sort of bird. *No matter,* she thought, *I've sung in a place named for an animal before,* and she began to wonder if there was a mysterious way that cabaret owners came by such names.

Yves knocked on the door at seven-fifteen. "I've got a cab," he said. This time, he was more formally dressed, in a white sport coat, a blue open-collared shirt, and navy blue slacks.

It took thirty minutes to get to the La Danse Jazz. Yves got out with his guitar case, and then helped Malena out. "Between you and Anna's butler, I'm getting used to such treatment," she said.

"Come on, let's go," he said. They entered a great room filled by dining tables with chairs sitting upside down on them. Beyond the dining room, there was a large stage. Malena pointed at it. "Is that where it happens?"

"That's it," he said, pulling a chair down. "Here. Sit down. I'll be back in a minute." He went to the stage and disappeared.

Malena saw his guitar on the ground, and called, "Hey, don't you want…oh, never mind." She crossed her legs and adjusted her red dress, then put her elbow on the table, cupping her chin in her hand, and waited. Ten minutes went by and still no Yves.

Finally he came out from behind the arras and sauntered over to Malena. He grabbed up the case, saying, "Here, I'll be needing this." Opening the case, he took out the guitar, then picked up a chair and plopped it down in center stage. He quickly sat down and started tuning his guitar, twisting here, plucking there.

In a clear voice he said, "Ladies and gentleman, we're gathered here today to pay tribute to a great singer and humanitarian, Malena Cårtobé. But before we proceed any further, I should play a little traveling music."

When he began a tune, the side curtain moved and Nicole appeared, curtsied, and walked over to Malena, who applauded and hugged her. "When did you get back?" Malena asked.

"Shush, you'll spoil the show." Nicole pulled over a chair and sat beside Malena. Yves continued the song and the stage curtain moved again, and Anna appeared. She came over and kissed Malena.

"What's this all about?" asked Malena, welling up.

"Shush, you'll spoil the show," Anna repeated. Malena threw up her arms in frustration.

As Yves continued, the curtain moved again, and a tall man with dark hair appeared When Malena recognized Kaarem, her jaw dropped. He walked over to her, and she got up and threw her arms around him, and they rocked back and forth. "You're back, you're back! But how? When?"

Kaarem smiled. "I've been here a few days. The helicopter came back after all."

"But all of you—you're in it together, the bunch of you." Malena said plaintively.

"It's all her doing," Nicole said, pointing at Anna.

Anna looked at Malena and shrugged, saying, "I thought you might like a little intrigue..."

Kaarem broke in. "Malena, I have a message for you. Someone you have known for a long time sent it."

"What is it?"

"Till sometime."

Malena raised her eyebrows, then smiled, saying, "Little Egypt."

Kaarem smiled broadly. "Yes. She was in charge of the group who grabbed me outside the cabaret that night. She said I was too late; you had gone and the others were coming. She had no choice."

"And all this time—are you okay? I mean did they treat you well?"

"Quite well. They protected me."

"Just the same, you're here," Malena said, "and I'm glad and grateful to you all." She approached Anna. "Thank you most of all," she said, kissing her.

"You're welcome."

19

CANNES 13 MAY 2009

Brad looked up at the frontage of Hôtel d'Anglais, bordering the Mediterranean; it so reminded him of another hotel in Nice: the Negresco. He and Maggie had played out a scene there at Christmastime, forty years earlier, having gotten properly drunk at a masquerade party on his last night in France. She was his girl then, and that was the last time he had seen her.

An onshore breeze lifts Brad's gilded robes and headpiece silks, flowing against the night sky as he strides onto the middle Promenade des Anglais. When he reaches the center of the boulevard, he turns and faces traffic, hands on his hips, feet spread apart, dagger hilt glistening.

With a flourish, he regally puts out his hand and stops the flow of oncoming cars. Horns instantly come alive, but the cars stop obediently. Turning, he stops the flow of cars from the other direction, with the same blaring reaction. When all traffic has stopped, he motions to Maggie, saying, "Now, fair lady, you may cross the street."

"Yes, your honor," she says with a feigned Cockney brogue, and starts unsteadily across. When she reaches him, she attempts a kiss.

"Not now milady," he exclaims, "everyone is watching."

Brad shook his head. *Time does exist.* Lifting his bag, he walked into the lobby of Hôtel d'Anglais.

He finished checking in, receiving a room two floors below Anna's suite. He barely noticed the elevator ride, he was so wrapped up in his memories, but shook his head when he got to his room, surprised that his flashback on the street had had such a sweeping effect. He dropped his bag and fluffed up the lush, green velvet bed pillows that matched the bed skirt. He lay on the bed, propping his head up on the pillow so he could look out onto the blue sea through the wrought-iron grates bordering the window.

He remembered the days after the flagship had settled on the homeport in Gaeta, between Naples and Rome. It was in Naples after the San Carlos that he had first met Anna. But it was later that they had become close, in Rome. And it was in Rome that they had parted. He hadn't known why; he wasn't sure he knew now.

"I need a drink," he said aloud, and called room service. He hadn't taken a drink for days preceding the first extraction, since he hadn't known exactly when it would happen. The second time in was planned; he had known he would have to be on his toes. Now it was all over, and he felt he had earned his drink.

When the boy brought up the bottle, he tipped him and opened it, pouring out three fingers of the sour mash. *Just like old times.* He took a good amount before picking up the phone to call Anna.

"Hi."

"Hi, yourself. Don't you have anything better to do than to bother me in the middle of my bath?" Anna said coyly.

"You haven't lost it."

"Lost what?"

"That tone like you want me in there with you."

"Oh, *that* tone. Hmm, not an original idea—nor a bad one; why don't you come up?" Anna asked.

"Whoa! Sorry. I thought I might ask you to the movies tonight—you game?"

"Only if you let me get you into the box office…box-office—you know like 'cockpit,' but with lady pilots…"

"Ha ha, very funny—and sexy. Well, if that's what you want…"

"I want," she purred.

"You got it." He laughed uproariously. "I love your games."

"Are you really game this time, Brad?"

"I'm not sure…I'm willing to try."

"Me too," replied Anna. "Uh, I did talk to June, who tells me you're wise to stay with me for a while, as a part of the import-export trade, if you get my drift."

"Because I'm being investigated?"

"No."

"Then…"

"Me."

"I should have a say in this."

"Well say it, dear."

"Umm, I shouldn't have disturbed you when you were taking your bath."

"Bravo! By the way, did I mention Nicole is accepting the Cannes Film Festival award for *Return to Algiers* on Reynard's behalf?" Anna asked.

"That's a good thing."

"—and you ought to know someone else is in town."

"Who?" asked Brad.

"Malena—staying at this hotel, and she's got her boyfriend with her," she whispered.

"What's the whispering about?"

"Shush, not so loud. I made a couple of calls and she's singing something before Nicole's presentation."

"The *chanteuse* after all."

"She says she loves her gigs in Paris, at a place called J'ai Bleu. Says to tell you she got most of her training from a place called The Black Owl. Do you believe me?"

Ignoring the "truth" ploy, he replied, "Sounds like she's for the birds. What's she going to sing?"

"Probably something French, but she likes Cinnamon Caruthers."

"I've been told."

"She has two of her old records she carried out of the desert. She tells me she thinks Cinnamon Caruthers sings like a nightingale.

She says once a nightingale came out sea to her, and perched on the rail of her boat bound from Rome."

"I thought you said she had never been out of Algiers."

"I asked her about that too. She told me...no, wait a minute silly, I'm not going to read you any poetry—give me a chance. Actually she sang it to me: *Only in my dreams.*

20

The Wedding Rite: Day Five

In the evening on the last day of the marriage rite, a fire rages outside the house where the brides have come to watch the Ahi duce, *a dance for men and divorced women.*

Attendants rouge red lambdas down each bride's cheekbones; rouge of deeper shades is applied to the lips and around the eyes. Their foreheads are dotted with blues and reds in a pointillist's tapestry of body paint. Three lines of dots extend from the middles of their hairlines to the ends of their noses. A solid line extends from each jawbone to the lambda at the cheek, forming an arrow upward.

The brides parade out in full costume, draped in long dresses and half-veils, their chins gleaming in the fire. Their faces show a range of emotions: smiles for the first marriages; fear from those who begin more permanent arrangements; and all varieties of joy, sadness, wonder, and hope, stirring among the sparks from the pyre they turn to face, their headdresses shimmering as if they were one bride.

† †

Samantha, curled amid the ampullae, was awakened by a shudder in the planks when the boat nudged the dock at Carthage. She stood and stretched her arms, shaking off the dampness of the sea. Peering over the bulwarks, she saw the dock filled with stevedores, already streaming onto the gangplank as merchants called out orders from their carts.

She thought of Augustine and wept.

In years to come, she would hear of him and how he saved his people from the slavers. From time to time, she met other Berbers who knew him outside the Church. They said he appeared to accept their way of worship, and had long since forgiven them their transgressions. They would say, "But Church law forbade him anything else but to seek redemption." He did this as Bishop of Hippo, as a Church official, and as a Roman.

He always loved them. It may never be known how much he was drawn to the tribal traditions of the Berbers, or how he respected their *nif* and need to be left to themselves. Perhaps the new Church Law he helped write somehow floated to the surface of tribal cohesion, stalked his mind, and embedded itself in him like a harpoon.

She remembered the last part of her dream, in which the girl appeared as a small red bird perching on the taffrail just above the bulkhead. Her feathers were wet and she struggled to keep her balance as the vessel rose and fell with the waves. Samantha didn't recognize the girl at first, and thought she was just a bird. But when she thought about her arrival, it came to her that this was the girl to whom she had spoken in her dreams.

In her dream, Samantha stroked the bird, and the bird gathered strength. Pouring some water from her flask into her hand, she offered it to the creature. The bird dipped her beak down into the liquid and drank, then ruffled her feathers, shaking the sea water from them. Stretching her wings up into the wind that washed down from the sails, she lifted into a hover above Samantha, caught an invisible wave of air, and slid over the ship's side and flew away.

Samantha watched the bird disappear into the horizon and touched her abdomen, which was beginning to show. *This is Milan, part of his love I shall keep. There's nothing left to forgive. From here I start, as has been done before,* like the girl—borne here by something inexplicable. She had stood at the rail long before the glimmer of Persian and Roman swords had flashed across the land, before the presence of any who had roamed into the reaches of North Africa, before this quay, this fire, in full view of her nation.

Epilogue

DIRECTION GÉNÉRALE DE LA SÉCURITÉ EXTÉRIEURE
PARIS, FRANCE

CLASSIFICATION:
MÉMORANDUM, NUMÉRO DE SÉRIE BB146, PAGE 1

21 FÉVRIER 2008
DE: DIRECTEUR GÉNÉRALE, LES OPERATIONS SPÉCIALES
À: DIRECTEUR GÉNÉRALE, DGSE
SUJET: RAPPORT FINAL D'OPERATION *NIAGRI*

1. It has been confirmed that the crux of the mission, the return of oil to France, is now concluded. According to special agent Nicole Soutane, the agent Jean Reynard, along with a subcontract operative, Malena Cårtobé, found the valve and opened it.

2. Regrettably, Agent Reynard, his cameraman, Lamar Talka, and his scriptwriter, Philippe DuPont, were killed in action during the escape phase of the operation. Agent Soutane's report states that despite precautions, Algerian Security forces were responsible for their deaths. Notwithstanding these losses, the mission is considered a complete success.

CLASSIFICATION:
MÉMORANDUM, NUMÉRO DE SÉRIE BB146, PAGE 2

3. Payment for Agent Reynard's service in Algeria was deposited in the usual Swiss account. We have discovered that prior to his departure from France, Agent Reynard named as his beneficiary Helen Demare, Nicole Soutane's stage alias. Subsequently, Agent Soutane has legalized the stage alias, so she is legally entitled to the payment. At this writing, Agent Soutane is out of country, in Tunisia, on a personal matter. It is expected that she will return and assist in producing the documentary, developed in Algiers during the accomplishment of the primary mission. The date of Agent Soutane's return is unknown.

4. The Department is in receipt of a statement from Hong Kong Helicopters, Limited, demanding payment for its part of the operation's rescue portion. Somehow the Department failed to negotiate a fee for these services prior to the operation. Aside from the nominal fees for the flight and maintenance crews, there's a charge of EUR 3,8 million for replacement of a helicopter. There are miscellaneous expenditures itemized for arms and munitions used in the extraction

5. There is a clouded issue of payment for the subcontract agent, Malena Cårtobé, who acted as a go-between, and was instrumental in deciphering the code on the poniards and actually helped open the valve. It is reported that she's here in Paris. I have requested her presence in our office for a proper recognition and for repayment. It is known that she received the Faberg reward for opening the valve. We feel she may prove useful as an

Classification:

mémorandum, numéro de série BB146, page 3

agent in future operations, and therefore feel it is important to solidify the relationship between the Agency and mlle Cårtobé.

6. Our channel to Algiers is intact, and the operative, code name, the Jeweler, is still under deep cover.

Respectfully submitted,
Claude Astride
directeur générale, les operations spéciales
End of Report.

A letter intercepted and on file in DGSE Headquarters
United States of America
Diplomatic Service
Tunis, Tunisia

September 5, 2008
Inter-Service Communication—Restricted Access
From: Intelligence Division
To: The Ambassador
Subj: French Filming Crew in Algiers; final report

1. Previous reports from deep cover stated possible SDECE involvement in French documentary, Return to Algiers, on location in Algiers and surrounding area.

2. Background of surveillance began when it came to our attention through our channels in France that Sun King Productions had been contacted by the SDECE to conduct special operations in Algiers. For purposes that remain unclear, since communication with our deep-cover agent in Algiers had been terminated, the production company was conducting a front for some deeper operation sponsored by the French government.

3. It may well be that French involvement in the undercover operation would have been eventually reported had it not been for the fact of the regrettable loss of the agent, code name Lytton Mallory, KIA by an explosion at a place called the Wadi of the Three Stones. It is known that the Algerian Security discovered the presence of the French operation; with the aid of a private helicopter company, HKH, based in Hong Kong, an effective operation was conducted to evacuate the French filming crew with three reported casualties. It is interesting to note that one of the principals involved in the rescue operation was an American, not a part of our service but working in the private sector, and known to us from a previous inquiry (See: Neary-Thomas Inquiry, HKH 1971, serial no. 045).

4. This letter will be made a permanent part of the Return to Algiers file, should you have need to use it in future reference.

P. J. Smith
By direction

A POEM APPEARING IN *LE MONDE*

Taken from the notes of Philippe DuPont; written on location in Algiers, during the filming of the documentary *Return to Algiers.* Published in fond memory of Philippe DuPont.

RETURN TO ALGIERS

Pour Albert Camus, pour l'Algérie

Life for him amiss,
In time, condensed itself,
Besieged the shore with words
In a strange convoluted rhyme.
At All Saints' Beach, a-wade,[1]
His vision cleared seven-fold—[2]
At last, the voice he gained,
Least absurd, remained unsold.
Of him, Jean-Paul would say,[3]
"Poor Bert's unraveled…
Hasn't been that way."
Unrebuffed, he swelled and roared,
Behaved as JP said he would:
"Let me state our valence,
Raise a voice to compare,
Breach the edge of silence,
Cross the precipice of despair."
JP rebuked his very reason,
No matter what he said,
The Reason, as the logic led:
"Too late in age, an age too late,
The 'Age of Reason' is already dead…"
—Philippe DuPont

1 All Saints' Day, Anniversary of Algerian Revolution, 1954.

2 References seven works by Albert Camus: *The Stranger, The Myth of Sisyphus, Cross Purpose,* and *Caligula,* in which he explored life's absurdity, The last three works, *Letters to a German Friend, The Plague,* and *The Rebel,* explain his rebellion against theatre of the absurd, that meaningful life is possible through human dignity and endurance.

3 Jean Paul Sartre

CPSIA information can be obtained
at www.ICGtesting.com
Printed in the USA
FSOW02n0514210616
21736FS

9 780615 334097